OF SONG AND DARKNESS

JESSICA SPRUILL

NIGHT PIRATE
PUBLISHING

To everyone who has ever felt like Dark Water is closing in from all around, may you find light in the darkness.

"And the light shineth in the darkness; and the darkness comprehended it not." - John 1:5

And to Mema, my light. May you rest in peace.

TRIGGER WARNING

Of Song and Darkness is an exciting fast-paced romantic fantasy that ends on a hopeful note. However, the story includes elements that might not be suitable for all readers. The death of a loved one, murder, blood, violence, mention of past rape, attempted sexual assault, and alcohol are mentioned in this novel. Readers who may be sensitive to these elements, please take note.

CONTENTS

CHAPTER I
RHEA

My father would fillet my tail if he caught me this far away from home. Just thinking about how long I had been gone this time sent shivers of fear down my tail fins. I'd been sneaking out for months, searching for the rumored Dark Water the refugees who fled to our home in Aquarius whispered about. With each venture, I swam farther, but so far, I hadn't found a shred of proof that it existed. A sensible part of me urged that I dismiss Dark Water as a tall tale, but I couldn't understand why my father would forbid any mention of it with the threat of banishment from the kingdom. For him to take it that seriously meant there had to be some krill of truth to the nightmarish tales, and I was determined to find out what it was.

I bit my lower lip, trepidation mounting with every passing moment. Hesitating in the water, I cast an uncertain gaze over my surroundings. Moonlit shadows swirled in the current, playing tricks on my mind and conjuring monsters where none existed, or so I hoped. The pink iridescent scales of my tail shimmered in the muted glow, a dead giveaway to my presence in these treacherous waters. A siren, especially a princess, had no business being this far out on her own. Still, curiosity had wrested control from my good sense, and I had blatantly put myself in danger over a rumor. Great—I was starting to sound just like my father. I crammed his words and my fear deep down and forced myself to regain composure as I pressed on.

The tension in my tight muscles intensified when I came upon a coral reef. Its presence signaled my proximity to land —a foreboding place where I should not be. I glided over to it, running my hand across its stunning orange porous surface. In our city, nestled in the frigid depths, coral like this could never thrive. I had only seen it a few times in my youth, long ago, before my eldest sister's death.

Just thinking of her shot a pang of sorrow through my soul. Valeria had been gone a few years now. Her death at the hands of humans had sent my father into a depressive state. Soon after, he passed a decree forbidding all sirens from going anywhere near land. A law I was breaking at the moment, and another reason for him to be angry with me.

When I saw coral reefs in my youth, crabs, colorful fish, and other species coexisted in harmony with the coral. So, where were they? I swam a little further, stopping abruptly when the foul scent of decay assaulted my nostrils. I hesitated before going further, not knowing what lay ahead. With a fleeting burst of courage, I cautiously circled the colossal reef. The hairs at the nape of my neck stood on end at the sight before me.

"No." I gasped as tears threatened to spill from my eyes and mix with the saltiness of the sea.

The vast area had been completely destroyed. The lush vegetation had turned black and floated in a slimy muck through the water. Shredded bits of dolphin fins, skeletal ribs of fish, and a stray crab claw floated before my eyes. The carnage was immense. My body trembled, and my mind screamed for me to swim away, to flee from the horrific scene, but movement in the looming shadows caught my attention, halting my escape. I flipped my tail fins once to glide closer, my eyes snaring on the unspeakable evil.

The swirling black water drifted closer. Slowly. Inexorably. The hum of death in the churning current froze my body in fear. I knew I had found what I had been searching for. Dark Water was not a myth; it was real.

The carnivorous Dark Water slowly churned through the ocean, consuming anything in its path. Common sense took hold and shook me from my stupor. I swam to the other side of the coral, turning back around as an evil hiss echoed through the water. I watched in horror as it floated over the beautiful piece of coral I had just marveled at. In a matter of seconds, Dark Water devoured the reef, and the living organism died instantaneously. I gasped as the darkness slowly consumed the crystal-clear water, tainting it with evil.

Tears burned the back of my throat as I turned around, putting as much distance between myself and the abomination I'd just witnessed. My people had to be warned. They had to know the truth. *Dark Water was coming.*

As I swam, a numbness overcame my mind, distracting me from my surroundings. A deadly mistake, I realized almost too late. Dark silhouettes shot through the current, forcing me to pause as my pulse drummed in my ears. My gaze swept across the open ocean, but I saw nothing. Doubt crept in, and I wondered if the shock of finding Dark Water had permanently damaged my mind.

I held my position, relying instead on my instincts. Something was out there—I could feel it. Precious seconds elapsed before I saw it again. Whatever it was moved with lightning speed, and I only knew one thing in the ocean that was capable of moving that fast. Sirens.

My breath caught in my lungs as they moved in closer. There had to be over twenty of them edging closer to me. I prayed they were friends and not foes. A large male moved from the shadows, and relief flooded through me. There was only one siren with flowing pale white hair rivaling that of a pearl and muscles that seemed to have no end.

"Orm!" I gulped as he rushed forward and latched onto my biceps.

His flashing green eyes scanned down the length of my body. "Are you hurt?"

"No, I'm fine," I assured him as I tried to pull from his embrace. His hand slipped to the back of my neck, the pressure increasing with my struggles.

"Do you know what you have done? You have put the entire kingdom in jeopardy. We should be protecting the palace, not out here searching for you." Shame burned in the pit of my stomach as he lashed out at me. "You know it is forbidden to come this close to land. You are the future queen of Aquarius. What if you had been injured or, worse, killed?"

His words stung like a physical slap to my face, reminding me of my daunting, unwanted duties. With Valeria gone, I was next in line for the throne, a looming future I did not want.

I pried away from his intense grip as my anger billowed up like a hydrothermal vent. "And as such, what makes you think you have a right to touch me?"

At my words, his anger waned, and his hands dropped

along with it. His eyes brushed across the ocean floor. "Forgive me. I have been worried sick, and I forgot myself."

I nearly scoffed out loud but managed to swallow it back down. He wasn't fooling anyone with his false pretense of caring. He had been engaged to Valeria, and now that she was gone, he believed he still had a shot at the throne through me. The mere thought churned my stomach.

"Forgive me," he said, attempting to reach for me again. I quickly evaded his touch, which brought a scowl to his otherwise perfect, angular face.

"We don't have time for this," I hissed. "Dark Water is real. I found it."

He glanced back, drawing his white brows together as doubt clouded his eyes. "Rhea." His voice held a subtle warning.

"You doubt my words? I saw it. We have to warn everyone."

"I believe you, but getting you back to safety is at the top of my concerns at the moment," he said as he ushered me toward a mass of armed warriors. They all eyed me, curiosity pulling at their facial features, but no one uttered a word.

For once, I agreed with him. We had to get back as quickly as possible to warn my people.

The swim back was unnervingly quiet. Orm kept close to my side, swimming in the center of our armed security. I snuck a glance at him a few times, but he did not seem interested in engaging me in conversation. As captain of the guard, it was his duty to always maintain tight control. A job he took all too seriously.

I bit my bottom lip as my nerves increased, and the silence stretched. The confirmation that Dark Water was not a myth gnawed at me, and I desperately wanted to speak to someone about it. For someone to alleviate my fears and tell me everything would be all right, even if I knew it wasn't.

"Do you think that Poseidon's death caused this?" Chills tingled across my scales as I spoke the words out loud.

Orm slowed his breakneck speed and stared at me. "I don't know."

His honesty was refreshing for once, putting a crack in his know-it-all demeanor, but it did very little to ease the quaking inside my chest. Poseidon's shocking death sent the Seven Seas into turmoil. There was no protection, no advisory for the creatures that dwell below the ocean's surface, and no one to contain the evil Dark Hydra that resided in the deepest part of the ocean. Without the might of Poseidon, the Dark Hydra had been unleashed, and its deadly Dark Water was spreading throughout the seas. A rumor I had just proven to be true.

"What should we do? Surely, my father will listen to me now that I have proof." I studied Orm's profile before looking around to the other males who swam alongside us.

"You shouldn't worry about it, just like you shouldn't have ventured out looking for trouble." He cleared his throat and swam faster to get ahead of me. Half the soldiers followed after Orm, and the other half crowded around me as if they feared I would disappear again if left unchecked. Given the chance, I probably would.

I stopped swimming, and Orm paused with a look of frustration.

"Shouldn't worry about it? How do you not worry about Dark Water? The entire existence of the ocean and all who live in it are in jeopardy!" I desperately looked around, staring into the faces of the other sirens, but they quickly downcast their eyes, refusing to meet my worried gaze.

Orm inhaled like he was trying to school his response. "I'll talk with the king. I don't want you worrying about it." He raised his hand as if he intended to touch my face, but I pulled back so violently that his hand stilled in the water before dropping back to his side.

I floated there in stunned silence, my mouth gaping open like a codfish. He couldn't be serious. How does one not worry about Dark Water? I was too shocked to speak to him again about it. What good would it do anyway? Obviously, neither he nor the soldiers intended to discuss the matter further with me. Anger surged through me like a raging storm. I continued toward Aquarius without another glance in his direction. He wasn't in charge, even though he liked to think he was. The one I needed to speak to was my father, King Manta. He could no longer dismiss Dark Water as mere gossip. It was real, and it was coming.

CHAPTER 2
RHEA

Fatigue settled in my bones like an anchor, but fear and concern for my people made me push through my exhaustion. The faster I could get home, the sooner we could form a plan to keep our people safe. Orm and his army had to increase speed to keep up with my intense pace. Relief washed over me like a calm tide when my home finally came into view. Orm left me behind and rushed through the shell-encrusted gates of Aquarius. That slimy eel was probably racing to inform my father about my discovery, but maybe that was for the best. He seemed to listen to Orm better than he did me. *Stupid male egos.*

As I entered the palace, a hushed silence greeted me. No one dared to meet my gaze as I quickly swam toward my father's throne room. The weight of shame gnawed at my insides, a reminder that my disappearance had stirred up turmoil throughout the entire kingdom. Well, they could be angry with me all they wanted. Now that we knew the threat was real, we could find a way to protect our people.

I threw the throne room door open without being summoned inside. I was already in trouble; what did the neglect of formality matter at a time like this? I eyed my father and mother as I rushed forward. Their faces were harsh and unforgiving. Orm was tucked close to my father's side, observing me intently as I approached the throne.

"What have you to say for yourself?" My father's voice boomed and echoed off the sand-colored rafters that held up the ceiling of the massive throne room.

My throat bobbed, irritation settling in my chest at his question. "Father, please. I had to know if the threat of Dark Water was a myth or not." My voice rang a little louder than I had intended, and the mere mention of Dark Water had the officials and court attendees gasping.

My father's eyes widened to the size of a dwarf pufferfish. Schooling his anger in the face of onlookers, he rose from his throne and approached me. He gripped my upper arm and pulled me closer so that he could whisper in my ear. "My patience with you is running thin," he warned. "You will not speak of Dark Water again, and if you dare to go close to land again, I will do much worse than simply taking away what little freedom you have."

My gaze shot to Orm's. The little seaworm had already squealed on me and told my father I had been close to land.

Tears leaked from my eyes as I yanked away from my father's grasp. "Someone needs to speak about it! We are in danger! Something has to be done! I saw it with my own eyes. It's real!"

I was near panic. Why could no one see the jeopardy we were in? Did my father truly believe ignoring the problem would make it go away? I glanced around as whispers broke out among the sirens at court. The wrinkles around my father's eyes intensified, and a vein throbbed on his forehead. His gaze bore into me, a silent storm brewing in the depths of his irises. The court hushed into an uneasy silence as he floated before me.

"That's enough, Rhea." My mother rose from her seat, casually interrupting the spectacle my father and I were about to make. "We are preparing a feast tonight to welcome you back home. The entire kingdom is looking forward to this celebration, and I will not allow you to be tardy." My mother pulled on my arm and ushered me out of the throne room, away from the piercing, disapproving glares of my father and Orm.

I bit my tongue so hard to keep from arguing with them further that the metallic taste of blood filled my mouth. This conversation wasn't over, but quarreling with my father in front of his court was disrespect of the worst kind.

How could they even entertain the idea of a party with Dark Water threatening everything in existence? I shoved the rising tide of my emotions back down as I rushed toward my room. I gently pushed my bedroom door ajar, hoping for a few moments of peace to figure out what I would do next, but my little sister pounced on me, leaving me with no respite.

"Where have you been? I have been worried sick," Meleea yelled, latching onto my arm and dragging me into the room.

"I…"

"Never mind," she interrupted, pushing me in front of the vanity mirror crafted from delicate conch shells and proceeding to shower me with her feminine wiles. She skillfully wove a comb through my auburn locks. Then she focused on enhancing my features, adorning my lips with a deep shade of crimson, and artfully etching intricate patterns on my skin using our celebration ink. I sat there, enduring her relentless attention, confused as to why she was so concerned with my appearance.

After she was content with her efforts, I gazed at my reflection in the mirror. My hair cascaded down my back in flawless waves, and the makeup and intricate skin art she applied were truly exquisite. I looked like a princess on the outside, but on the inside, I was a fraud. I wasn't like Meleea, who reveled in the glam and attention of our court. She embodied the word princess, and I, the rebel who never did as she was told and never lived up to my father's hopes.

As I sat there, the weight of expectation pressed upon me like an invisible pearl crown. The court would soon be filled with nobles and sirens of import, all expecting the poised princess they believed me to be. Little did they know that beneath all these layers of shimmering paint was a spirit yearning for freedom.

"You look beautiful." Meleea smiled, brushing her hand against my cheek. "Even I can see that you do not want this, but we can't choose the life we are born into. It's time you lived up to your duties and stopped running off."

My eyes rose to meet her emerald ones, and then swept over her beautiful sandy-colored hair, so much like my mother's and Valeria's. "You sound just like father."

She nudged me playfully. "I'll take that as a compliment."

A knock at my door brought my head back around. "Enter."

Our mother floated in, looking every bit the queen she truly was. She stopped behind me with a sad smile tugging at the corners of her lips. "You are going to be the death of me," she said, her words wrapped in a mixture of concern and affection. Running her fingers through my hair, her laugh lines became even more evident with her smile, betraying her years and wisdom. "When will you learn that these little excursions of yours are foolish and dangerous?" She offered me her hand, and I took it, letting her pull me from the chair.

She grabbed Meleea's hand with her other. "Come my lovelies, we have a party to attend."

As we ventured through the grand halls of the palace, I felt a twinge of guilt for the worry etched on her face. Worry I was getting ready to intensify. "Mother?"

Her eyes sparkled with a warm smile as she motioned for me to proceed.

"I was not lying when I said I found Dark Water." She stopped immediately, casting a cautious gaze to Meleea, who had paled at my declaration. I silently cursed myself for not guarding my younger sister against such horrifying news. "Father refuses to listen to me. We have to do something," I rushed on before she could reprimand me.

Mother, ever the composed ruler, broke her silence with a measured tone. "You have always been just like him. That's why the two of you do not get along." She paused so long I feared she was done with the conversation. "Your father does not plan on staying long at the party. When he makes his move to leave, I suggest you speak to him about it." She smiled, pulling a gaping-mouthed Meleea behind her and into the mass of sirens waiting outside.

"Believe me, I will," I promised as I composed myself and ventured into the crowd.

The sirens were in an uproar, and I tried to muster a smile

as I made my way through the multitude. On a raised platform, my family awaited my arrival, so I glided toward them with deliberate grace. In my paranoia, I kept stealing glances at the horizon, expecting to see Dark Water descending upon our city at any second, but the water remained clear.

I paused, hovering in the current as my mind jumbled with confusion. Why was Orm up on the platform with my family? Even as the captain of the guard, that status did not afford him such privileges.

My pulse jumped as Orm reached down, drawing me to his side on the platform. His touch tingled against my skin, stinging like the tentacles of a jellyfish. I started to pull away, but my father's heated gaze shifted in my direction, shutting down that thought.

He glanced across the mass of sirens and spoke in a commandeering voice. "It is with great happiness that I announce the betrothal of my eldest daughter, Rhea, to the captain of our guard, Orm. The future of our kingdom."

A wave of cheers reverberated through the ocean, drowning my senses in a paralyzing numbness. The celebration clashed sharply with the churning turmoil within me. Bile surged up the back of my throat, threatening to undo my composure. With a determined swallow, I suppressed the rising discomfort, refusing to embarrass myself in front of the entire kingdom by spewing the contents of my stomach.

"Smile," Orm hissed in my ear, penetrating my shock.

I plastered on my best fake smile and raised my arm to wave to the well-wishers. For now, I was forced to play my role, but later, I would give my family a piece of my mind. So, this was the reason behind Meleea's makeover and my mother's saddened eyes.

In seconds, the entire court was busy with servers who carried mounds of food. The celebration quickly died down as the sirens stuffed their mouths. I would normally join them; the fare of fresh fish and seaweed rolls looked delectable, but my father's announcement of my unexpected engagement had soured my stomach.

I pulled my hand from Orm's as I sought my father. Finally, I found him hiding in a dark corner away from the mass of sirens. I started toward him but was stopped by Orm grabbing my wrist.

He smiled down at me. "I hope the news of our engagement is pleasing to you." He had the audacity to touch his slimy lips to the back of my hand.

My skin crawled beneath his touch. With practiced grace, I slid my hand from his grasp, even though my mind screamed for me to peel the lips from his face with my claws. "It sickens me, to be quite honest, and I will not allow it," I whispered, baring my teeth at him, hoping it appeared as a sweet smile in front of the people who crowded around us.

Orm gently slid a finger beneath my chin, forcing my gaze back to his. "You have no choice in the matter," he purred, bending down to kiss my brow. My body shook all over as hot anger coursed through my extremities. "Don't forget to save me the first dance." Orm's smug smile did unspeakable things to my already queasy stomach.

I crammed my raging emotions down as deep as they would go before lifting my eyes and frantically scanning the mass of sirens, searching for Father. When I feared that he had retired for the night, I caught a fleeting glimpse of his tail as he ducked back into the palace. I smiled to myself at my luck as I swam off after him.

I paused at the door, casting a cautious glance around to ensure no prying eyes were watching, and then discreetly followed him inside. The impending argument weighed heavily on my conscience. Whenever he and I clashed, it rarely ended well. Hopefully, the noise from the party would drown out our fighting.

"Father," I called to him, and he stopped and turned toward me.

He swam closer to me, and I swallowed past the lump forming in my throat. He blew bubbles out of his nose and slowly floated back toward me. "Rhea, please. At least let me have one good night's sleep before we go head-to-head about your engagement to Orm."

"Surprisingly, that is the least of my concerns at the moment."

He gritted his teeth. "Before you start, let me warn you: if you mention Dark Water again, I will not be held responsible for my actions."

"But…"

"Besides, Orm has told me everything I need to know."

After he rudely interrupted me and then turned away as if dismissing me, my anger surged another notch. Fueled by frustration, I swiftly maneuvered to block his path with a quick swish of my tail. I was determined to make him listen, even if it meant arguing with him for the rest of the night.

"I want to know what you intend to do about Dark Water. It's real, Father!"

"Rhea," he warned and glanced around, as if ensuring no one was around to hear me.

"I have a right to know, as does the rest of the kingdom. It will bring everyone peace if you just tell us what you intend to do!" My emotions were all over the place and I was having a hard time keeping them in check.

My father's face softened as he met my eyes. "There's nothing I can do." As his words took root, a sudden burst of coldness expanded in my core.

I blinked at him a few times, and he pinched the bridge of his nose. When my gaze rose to meet his again, he continued, "There's nothing I can do, Rhea. I have tried. Not even my trident fazed the Dark Water." My hope sank like a ship going down in a storm. He knew all along that Dark Water was real. "That's why I have been so tight-lipped on the matter. It cannot be stopped. I didn't want everyone living with the fear of knowing that we would all die soon. It's your responsibility now to hold your head high and continue on as if nothing is wrong—to uphold morale."

"Nothing can be done..." I repeated, my mind struggling to fully grasp his words.

"Rhea." He gripped my shoulders and lightly shook me to gain my attention. "You have to be strong. As the Princess of Aquarius, it is your responsibility to shoulder the burden of the people so they don't have to. I don't want anyone else to know about this. I tried to protect you as well, but you are so stubborn." His eyes reflected his unspoken emotions, and I knew his words were true. He inhaled a sharp breath. "If only..."

"If only what, Father?"

"Nothing. I'm sorry you learned of this on the night of your betrothal celebration. I wanted you and the rest of the kingdom to have something to look forward to." He turned to leave again as I idly floated in the current.

There was something he wasn't telling me. I felt it. He

might be more mature than me, but I would not accept a doomed fate and simply belly up and die. I glanced at his retreating back and swallowed past the dryness in my throat. Sirens could not be swayed by another's song, yet I had discovered years ago that my song held unusual power. I had carefully guarded this secret, keeping it hidden from all. But now, if I were to uncover the truths my father was so unwilling to share, I had no choice but to take the risk.

My lips parted, and my siren's melody filled the dimly lit hallway. As my father turned, his eyes immediately clouded with enchantment. I couldn't predict his reaction if he uncovered my actions, as I was breaking sacred siren laws just by attempting to influence another of our kind.

I held my breath, praying that my deceit would be worth the risk and he would answer me. "Tell me everything you know about stopping Dark Water."

Confusion washed over his face, and I could tell he was trying to fight my melody, but then the words tumbled from his lips. "There is a rumor about a locket around the neck of a gorgon. It contains a piece of Poseidon's heart. With it, there might be a small chance of stopping Dark Water."

Hope dared to flare in my chest at my father's words. Could it be possible? Was a small piece of Poseidon still in this world? "Where?" I could barely contain the urgency in my voice.

"Eel Cavern. The sea witch, she is the only one who might know where to find it. She knows more about the upper world than anyone I know."

His response sent a chill coursing through me and ignited my curiosity. The legends painted the sea witch as the epitome of evil. Her dark magic was both forbidden and feared. In truth, I wasn't entirely convinced of her existence, until now.

"She's real?"

I did not realize I had spoken the words aloud until my father spoke. "She's very real and dangerous. I banished her from the kingdom for practicing forbidden sorcery before you were born."

I wanted to know more, but his hazy eyes were becoming clearer and I knew I was running out of time. I had the information I needed anyway. As my siren song gradually subsided, my father blinked several times until his eyes regained clarity. Once I was sure he was back to his usual self, I lightly brushed a kiss on his cheek and started off toward Eel Cavern before anyone realized I was missing.

I managed to slip past the crowd and reach the gates without anyone noticing me. A quick glance over my shoulder revealed the looming figure of my father, engaged in conversation with his subjects, seemingly oblivious to my deceit. Anxious, I gnawed at my lower lip as I slipped through the gates. I watched the top of the imposing structure, careful not to let the guards see me.

"Where do you think you are going?" Dread gripped my stomach as I turned to see Meleea stalking from the shadows.

I rushed to her side, shoving her back inside the safety of Aquarius's walls. My heart raced, and I spoke in hushed urgency, "Eel Cavern. I have to stop Dark Water."

Meleea's eyes narrowed, a mixture of concern and disbelief flickering in their depths. "It's not your responsibility to save everyone. It's too dangerous."

"I know," I interrupted, the weight of my choices pressing

on me. "But I have to try." With those words, I turned away, desperately hoping that she wouldn't try to stop me.

The cool current hung heavy with uncertainty as I slipped beyond the city walls, leaving behind the safety of Aquarius. The looming threat of Dark Water echoed in my thoughts, a relentless hum urging me toward Eel Cavern.

CHAPTER 3
RHEA

A s I drew nearer to Eel Cavern, the ocean's chill seemed to intensify. A shiver coursed down my spine, extending to the tips of my fins. At that moment, I couldn't tell whether it was caused by the icy embrace of the water or the apprehension of encountering the sea witch. It was likely a potent mixture of both. My heart banged loudly against my ribcage at the mere thought of defying yet another of my father's rules, but what did it matter? I had already broken the most sacred law of the sirens. How much more trouble could I be in by going to parlay with a sea witch?

The lush, vibrant vegetation gradually surrendered to a grim terrain of jagged rocks and menacing boulders. The waters grew somber, as if the sun itself refused to cast its light upon this forsaken part of the sea. My certainty in being on the right path deepened as eels cautiously emerged from the rocky crevices, their dagger-like teeth gleaming menacingly. As much as I tried to avert my attention from them, I couldn't help but be drawn to their disturbing presence, their beady black eyes fixated on my passage.

Finally, I came upon the entrance of a colossal cave, an

unmistakable sign that I had arrived at my destination. I drew in a deep breath, attempting to summon the remnants of my courage before daring to enter its dark maw.

"Hello?" My voice shook as I was swallowed by the cave's darkness.

A sudden movement to my left caused a tight constriction in my chest.

"To what do I owe the pleasure of your visit, princess?" a voice called from behind me.

Terror crept up my fins. The speaker had stealthily approached from behind, effectively cutting off my escape route. Summoning a deep breath, I slowly pivoted, my eyes fixing on a silhouette drifting through the murky water. The dim light failed to unveil any details.

"How do you know who I am?" I asked as the being drifted closer to me.

A sigh of relief escaped my lips as the figure swam past me and deeper into the cave. With its departure, a profound sense of ease settled over me, now that it no longer blocked the entrance.

"I am Morgana, the sea witch, dear. Ask me a harder question," she singsonged.

I nervously gnawed on my lower lip, my apprehension growing by the second. "Very well. How do I find the gorgon that has a piece of Poseidon's heart in its locket?" With a sense of urgency, I plunged headlong into the matter, for there was no time for pleasantries or idle talk.

At my inquiry, she stopped moving. "Now, that is an interesting question."

I didn't miss the sarcasm in her voice.

I gasped as a spark of magic surged through the cave. The

eerie, dim cavern transformed, bathed in an otherworldly green glow. Blinking rapidly, I allowed my eyes to adapt to this newfound brightness.

I struggled to keep my mouth from falling open as I could now see her features. Inky black tentacles drifted around her, forming a twisted, aquatic halo. She appeared elderly and frail, with a sickly paleness. Her skeletal frame made it all too easy to count each rib along her side. With a graceful flick, she swept her flowing mane of white hair over her shoulder, unveiling more of her pasty gray skin.

I caught myself gawking at her and quickly averted my eyes. My attention shifted to the smooth cave walls, which were adorned with countless shelves, each crammed with an assortment of potions and mysterious objects I did not recognize. With measured movement, I eased closer to a particular shelf adorned with glowing magical bubbles. There had to be over fifty of these shimmering orbs.

"Gorgeous, aren't they?" she asked, plucking one from the shelf and holding it out for me to see.

I leaned in closer, captivated by the enchanting spectacle. The lower portion of the bubble was filled with water, while a miniature ship floated serenely on top, mirroring its existence on the ocean's surface. Startled, I shifted my gaze back to hers. She offered me an insincere smile, her jagged, razor-sharp teeth grazing across her blood-red lips.

"Are these real?" I asked in awe as the tales of her escapades came flooding back to me.

I had heard fables of how she sank ships and of her deep hatred for the above dwellers, but it looked as if she had been collecting them, not sinking them.

"Of course. Can't you see the skeletons of the sailors who shriveled up to nothing after I trapped them in my magic?"

I peered inside the bubble again and then reared back, disgust pulling at my lips. I hadn't noticed the bodies before. They were nothing but skin and bones scattered among the ship. She must be more powerful than I could have possibly imagined to cast a spell like this.

"Enough of my treasures. Tell me why the princess of the sirens seeks information about a gorgon and a locket?" she asked as she delicately laid her trinket back on the shelf.

I held my breath and tried not to move as she reached up and ran her bony fingers through my hair.

"My father told me that with the locket, there was a chance of stopping the Dark Hydra and its Dark Water," I said barely above a whisper, observing her with careful eyes.

Something dark and menacing flashed across her face. I desperately wanted to pull away from her touch but refused to show her my unease. The sea witch smiled at me, dropped the strand of my hair, and returned to the darkest corner of the cave.

"Is any of this true about a gorgon and a piece of Poseidon's heart?" I asked again, summoning additional courage as I ventured further into the shadows. My confidence grew with each passing moment, for it seemed she had no intention of harming me. At least, not at the moment.

"The king told you this?" she asked, interest lining her tone as she ignored my question a second time.

My hesitation did not go unnoticed, and her eyes darted to mine. I sensed a pulse of something I could only assume was magic, weaving through the water. It delicately glided along the currents, its ethereal touch lightly brushing against my skin.

"You are a wicked little thing, aren't you?" She smiled and ventured closer to me from out of the shadows. "Don't you know it is punishable by death for a siren to influence another with her song?"

My spine stiffened as she revealed my sin. Fear lodged in my throat, preventing me from speaking a single word. I wanted to deny her accusation, but what good would it do? Her magic had already brought my treachery to light. I swallowed past the dryness on my tongue as she continued to venture closer.

"How powerful you must be to influence the King of the Sirens. Never have I heard of such." She stopped a few inches before me and touched my hair again. I could not fathom her fascination with my hair, which made me uncomfortable. She stared into my eyes as if considering me.

"Hades created the Dark Hydra to terrorize the oceans," she said. "Poseidon trapped it centuries ago in the deepest part of the seas. Only he could stop the Dark Hydra."

My muscles quivered as I anxiously awaited her next words. I remained perfectly still, fearing that any movement on my part might cause her to cease speaking.

"Your father was correct, of course. There is a small piece of Poseidon's heart left in this world." She released my hair and leaned back against the cavern wall.

"Where?" I exclaimed, drawing nearer to her.

"That first bit of information was a free history lesson. The next will cost you." Her voice was sinister and filled with hate. The little glimmer of hope she baited me with was instantly snatched away.

"What is it you want?" I asked, watching her every movement.

She eased from her spot and edged closer toward me, stopping when she was inches from my face. "Once you get the locket and use it to stop the Dark Hydra, you are to bring it to me." She held out her hand, intending to shake mine.

I immediately retreated a few feet. "What do you want with the locket?"

"What difference is it to you?" she gibed.

"It will do me no good to stop one evil only to create another," I answered, forcing calm into my tone. I knew she was cunning, but I would not allow her to trick me that easily.

"Smart and beautiful. How refreshing." She paused and considered me again before she continued. "Did you know I was once a beautiful siren?"

Shock rendered me speechless as I absentmindedly shook my head. My eyes wandered over her form and tentacles in disbelief.

"I want that piece of Poseidon's heart to turn me back into my true form."

"How is that possible?" I sputtered.

"Let's just say playing with dark magic has its consequences." She turned away, indicating she was done with the conversation.

Panic welled up in my chest like a sponge soaking up water. Was it really such a terrible idea to let her return to being a siren? Maybe. I couldn't begin to comprehend how her magic could be so vile that it had transformed her into such a monstrosity or if that was the true reason she wanted the locket.

"You will perish as well if the Dark Water reaches you." I

was desperate at this point, trying to threaten her with the approaching Dark Water.

She threw her head back and laughed. Her evil pitch sent a shiver down to my soul. She straightened up and lashed out at me with her tentacles. I moved to avoid her, but she had much more speed than I would ever credit her for. She grabbed both of my wrists and pulled me close until my nose touched hers.

"I have been exiled in this cave for eons, wasting away to nothing. Do you not think that I long for death?" She hissed in my face. "Besides, Dark Water has no dominion over me. I am too powerful."

I held perfectly still, refusing to flinch, even though the pressure she applied to my wrists threatened to snap them in two. Her eyes bored into mine, but I refused to relent. This monster would not terrorize me. She slowly pulled her tentacles from my wrist, leaving the embossment of her suckers on my skin. She threw out her hand again.

"Do we have a deal, princess? Or will you allow everyone to suffer because you are afraid to make a deal with a sea witch?"

I stared down at her hand like it was a great white shark. My gut told me to leave this place at once and forget all about this nightmare, but I could not let everyone perish. I wondered for a fleeting second if my siren song would work against her, but something within warned me not to try. I could always lie. Once I had the information I needed and left here in one piece, would she truly seek me out for vengeance? The answer to my question stared me in the face.

"We have a deal." I reached up, clasped her hand, and gave it an unsure squeeze.

A smile pulled at the corners of her mouth. "Around the

neck of the gorgon, Medusa, hangs a locket, and in that locket is a piece of Poseidon's heart, just as your father said. It's the only piece of Poseidon left in this world. Get the locket, find the Dark Hydra, and kill the thing with it." She smiled, shrugging her shoulders. "Then bring it back to me, as per our deal."

I scoffed. She made the task sound like a leisurely swim on a warm summer day. I was not so naive that I had not heard the name Medusa. When I opened my mouth, nothing came out. I had so many questions that they all jumbled on my tongue.

"How exactly am I supposed to find Medusa? She is more myth than legend. No one knows her whereabouts. No one has ever seen her and lived to tell about it." With each word I spoke, my voice rose an octave as my panic reached new heights.

"Never say never." She smiled. "There is a rumor floating around the human world that one man encountered Medusa and lived to tell about it."

"A man?" I repeated in disbelief. "How do you know this?"

"I've been known to walk among the humans," she answered vaguely.

"Who is this man, and where do I find him?" I eased toward her, refusing to ask what she meant by walking among the humans. Some questions were best left unanswered.

"Blackheart Kai," she said, and my heart flopped in my chest like a fish on dry land.

"The sea monster hunter?" I sputtered. Bubbles flew from my nose as I tried hard to breathe.

Blackheart Kai was a living nightmare for all creatures beneath the ocean's surface. His kind was the very reason my father prohibited anyone in Aquarius from venturing to the surface. People like him had wreaked havoc, leading to the mass slaughter of hundreds of our beautiful sea brethren. Since we, as sea creatures, lived longer and were slow to reproduce, they were single-handedly pushing all of us toward extinction. The malicious smile on the sea witch's face only grew wider, relishing in my distress.

"There's no one else who knows Medusa's whereabouts?"

"No," she answered, easing back into the shadows.

"Where can I find him?"

"He sails the Caribbean Sea, or so my pets say." An enormous eel eased its way from the shadows, and she lovingly stroked her long nails down its body. A tremor rippled down my scales as its beady eyes watched me.

I started easing my way out of the cave before the situation became grimmer. "The Caribbean Sea is massive. How will I find him?" I stopped at the entrance of the cave, peering back at her.

"Don't worry, dear. If you enter his territory, he will find you and most likely kill you before you even have a chance to speak."

Her wicked laughter lingered in the currents as I rushed from the cave. Fear clung to my every movement just thinking about facing Blackheart Kai, the terror of the seas. Yet, driven by the urgency to protect my kingdom, I ventured into the unknown waters, even though my determination flickered like a luminous jellyfish about to burn out.

CHAPTER 4
KAI

The man before me squirmed in his seat as I narrowed my gaze on the worn leather bag with coins.

"You insult me if you believe I will hunt down a leviathan for that amount of coin," I scoffed, sliding that bag back toward him.

Everyone in the dimly lit tavern seemed to hold their breath as my words hung in the air. The clanking of tankards stopped and the distant chatter fell into a hushed murmur, all attention now focused on the uneasy exchange between the man and me.

He nervously licked his lips, realizing that my services didn't come cheap. "Please, it's all I have. No ship has been able to get to Andros without that damned monster attacking it. It's costing me and several men our livelihoods." He slammed the tankard of ale down on the table, sloshing the golden liquid over the edges.

I pushed away from the table, the chair legs scraping across the shabby wooden floor. "Tell your sob story to someone who cares. My price is double that."

The man stood abruptly, gripping the bag between

29

whitened knuckles, and my hand instinctively went to the hilt of my sword. He quickly realized his error and slowly sat back down. "I'll be able to pay you the rest once I can get my merchant ship to Andros." His hands shook as he desperately pushed the satchel back toward me.

A fight broke out in the corner of the tavern. Hoots and hollers followed shortly after as my attention was pulled from the pitiful man before me. Two men were brawling in the center of a makeshift circle of onlookers. I watched in fascination for a few seconds, only to realize it was one of my crew members, Flynt. Sprays of stale-smelling alcohol sprinkled across my face as the surrounding men became increasingly unruly while they cheered on the fight.

I glanced back at the man sitting at my table, who had gone stark white with fear. His clothing was a patchwork of tattered garments stitched together, but he was clean and seemed well-fed. Based on his meager attire, I had my doubts about getting the rest of my money. His trembling hands clutched the frayed satchel. Despite the weariness in his clothes, a glint of resilience lingered in his eyes, a spark that refused to be extinguished by the shadows of his circumstances.

Snatching the bag from the table, I shoved it into my coat pocket. "Be gone with you," I said, stepping toward the fight.

"Does that mean you are taking the job?" His voice trembled as I turned back around.

I met his gaze with steely determination. "I expect the rest of my money the next time I am in port."

"How will I know when you have re-returned?" he stuttered.

"You'll know," I replied cryptically, turning my attention back to the brawl.

The instant the fistfight turned deadly, blood drummed in my ears. I pressed closer to the show as the man who was losing to Flynt pulled out a dagger. He dove for Flynt to rip him from stem to stern. His hand came crashing down, but I caught his arm in midair.

As I squeezed his wrist without mercy, the man holding the knife yelped in pain, went down on his knees, and dropped the blade he had clutched between his whitened knuckles.

The dim light flickered over the tense faces of the onlookers, their eyes shifting between me and the man on his knees. The man struggled against my grip, his eyes widening with a mixture of surprise and fear. Caught off guard, Flynt took a step back, his gaze darting between the dagger and the unexpected interference.

I stared down at the miscreant before me. "We may be pirates, but we do uphold some decorum in our fights, and it appears to me that you tried to win by cheating." A sudden hush enveloped the tavern, a collective gasp lingering in the air as I held the assailant's wrist in a viselike grip.

"Please," the man begged as I further twisted his wrist. The snapping of bones and the man's cries rang in my ears.

"Have some decency. Don't beg. Die like a man." I struck out at the man and slit his throat with my cutlass. His body fell and struck the floor with a loud thud. "Clean up this mess," I thundered and retreated back into the shadows.

Two men rushed forward and dragged the body outside while everyone else continued on as if a man had not just been slain before their eyes. Once back at my table, I noticed a spindly woman attempting to press her way through the dispersing crowd.

I usually wouldn't pay anyone like her any attention, but something about her sparked my curiosity. The haggard woman navigated through the remaining men with an air of determination. Her worn clothes suggested a life of hardship, but something about the unusual glow of her otherwise wrinkly skin held my attention.

As she reached my table, she cast a sneaky glance around before leaning in, her voice barely above a whisper. "I wish to parlay with your captain," she said plainly. "I have a proposition for him."

My eyes rose to meet hers over the tankard of ale at my lips. With a quick jerk of my head, I motioned for her to be removed from my sight. I had no patience for any more begging or pleading this night.

"Wait!" she called as one of my men tried to shove her toward the door. "At least hear my proposition. You won't be sorry!" she screamed as she hopelessly leaned all her meager body weight against a man who was double her size.

With a frustrated huff, I sat my cup back on the wobbly table. "Very well, Cael. Let her pass."

She rushed forward and plopped down in the chair across from me. My eyebrow shot up at her audacity.

"I have a job for you—" she started, but I immediately cut her off.

"I don't take jobs from sea witches." I waited to see if she would confirm or deny my suspicion.

Her eyes gleamed with a mixture of mischief and frustration. "How could you possibly know that I am a sea witch?"

She glanced down at her tattered clothes as if to ensure her disguise was still in place.

I regarded her with skepticism, surprised that she so readily admitted to me what she was. My fingers drummed rhythmically on the table as I attempted to control my anger. The reputation of sea witches was rife with deceit and treachery, their motives often as murky as the depths they hailed from. But a flicker of curiosity danced within me, urging me to hear her out. "I haven't survived this long by being naive. I know more about your world than you could possibly imagine." An evil smirk pulled on my lips, and she sat back in the chair, completely flabbergasted.

"I'll pay you well," she insisted.

"I don't want your money." I motioned for Cael to step forward to throw her out.

"Wait! I don't offer money!" With swift hands, she reached into a bag made of seaweed and pulled out a glowing orb filled halfway with sparkling sea water.

My eyes latched onto her offering, and I held up my hand, stopping Cael. "You offer me a trinket?" I growled.

"This is no trinket. Take a closer look, pirate." She shoved the magical bubble before me, and I peered closer. A victorious smile brushed her lips when my eyes widened with wonder. She knew she had ensnared my attention.

"The Wraith." She supplied the answer to the question burning on the tip of my tongue. "They say the hull was carved from the bones of the leviathan, making it impenetrable to Dark Water." She ran her fingers lovingly along the smooth surface of the bubble, as if caressing a cherished relic.

"Dark Water is a myth," I scoffed, attempting to quell the unease that crept into my thoughts.

A wicked smile twisted the corners of her lips. "Oh, it's real, and it's coming."

I leaned back into my chair and crossed my arms over my chest as she continued.

"Think about it. You will be the only human capable of sailing the Seven Seas once Dark Water takes over." She let a cackle slip from her lips and placed her hand over her mouth to stop it. "Think of the power. If you do this little job for me, I will release the Wraith from my enchanted bubble, restore it to scale, and it will be yours."

Something akin to excitement drummed in my veins as I leaned forward. "What's the job?"

"Nothing a grand hunter like you couldn't handle in his sleep. I just want you to kill a siren," she said as innocently as possible.

"That's it? Just kill a siren, and you will give me this legendary ship? I'm not buying it," I answered while sipping my ale. If she thought to pull one over on me, she had another thing coming.

"Fine, she may be the Princess of Aquarius…"

I set my tankard back on the table.

"And I want you to take her to Medusa…"

For a moment, shock rippled through me, a jolt that I tried to conceal. My eyes widened before I could regain control, and I took a steadying breath, attempting to cloak my surprise with a mask of indifference.

"And I believe she is the only being who could steal Medusa's locket. I want you to take her to Medusa, let her get the locket, steal the locket from her, kill her, and then bring the locket to me." She smiled as if she hadn't just requested that my crew and I accept a suicide mission.

I threw my head back and laughed. The rich rumble echoed throughout the tavern, drawing prying eyes in our direction. I reached across the table, picked up the bubble, and held it closer to my face. I marveled at the stunning ship gliding over the entrapped waves within the iridescent sphere.

"An illusion." I chuckled, skepticism lingering in my eyes. "You'll need more than pretty tricks to sway me."

The sea witch's expression remained composed, though a glint of frustration flickered in her eyes. "Appearances can be deceiving, but the power of this ship is very real. Take the offer or leave it, but time is not on your side."

The noise in the tavern gradually subsided, leaving a charged atmosphere in its wake. I leaned back in my chair, the tankard of ale now forgotten. I was known for my brash decisions and could not deny that her offer was more than tempting, no matter how outlandish the job seemed.

"You have a deal, witch," I said, placing the bubble on the table before her. She collected it and shoved it back in her bag. "But I warn you…if you even think to double-cross me, I will hunt you down, decapitate you, and hang your head on the bow of my ship for all to see." I held out my hand, intending for her to shake it.

The sea witch studied my outstretched hand for a moment, her calculating gaze meeting mine. After a tense pause, she extended her hand, a sly smile playing on her lips.

"Deal," she replied, the echo of our pact settling in the air like a deep-sea current.

As our hands clasped in a shaky alliance, the atmosphere in the tavern shifted. Having witnessed the exchange, the onlookers returned to their drinks and conversations, oblivious to the agreement unfolding between us.

She rose to leave, but I stopped her. "How will I find this princess?" I inquired, curiosity lining my tone.

"Don't worry, Captain. When you see her, you will know. You have never seen anything that looks quite like her, and besides…" She stepped closer to me. "She is on her way to you as we speak."

CHAPTER 5
KAI

A sneer pulled at my lips as I watched the witch slink out of the tavern. Allowing her to leave this wretched place in one piece was a miracle in itself. Sea witches, with their eerie powers, made my skin crawl. The moment she revealed her ship encased in a bubble, I recognized her as the sinister creature who had plagued sailors and their vessels for longer than I'd walked this Earth. She was the stuff of legends and nightmares, a terror of the Seven Seas. I never anticipated she would seek me out, bearing a request.

I must have been the greatest fool ever to have entertained an offer from a sea witch. However, when she dangled the Wraith before my eyes, my mouth began to water, and all reason and caution sailed away with the wind.

The Wraith was a legend, a ship whispered about in hushed tones, long believed to be lost to the unforgiving sea. Yet, there she was, presented to me as if on a silver platter. So what if I started a war with the siren king for slaughtering his daughter? With the Wraith, he would have to catch me first. The prospect of possessing such an elusive ship had ignited a fire in my soul, one that no threat, no matter how ominous, could extinguish.

Cael came up beside me with a stern look on his face. "Do you truly intend on accepting this suicide mission?"

"I intend to get my hands on that ship," I clarified. "Now, whether or not I do everything else she requested of me is yet to be seen."

Cael sat down in the seat the witch had recently vacated and stared into my eyes. "Seems to me she's got you over a barrel. That one is cunning. I don't know how you intend on tricking her into giving you that ship without following through on her other demands."

I usually would not allow any of my crew members to question my motives, but Cael had been my friend long before we knew how to sail, and I trusted his judgment, not that I intended to listen to it. He was also my first mate, which allowed him some leeway.

Cael's skepticism was evident as he leaned back in his seat. "Tangling with Medusa sounds like nothing but trouble," he remarked, shaking his head.

"We'll cross that ocean when we get there." I stood, and when I did, all my crew members' eyes shot to me. No one grumbled or dared complain when I motioned for them to move out. It was a day ahead of schedule, but we had a new job to do, so I planned to set sail with the tide.

My boots thumped across the pier as I headed for the dinghy. Several of the small boats were piled high with my men, and in a matter of seconds, we paddled back toward the ship. I scaled the rope ladder and started yelling orders as soon as my feet hit the deck of my ship.

"Weigh anchor and prepare to sail," I boomed across the deck.

"Heading, Cap'n?" Cael yelled from the helm.

My gaze swept across the vast expanse of the ocean, tracing the ship's graceful progress as it effortlessly cleaved through the rolling waves. "A hefty sum has been offered to kill a leviathan that has been lurking around the Bahamas. It was last sighted near the island of Andros." I could see the greed and excitement in the crew's eyes as I announced our next target. "And if we happen to run into a siren on the way, we will take her as well," I said with a devious smirk.

"A siren this far north?" Flynt scoffed as he tightened the jigging.

"That's what I've been told." I looked toward Cael, who still wore a sober expression on his face. I had no intention of telling anyone else about my encounter with the sea witch and what she wanted us to do. Sometimes, the less my crew knew, the better.

My gaze danced across the surface of the water once again. The sea witch didn't give much detail on the whereabouts of the siren princess, only that she was looking for me. I had to stay on my toes. I despised surprises, especially when they took the cunning form of a siren. With a mere song, she could lead my entire crew to a watery grave, a fate I was determined to avoid.

As the ship ventured deeper into the boundless expanse of the ocean, well on its course toward the Bahamas, I retreated belowdecks. The serenity of my cabin beckoned, a sanctuary from the unknown perils that lay ahead.

Leaning over my desk, I surveyed the chaotic mess of maps, compasses and calipers, musty books, and a tarnished spyglass. With a swift, impatient sweep of my hand, I cleared the clutter aside to reach for a map hidden in the depths of the mess. It was a tucked away, cherished secret.

Unfolding the yellowed, creased parchment, I gingerly spread it across the worn surface of the desk before taking my seat. This map was a coveted relic among sailors, a treasure hunted by those who shared my perilous profession—sea monster hunting. The map was a masterpiece, years in the making, adorned with cryptic lines and symbols and highlighted regions where sea creatures prowled. My gaze settled on the small islands of the Bahamas, Andros nestled among them. It was there we set our course, heading toward the depths of the deep blue waters just off the coast.

Leviathans were elusive sea monsters that had a fondness for lurking within the shadows of the Earth's undersea craters. If there was a leviathan haunting the waters around Andros, that was precisely where it would lie in wait, hidden within the heart of those dark, bottomless chasms.

I smiled to myself as I rolled up the map and tucked it away in a safe place. It had been a long time since I last encountered a leviathan. My blood sang with the possibility of battle and the kill.

"Storm a'brewing off the starboard!" Rat's voice rang out over my jumbled thoughts.

I took the coins from my pocket, securing them in a hidden place, and then ventured back up to the deck.

As I stepped onto it, the salty sea wind rammed me hard. The ocean was an unpredictable and moody mistress. She would turn on you in seconds without a moment's notice, and she had little regard for those who dared to cross her.

I looked in the direction that Rat indicated from high up in the crow's nest. The dark sky hung low, and the crack of thunder was so loud it rattled my teeth. Sheets of rain scurried across the vast expanse of the ocean, a warning of the tempest that lay miles ahead, lurking in the dark, brooding depths.

Within minutes, the rain pelted my skin, drenching me to the bone. I shoved my unruly wet hair from my eyes and strode toward the helm, where the ship's wheel groaned under the strain of the squall.

"Batten down the hatches, boys! It looks like we're in for a wild one!" I bellowed, my voice lost in the roar of the storm. The wind howled, and the rain stung like a swarm of angry bees as we charged headlong into the squall, a relentless force of nature that threatened to consume us.

RHEA

THE CLOSER I ventured to the Caribbean Sea, the more the water warmed around me. The rising temperature was an unwelcome change, far removed from the comforting coolness of Aquarius's dark ocean floor. Exhaustion weighed heavily on my shoulders, and fear gnawed at the edges of my resolve. A relentless ache in my belly constantly reminded me of my hunger. It was a perilous combination for a siren, especially one already teetering on the edge of her wits.

I had traveled for days to reach the Caribbean Sea, and I was calling myself a fool with each mile I swam. Doubt festered within me, a nagging suspicion that the sea witch had sent me on a self-destructive mission. How I would ever convince a heathen, a hunter of my kind, to take me to Medusa was a mystery as vast as the ocean itself.

I pondered the option of using my beguiling song to persuade him, but I knew I couldn't sing the entire trip. The odds were stacked against me, and the weight of the task ahead was crushing, like the depths of the sea.

A sunken ship resting on the ocean floor ensnared my attention, pulling me away from my thoughts. I cautiously approached it, marveling at the new residents of the boat. The ship had become a vibrant ecosystem of its own, swarming with fish of every imaginable shape and color that swirled around its sunken hull. Crustaceans scurried across the decaying deck, breathing life into this forgotten vessel.

My pulse increased as a tiny octopus shot out of a circular window, ink trailing in its wake, fleeing the scene as I drew closer. The shipwreck, with its thriving life, offered a stark contrast to the solitude and uncertainty of my mission, and I found a moment of comfort in this submerged world.

A smile tugged at my lips. I should have kept going, but my curiosity got the better of me. I ducked into the porthole that the octopus had just vacated. Darkness engulfed me as I edged deeper inside the ship. Rays of sunlight peeked through the rotting floorboards, disrupting the gloom and offering glimpses of the ship's interior. I was giddy with excitement. These human objects held a certain allure, something I had never witnessed before in the world of sirens and sea. My father would have a fit if he knew I was this close to *human* objects.

I continued down, winding through the debris and destruction. A small cry of surprise escaped my lips, shattering the eerie silence as I came upon the skeletal remains of a human. Foolish curiosity had my hand lifting as my fingertips brushed across the smooth bone of the skull. My eyes traveled down the form, brushing over the material that swayed in the current, covering the bony extremities.

Humans really weren't that different from us, except for the legs.

I left the sailor behind, continuing deeper, slowing when the ghostly creak of the wood echoed through the water. I nervously chewed on my bottom lip. This whole vessel could collapse at any moment. Good sense begged me to leave, but thick wooden barrels caught my attention, pulling me deeper into the darkness. I approached one and pulled until the waterlogged boards gave way. Hissing in pain, I pulled my hand to my chest as a splinter of wood lodged in my palm. I yanked the offending piece out, waving my hand through the current as my blood tainted the water. Ignoring my minor injury, I glanced into the barrel, studying the contents. My stomach heaved as a sour scent invaded my nostrils. Whatever this was—or used to be—was pungent. A quick glance revealed an array of barrels, each bearing identical symbols on their sides. I had no desire to investigate them further.

I hurried from the ship, hoping that the stench of whatever was in those barrels did not linger on me. I squeezed out of the porthole, stalling in the water before I noticed that the inhabitants of the sunken ship had vanished and the sea was eerily quiet. The hushed silence made my pulse race, hinting at the danger.

A dark, shadowy figure ahead of me caught my attention, and I immediately scolded myself for becoming distracted and not paying closer attention to my surroundings. I glanced down at my palm, which was still bleeding, cursing myself for not being more careful.

The silhouette stalked closer and became more apparent, exposing itself as a threat. My heart increased tempo as a giant shark swam closer, battle scars etched in its gray skin. It circled me with a predatory grace, its cold, unrelenting gaze sizing me up. I'd had minor dealings with sharks. Aquarius was too deep and far from the mainland for sharks to frequent. Whenever one ventured that close, Orm and his army dealt with it. This shark was massive in length and inched closer to me with each pass it made. I was an easy bite-sized meal for it, or so it thought.

My lips parted, and my siren song hummed through the ocean. I prayed that it would work against this shark. If not, I had already made the grave mistake of letting it get too close to me. I would have to flee if my song didn't work. Sirens were one of the fastest creatures in all the oceans, so hopefully I could get away. The shark instantly paused. Its body slowly started to drift to the bottom of the sea. I stopped my song immediately. When a shark stopped swimming, it stopped breathing. I didn't want to kill it, even though it was trying to eat me. It was just doing what sharks did.

Even after stopping my song, the shark sank to the bottom. Against my better judgment, I swam toward it, grabbed its fin, and started pushing it. A small trickle of relief filled me as the shark's gills began flapping in the current. In a matter of seconds, it bucked and thrashed. I released it and retreated a few feet. It finally got the message that I was the more significant threat and swam off in the direction it came. My father had always told me that my big heart would get me killed, and based on my current situation, he was probably right. The shark may not have been my doom, but the mission I was on now likely would be.

I collected myself after my shark encounter and continued on my journey. As I swam, the ocean darkened. I braved going to the surface and eased my head above the waters. Night had fallen, and only a few twinkling stars were visible, along with a big moon high in the sky. It was rare that I broke through the surface of the water, so I just floated there for a while, enjoying the beauty of the night sky. A loud cracking sound had me swinging my head around, and I looked to the sky, where an angry storm had built in the distance. Lighting struck again, this time closer and louder than before, and soon after, rain started splattering across my skin. I ducked below the surface. I would be safe from the squall under the water, or so I assumed.

I dove deeper as the waters became rougher. No matter how far I ventured down, the storm seemed to follow. I was using all of my strength to keep from being tossed around. Never had I seen a storm churn the waters this deep before. My body was roughly thrown through the ocean as a whirlpool swallowed me. My lungs threatened to collapse in on themselves as the swirling pool of death suffocated me, its icy grip pressing against my chest...

I INHALED DEEPLY, expecting the cool ocean water to pass through my lungs, but instead, I nearly choked to death as I breathed in sand. I sputtered and coughed, trying to rid the offending substance from my mouth and throat. My body ached, and my skin and scales felt parched and dry. I dared to pry my eyes open, only to be blinded by the bright, blistering sun as it bounced off the pristine beach.

Dizziness enveloped me, my head swirling, as an intense, searing pain surged through my fins. Agony gripped me, and a screech escaped my lips as the torment heightened. I raised my head, sweeping tear-saturated eyes across the tattered remnants of my tail fin. Panic consumed every inch of my being. The extent of the damage left haunting uncertainty of whether I would ever swim again.

Spots danced across my vision when I saw how far the storm had tossed me from the ocean. How would I ever maneuver my mutilated body that far to get back into the sea? I was hopelessly beached.

I laid back down as I tried to calm my hysteria. I just needed to rest for a minute to catch my breath, and then I would claw my way down this massive beach and back into the safety of the ocean.

I struggled to keep my eyes open as my hope plummeted like a ship in a storm. Seagulls cawed in the distance, circling overhead as if waiting for my eyes to close. No matter how hard I fought, I was losing the battle against consciousness. My head buzzed as darkness crept in from all sides. My head dropped onto the scorching sand as my eyes rolled back. An eerie voice whispered, its sinister tone beckoning me to follow it to my death.

CHAPTER 6
KAI

Cael jumped down from the splintered mast, his boots scuffing against the deck as he approached me. "Cap'n! The rigging is badly damaged. It will take all day to fix it."

I closed my eyes as anger bubbled up inside me. The storm last night had wreaked havoc on my ship. We should have been halfway to Andros by now, not stuck on some godforsaken island repairing our rigging and mast.

"Then I suggest you get to it instead of standing here telling me about it," I grumbled.

Cael shot me a lopsided smile and started yelling orders. He knew to avoid me when I was in one of these moods. I grabbed my scabbard, attached it to my hip, and joined my men in one of the dinghies. My anticipation swelled with each stroke of the oar, and an exasperated groan escaped my lips. We had two tasks to complete, and I was already lagging behind. Despite being a pirate, I prided myself on punctuality when it came to completing a job.

The small boat gently grazed the sandy shore, and my crew eagerly scrambled toward the untamed wilderness to gather supplies. I stopped midway as a mass of seagulls in the distance caught my attention. It was stupid and not time-efficient to go investigate whatever it was, but something about the scene bothered me.

"Carry on," I instructed my men as I headed down the beach.

Whatever was washed up had to be sizable for that many gulls to gather. My boots sloshed in the soft sand and sea spray, and my gaze fixated on streamers of seaweed as they danced in the surf.

I rounded a beachside boulder and came to an abrupt halt as I spotted the source of the gulls' excitement. There, stretched out on the sand, lay the lifeless form of a siren. As I approached, the gulls scattered into the sky. It had been years since I had seen a siren, so I leaned in for a closer look. Was this the siren that the sea witch had informed me was on the way? It had to be. The timing was too perfect.

I cursed under my breath and gritted my teeth in aggravation. The death of this siren also meant that my job of taking her to Medusa and then killing her was void, and so were my chances of getting the Wraith.

I glared at her, my eyes sweeping over her form. Her body was face down in the sand, and she had been through hell by the looks of it. Her tail fin looked like someone had taken a blade to it. It was probably a good thing she was dead because she wouldn't swim again anytime soon with that kind of damage to her tail.

I cautiously advanced and shoved her with the toe of my boot. *Nothing.* I turned to head back to my ship to rethink the situation. Maybe the sea witch would still give me the Wraith for just producing the siren's body? I needed to return to my ship and find something to wrap the remains in. I didn't want my crew members to see her, or they would become suspicious as to why I was carrying around the corpse of a siren.

Moaning stopped me in my tracks, and I slowly turned back around. *Sink me*! She was still alive. She seemed stunned as she wiggled until she flipped over and blinked up at the sun. Despite the veil of seaweed and sand, her features were striking. The sea witch said that I would know it was the princess when I saw her, and she was right. Nothing in my lifetime had prepared me for this sight. Sirens ensnared you with their mesmerizing beauty, which made them perilous, but this siren surpassed any description.

I remained vigilant as I approached, keeping my hand on the hilt of my sword. Her chest rose and fell rapidly. Panic was evident in her demeanor. Might as well give her something to panic about…

I leaned over her, and our eyes met. "Well, well, what do we have here?" I gave her a rakish grin.

She writhed on the ground, hissing in my direction. She opened her mouth, but all that came out was a spew of sand. She began to sway slightly and then leaned over, expelling seawater and the contents of her stomach all over my boots.

"Bloody hell!" I cursed and stepped back, scraping my boots across the sand to rid them of the offending vomit.

When I glanced at her again, it was evident she wouldn't survive; maybe it was merciful to end her suffering. I drew my sword from its scabbard, and the sharp hiss of metal against leather halted her frantic motions. Our gazes locked. Her dark, honey-swirled eyes momentarily captivated me, drawing me into a trance. They shimmered with unshed tears before a glint of something indescribable—something akin to bravery—flashed within them.

I should be glad that she was still alive and I could now uphold my bargain with the sea witch, but that meant I had to deal with a siren aboard my ship. That was something I should have considered, but I had no idea I would find her this quickly. I cursed and slowly slid my sword back into its scabbard.

A few moments ticked by as I tried to decide what to do with her. The siren cried out in pain, and I stepped back as her tail split, separating into two distinct limbs. A radiant light enveloped her as her tail morphed into legs. Her anguished cries reverberated, nearly shattering my eardrums. Eventually, she collapsed back onto the sandy shore, unconscious. As her wails ceased, a sense of relief washed over me.

I glanced back down at her, my curiosity piqued by the magic I just witnessed. She was now fully a woman, and I could not help but stare at her like a lecher. Let's be honest—I was a pirate, not a gentleman. I reached down to touch her hair. The hue was unlike any I had seen before. It reminded me of the rich interior of a ripe pomegranate. The sound of my crew rushing down the beach finally snapped me out of my haze, and I stood.

I quickly unbuttoned my shirt, pulled it off, and bent toward her. My crew did not need any more enticement. A lone woman on a beach was enough to cause a ruckus, but a naked woman on a beach would likely end in someone or something dying. I awkwardly sat her up. She flopped in my arms like a rag doll as I held her by the neck and tried haphazardly to push her arms through the sleeves of my shirt. I managed to get it on her and buttoned as Cael and the rest of my men rounded the beach and stopped dead upon seeing me.

"What goes, Cap'n?" Cael asked as he ventured closer, staring down at my newfound prize. I met his gaze and gave him a knowing look. It didn't take long for realization to dawn on him. He responded with a swift nod.

Flynt weaseled his way through the pack of men and reached for her. "Look at that fresh piece of meat."

"Stand down." My voice was calm but had an edge of warning and death to it, and he immediately straightened and fell back into the horde of men.

"Seems to be a wash-up," I answered before scooping down and lifting her in my arms.

"What are you going to do with her?" Cael played along with my story as I started back toward the ship.

"Look at her hands."

Cael lifted her swaying palm and inspected it closely.

"They haven't seen a day's worth of manual labor in their entire life. That means she could be worth a hefty price," I lied, and Cael nodded his head in understanding as I wove a tale through my crews' minds.

One thing about my men was that they valued money over a woman any day, so I was hoping that would deter them from her. Probably not, but it was worth a try. I certainly was not ready to announce to them that I was bringing a sea demon aboard my ship. Not until I had a chance to think the situation through. They would find out soon enough about the job I accepted.

"No one is to touch her until we find out how much she is worth." My voice rang loud and clear for all my men to hear as I reached the dinghy, sat down, and readjusted her in my lap. She flinched in my arms, prompting me to glance down at her face once more. It was a mistake, as I found myself immediately captivated by the flawlessness of her skin, the harmony of her facial proportions, and her petite, yet distinct, nose. Undoubtedly, she was destined to become a source of numerous headaches in the days ahead. Her presence posed a distracting complication that my crew and I couldn't afford.

My men rushed to load the supplies needed to patch the ship. It would serve as a temporary bandage until we could reach a port and mend the damages. Yet another delay in my plans. At least one thing had gone my way this day. I had the siren I was supposed to find. I would not be surprised if the sea witch had caused the storm to wash us both up on the same island at the same time. If that were true and she was the one who caused the damage to my ship, my anger would increase tenfold.

Once we were back on the ship, the men crowded me in hopes of holding the woman while I climbed the rope ladder. They eagerly held out their outstretched arms. I walked past them in the swaying boat without so much as a word, slung her over my shoulder, and quickly scaled the ladder. They all watched me like a bunch of buzzards as I repositioned her in my arms and headed below.

Bringing a woman aboard, especially a siren, was a hazard waiting to happen, but if my men valued their innards, they would obey me no matter how tempting this little morsel in my arms was. I booted the brig door open, walked inside, and laid her on the rickety cot. Her mass of red hair fell across her face, and I brushed it aside. Cael cleared his throat behind me, and I quickly pulled my hand away from her.

"Watch her like a hawk," I instructed him as I walked out

of the cell and closed the door behind me. The creak of the bolt-action lock slid into place, and I put the key in my pocket. "I don't want anyone else down here, and the minute her eyes open, come and get me."

"Aye, aye, Captain," Cael answered, standing up straighter, obviously still pissed with the whole situation.

"Don't be a smartass. We cannot afford any mistakes," I warned. "You know as well as I do that sirens are devious creatures. There's no telling what a princess is capable of."

"Which is why this whole thing is a bad idea," Cael snapped as I started ascending the stairway.

"Your concern is duly noted." I smirked and continued up to the deck to help my men repair the ship so we could get underway as soon as possible.

"Look alive, ingrates! We're wasting daylight!" I thundered just as soon as my feet hit the deck.

Suspicion lingered in the glances of my men, their curiosity smoldering, eager to inquire about the girl. I scanned each of their faces, my posture and aura daring them to broach the subject. Swiftly, they averted their gazes, refocusing on the preparations needed to set sail.

"Tie it tighter, Rat," I bellowed, my voice carrying on the cool morning breeze.

"Aye, Capitán," he answered and quickly retied the rigging.

Minutes turned to hours before the ship was ready to sail. The intensifying heat of the day only served to stoke my mounting impatience and aggravation. After I inspected the crew's work and was satisfied that it was seaworthy, we hauled up the anchor and easily sailed through the surf break.

I cast a cautious gaze over the expansive, open ocean. I didn't trust that sea witch or the little siren she supposedly wanted me to kill. The thought had crossed my mind that this entire thing was a trap, and their sole purpose was to end my crew and myself to rid the world of another human that hunted their kind. I chuckled inwardly at the notion. They would have to do better than sending a little siren princess if they wanted to get rid of me.

CHAPTER 7
RHEA

My body was swaying back and forth in a rhythmic motion. I was on something solid, dry, and warm. It was not totally unpleasant. I snuggled deeper until my brain caught up with what my body was feeling. I wasn't in the water. I was dry, too dry! Startled, I surged upright, my head spinning and my vision ablaze with swirling stars as I struggled to adapt to this unfamiliar environment. A veil of darkness enveloped me, punctuated only by the soft, swaying glow of a distant light.

Panic threatened to overtake me. I had to breathe deeply to calm my rapid pulse. My eyes darted from the wood plank floor to the bars of what appeared to be a cage. The swaying motion was making me queasy. I had to be on a ship. The lower half of my body throbbed with pain, and it felt strange and foreign. I glanced down, confusion clouding my brain. A scratchy fabric covered my tail. I yanked the material from my lower half. My mind went dead after that point. I reached a shaky hand toward where my beautiful tail used to be.

When I touched the offending legs, a cry ripped from my throat. This was real! They were real. I had legs! I thrashed until my body hit the floor. Panic swelled in my breast. I couldn't breathe; I needed water and my beautiful tail. What had happened to me? What sort of magic was this?

A dark silhouette stalked from the shadows but stopped when the door to the room crashed open and the man from the beach walked in. As he approached, I scooted away until my backside collided with a wall.

"Your timing is impeccable," the man in the shadows said.

"I was on the way down when I heard her screeching," the one who just entered said as he approached the bars.

"Stay away!" I hissed.

He stopped and glanced back at the other man. "You head on up. I will take it from here."

With a swift nod, the man left, closing the door and leaving me alone with the one who was looking at me menacingly.

"What did you do to me?" I cried as a tear slipped down my cheek. Even something as simple as a tear felt foreign. I would have never felt it on my cheek in the water.

"I picked you up off the beach, clothed you, and put you in the brig. I wouldn't complain if I were you. At least you're still living," he thundered in a voice filled with disdain.

"What are these? Where did they come from?" I motioned toward my legs as they bent unnaturally and started flexing the ten little nubs at the end.

"Those are legs..." The dark-haired one eyed me up and down with a scowl on his face.

"I know what they are... I want to know how..." I stopped mid-sentence and slammed my mouth shut.

Why was I accusing this human? He couldn't have done this to me. The sea witch... My mouth fell open again, but no words came out. She did this to me, but why? I looked at the stranger again, and one of his dark eyebrows shot up in questioning.

"Water!" I gasped. "I need water!" I tried to make these accursed legs straighten, but I didn't know how the things worked and ended up on my side.

"Do you plan on drinking the water or drowning yourself in it? I'm fine with either if it stops your screaming." His deep voice boomed, and he crouched down before me so that he was level with my gaze.

Fuming, I locked my gaze on his, and a surprising sense of calm washed over me. His eyes, swirling with shades of blue, reminded me of a tranquil summer ocean. I blinked a few times, still coming to terms with the fact that a human was hovering right in front of me. I had rarely encountered humans, let alone been in such close proximity to one. The rumors I'd heard painted them as feeble beings, lacking both physical strength and intellect. Yet the figure before me defied that description. He stood tall and broad, exuding strength and confidence. His wispy white shirt hung partially open, offering a glimpse of his well-defined chest as he leaned closer.

"See something you like?" His deep voice rumbled with laughter.

My gaze quickly darted back to his face, and a shiver of goosebumps rippled across my skin. I straightened, running my hands along my arms to dispel the sensation. As my eyes were tempted to wander lower, I fiercely resisted the urge to let him catch me ogling his muscles again. One side of his mouth curled upward in an arrogant grin, and I couldn't help but admire his striking facial features. He had a strong face with defined cheekbones and a neatly groomed, dark-brown beard that harmonized with his untamed shoulder-length curls.

It was difficult, but I pulled my attention away from him and focused on my surroundings. I was in some sort of cage in a dark, musty room. "Why have I been locked up?" I tried to act innocent, desperately hoping that he would let me out.

"Let's not play coy, siren. I don't trust you, and I am sure you don't trust me," he answered as he straightened back up.

I glanced down at my legs again in momentary shock. How did he know that I was a siren when I clearly looked like a human?

"Who exactly are you?" I tried to gain my footing but only managed to make it to an upright seated position with my legs tucked under my body.

"Kaiden Alexander, but most people know me as Blackheart Kai."

His response hit me like a surge of icy water, causing my thoughts to run sluggish as I maintained an unwavering gaze. He was the one I had sought, yet deep down, I had hoped to never find him. I swallowed hard, attempting to dislodge the lump in my throat, and observed him with a fresh perspective. In that moment, he embodied everything I had ever dreaded in my darkest nightmares. It was then that my scrutiny fell upon the array of weapons strapped to his body, each sword and knife undoubtedly bearing the permanent stain of the blood of my kind.

He smirked at me, obviously pleased with the fear his name invoked. Anger seared its way through my bloodstream as I fought to balance on these wretched legs. After several failed attempts, I managed to stand upright.

"Bravo." He mocked me with a clap of his hands and another devious smile.

I wanted so badly to reach through the bars and wipe that smirk from his face with a quick slice from my claws.

Would my siren song still work? It couldn't hurt to try it. My song strummed from my lips in perfect harmony, just like it always had. I was so happy that I still had my song that I almost missed hitting a note, but I quickly corrected myself and continued to sing. A victorious smile graced my lips as the murderous captain's harsh gaze shifted to me. He emerged slowly from the shadows, steadily advancing in my direction, his unwavering gaze locked onto me. His proximity caused a knot to tighten in the pit of my stomach as he drew nearer, eventually standing just inches away on the other side of the bars.

"Back up," I instructed him through my song.

"Make me."

A surge of icy dread coursed through my body as that familiar, smug grin etched itself across his face. Swift as a sea snake's strike, he lunged, seizing the back of my neck, and forcefully thrust my body against the unyielding bars. My head and face collided painfully with the frigid metal. In shock, my song died on my quivering lips.

He leaned in closer and whispered in my ear. "Now what, siren? What happens when you cannot manipulate a man into doing your bidding?"

I was so stunned that my siren song didn't work on him that I could not move. Mine was the most powerful in all of Aquarius. How was it possible that it failed me now? Had my song been diminished by the sea witch when she turned me into a human? I finally met Kai's eyes as the swirling blue depths stared down at me. With a sinister sneer, he released me and returned to his spot in the shadows. A trickle of something wet dripped down my forehead. When I reached up to touch it, I winced at the pain. As I examined my fingertips, I discovered them smeared with blood. A swirl of emotions, blending rage and fear, overwhelmed me.

"You…" Anger surged from my depths so hot that it threatened to burn me from the inside out. "You slimy son of an eel," I sputtered, finally managing to make my mouth form words.

"Is that the best you can do?" Kai asked, leaning against a nearby barrel.

My body shook with rage, and my eyes misted over with angry tears. I breathed deeply a few times and stepped toward the bars to collect my scattered emotions. "I need your help," I stated plainly, trying to hide how my voice shook with trepidation. I wanted so badly to drown him and watch his body seize as his lungs filled with seawater, but that would have to wait, at least for the time being. Much to my dismay, he was the only one who could get me to Medusa.

"So now you ask," he answered smugly.

When a hiss slipped past my lips, he smiled.

"Speak up, sea demon. I will hear your request."

As fierce as the swirling sea, my fury surged once more, stirring tumult in my depths. How was it possible for one man to burrow his way so deeply under my skin and make me so furious?

"Dark Water." I seethed, clenching my teeth.

His muscles tensed, but he never looked up at me. "It's not my concern. It's not in my waters."

"Yet," I added, peering around at him.

"What is it you think I can do?" He shrugged his shoulders like he didn't have a care in the world. What was with the males? Why could no one see that we were all in danger?

"I need you to take me to Medusa..."

A fleeting smile brushed his lips, and then it disappeared like it had never been there. "What do you offer me in return?" He stood from the barrel and stepped closer to the bars.

I did not miss how his eyes raked down the length of my body and stopped on the hideously bare human legs. Were legs something that human men found attractive?

I glanced down at my body. I may be a human, but from the waist up, I still looked exactly the same as I did before, or at least the parts I could see. I was well aware of what the siren males thought of my body. Perhaps I could use my feminine wiles on this killer as well. I pulled on the fabric around my neck, further exposing my breastbone. His eyes immediately followed my every movement. The mental image of him intimately caressing my skin summoned an intense feeling of disgust. I swiftly let go of the fabric and retreated deeper into the cell.

"Changed your mind?" His laughter was gruff and filled with malice. "Probably for the best. I wouldn't mind a show, but I can promise you, I will never touch a creature like you, not in that way." His voice was filled with just as much hate as I felt for him.

As he headed toward the stairs, desperation clawed at my throat.

"Wait!" I rushed forward and gripped the iron bars so hard that the metal bit into my skin.

He paused but never turned back around. My mind scrambled for anything to keep him talking. Anything to make him agree to take me to Medusa. What did I have that he could possibly want?

"Treasure…" I sputtered the first word that I believed a pirate like him would be interested in.

Relief washed over me when he slightly angled his body to face me. I swallowed past my rising hysteria as his eyes bore into mine.

"If you take me to Medusa, in exchange for your help, I will offer you the treasure of a sunken ship that went down off the coast of Brazil."

It wasn't a lie, exactly. I had discovered that ship on the way to the Caribbean Sea. I wasn't about to tell him that the ship was loaded with barrels of slimy gunk that smelled worse than something that had died.

He stepped closer to me. His scent assaulted me full force at his nearness, and I couldn't help but breathe him in. He smelled of the salty sea air that I longed for, with a mixture of masculinity and spice.

He stalked closer to the bars like a predator and rammed his hand through them. "You have yourself a deal, siren."

I looked down at his hand like it was a shark preparing to amputate my arm if I ventured too close. The last time he touched me, I ended up with a split forehead. I had no intention of repeating that mistake.

"Smart little fish. You might make it after all. But let me warn you, if you ever try to use your siren song on me or any of my crew members again, I will carve you into tiny pieces and use you as shark bait." His voice boomed and bounced off the walls as he walked up the stairs and left me behind in the darkness.

CHAPTER 8
KAI

Cael noticed the smile on my face as I ventured up from the dark hole and back into the fresh, salty air. With a quick jerk of my head, I motioned for him to relinquish the wheel to me. He complied, taking his place to my left, feet apart and arms behind his back. I quickly checked our heading, and I was not at all surprised that we were right on course. Cael could sail just as well as I could.

My mind drifted back to the siren I had locked up tight in the brig. She fell headfirst into my trap. Now she believed she was paying me to take her to Medusa, unaware that a sea witch had an alternative agenda and a prize that I valued above treasure.

"We should arrive in Turronto Port by midmorning tomorrow." Cael cleared his throat, stating the obvious.

I turned my attention to him, waiting for him to reveal what he actually wanted to say versus this idle small talk.

"If you have something to say, spill it," I said harsher than I intended, but between my handicapped ship, a siren aboard, and the fact that we were behind schedule, my patience was long past expired.

Cael's gaze darted around, as if ensuring no one was

around to overhear the conversation. The ship was quiet at this point. It was smooth sailing once we were in open waters, except for a few minor rigging and sail adjustments. Most of the crew had retired for the evening in search of much-needed food and rest.

"I take it by the look on your face that your first encounter with the siren went well?" Cael raised a questioning eyebrow at me, obviously hinting at the smile that was on my face when I came from below.

The mere mention of the siren immediately had my mind conjuring up her image, making me hot beneath the collar. The uncomfortable sensation had me reaching up and tugging at my shirt to let in the cool sea breeze. She was beyond dangerous and borderline deadly. If she could make someone like me, someone who hated every fanatical creature that swam below the surface, to be lustful, then she was a force to be reckoned with.

"Well?" Cael pressed when I did not answer him immediately.

"She offered us the treasure of a sunken ship if we agreed to take her to Medusa," I said barely above a whisper. The name Medusa would have my men jumping ship if they overheard me.

"Pity we will never see it," Cael stated the obvious.

"We won't need it after I get my hands on the Wraith." Thinking about that glorious ship had my skin tingling with anticipation.

"How are you going to keep her in check until we reach Medusa? She is a siren, you know. Not all of us can withstand the song." Cael's worried gaze washed over me, and then he turned his eyes back to the ocean.

"She's already tried her song on me and quickly discovered it did not work. I also told her that if she tried it again, I would chop her up into shark bait."

"Do you think that threat will deter her for long?" Cael asked without taking his eyes from the horizon.

I followed his gaze to the skyline, admiring the sunset as the last orange rays danced across the sky before twilight gave way to the stars. The colors reflected across the darkening blue sea, setting our faces aglow with the waning light. This was my favorite time of day and the most peaceful, but Cael was messing that up with his constant worrying.

"Probably not, but I think it took her confidence down a peg when her song didn't work on me. It will probably be a while before she tries it again," I stated honestly. I learned long ago that I was not affected by siren songs, which possibly added fuel to my rampage of sea monster slaughtering. If sirens, the predators of the Seven Seas, couldn't take me down, what beast could? Was I too cocky? Probably, and it would likely be the death of me, but I wouldn't go down without a fight.

"Hmph," was Cael's response to my oversized ego.

"I can keep the siren in check. You just make sure that the crew doesn't learn the truth about any of this until there is no turning back," I warned.

Cael's gaze drifted to me. "Do you want me to watch her tonight?"

"No need. I locked the room to the brig, and I have the only key. She's not going anywhere, and no one can get to her in there. I say we retire for the night; it's been a long day." I stretched my tightly wound muscles. "Call that new helmsman and have him take over steering," I instructed as I headed for my cabin and, hopefully, a restful night's sleep.

"WHAT IS THAT BLOODY NOISE?" When I slung my cabin door open, I nearly tore the hinges off it. I stormed out of the room only to be met by Cael.

"There seems to be something wrong with your prisoner. Her screeching would wake the dead!" Cael met me in the doorway and motioned below to the brig.

"I'm going to kill her before we even make it to our destination," I grumbled as I slammed the cabin door closed behind me. I wanted to wring her scrawny neck for disturbing my peaceful sleep. "Tell the crew to return to their barracks," I thundered as a crowd gathered around the door that led below. If this was a new trick of the siren, I didn't want my men anywhere around her.

"Yes, Cap'n." Cael wrinkled his brow at me and then started yelling orders to the crew.

As I made my way down to her, my pulse increased in tempo, which was odd. Why should I care if the siren was in distress? I didn't. I willed myself to calm my rapid pace. I didn't know what her wailing was all about, but she couldn't be in danger. More than likely, she was laying a trap for anyone who dared pity her cries for help. I slowly descended the two stories to get to her.

Her screaming got louder the further I went down into the hold. When I opened the door, darkness engulfed me. The bloody lantern had gone out. I fumbled around in the dark until I lit it again. Light flooded the room, and I looked at her. Her screaming momentarily stopped as I walked up to the cell bars.

"Let me out," she wailed, and I took notice of the tears streaking down her face.

"Not happening, so you can stop this display. If you don't stop all of this screaming, I'll come in there and give you a reason to…" My threat died on my tongue as I looked down at her, and so did my rage.

She was unusually pale and quivered all over. She wasn't pretending. I had seen that look before, usually right before I ran my blade through someone. *The siren was terrified.* I shoved the key into the lock and cautiously entered the room. Sirens were as cunning as they were beautiful, so I was fully aware that she could be setting a death trap. I put my hand on the hilt of my sword as I stopped in front of her.

"Please… I can't breathe." She panted as another tremor overtook her body.

Against my better judgment, which was clearly lacking at the moment, I reached down and picked her up off the floor. Her skin was cold to the touch, and she reeked of vomit. I glanced down at the cell floor where she had spewed the contents of her stomach again. *Sink me!* My mission would be moot and void if I killed her in the process. She quaked in my arms as I carried her up the rickety wooden steps that led to the ship's deck. I sat her backside on the railing while still holding tightly to her midsection so she didn't fall off the ship. In her condition, I doubted she could stand on her own.

"Breathe, lass." Her back was flush against my bare chest, and she leaned her head against my shoulder and breathed deeply.

I glanced down at her as she closed her eyes and took in several deep breaths of air.

"That's right. Calm yourself." I was soothing a bloody siren. My brain had definitely leaped over the railing right along with my good sense.

After several minutes ticked by, she slowly pried her eyes open.

I shook my head and pulled her from the railing. Showing any form of goodwill to one of her kind sickened me, and yet here I was, helping her calm down from what appeared to be a bout of claustrophobia. This siren was obviously more powerful than I initially thought. She was making me do stupid things like releasing her from the brig and bringing her on deck without even using her siren song. She steadied herself against the railing, and I retreated a few steps from her to regain my senses.

Her gaze swept longingly over the sea as it twinkled in the moonlight.

"You'll drown if you jump overboard," I reminded her of her human form.

I leaned beside her against the railing, allowing a glance down the length of her body.

"A siren, drown?" She huffed in disbelief.

"You're not a siren anymore. Remember?" To prove my point, I brushed the toe of my boot against her calf. "Hence the reason why I said if you jump ship, you will die. We're miles from land now, and you no longer have the ability to swim or breathe underwater. Like it or not, *sea demon*, you are stuck on my ship."

Touching her was a mistake because my eyes immediately followed where my boot brushed her skin. For someone who had just recently grown a pair of legs, she had some nice ones.

"My name is Rhea, not sea demon," she hissed. Her color

was returning, and so was her fiery temper. "Princess of Aquarius," she added, as if it would make any difference to the fate she faced.

"Would *Her Highness* like to wash the vomit from her hair? You reek." I mockingly bowed before her.

"I hate you," she hissed between clenched teeth.

I walked back toward the lower deck. "The feeling is mutual, sea demon."

I did not hear footsteps following behind me. She was still staring out into the dark blue sea that swirled against the ship's hull. I hesitated for a second, thinking she might actually try to jump, but I guess my warning about drowning had stuck. With a sorrowful sigh, she turned and followed me below.

I kept glancing over my shoulder, ensuring she was keeping her distance. Having a siren to my back was not an ideal situation, but it seemed as if the fight had temporarily been wrung out of her. I opened my cabin door and gestured for her to proceed.

"You have until I return to wash yourself off and change into this." I motioned to a warped wooden bucket of water in the corner, pulled out another one of my shirts from the wardrobe, and tossed it on the bed.

I stepped out of the room and closed the door behind me, satisfied when I heard the slosh of water. I needed a shot of rum, but I didn't think leaving her alone in my cabin was a good idea. To ward off an impending headache, I pinched the bridge of my nose. I stood outside the door like a watchdog.

When the splashing of water ceased, everything went quiet. I opened the door and walked back in. She was waiting in the middle of the room, somewhat clean with a fresh shirt on. Her long, damp hair dripped onto the white shirt, making it nearly see-through.

She flinched when I stepped toward her. "Don't make me go back down there."

The words "like hell" were on the tip of my tongue, but a tremor in her voice had me hesitating to speak them out loud. "Are you asking or threatening?" I couldn't keep the anger from my voice from the sheer inconvenience she was causing.

"I am asking." She held her head higher and looked me directly in the eyes, slightly impressing me with her strength and dignity. "I am asking. Nicely, I might add," she said with something that barely resembled a smile. Her golden eyes twinkled in the slight sway of the lantern that lit the cabin.

I cursed under my breath as I walked around her and snatched the covers and my pillow from the bed. She watched my every move with precision.

"Don't just stand there. Get in the bed," I said between clenched teeth.

The thought of a siren beneath my sheets made my skin crawl, but like it or not, she was my responsibility and my cabin was the only other place except the brig that had a lock on the door. I groaned as the realization sank in. I had to ensure she was safe and sound until we reached our destination. Then I could kill her.

Her haughty stare never left mine as she slowly approached the bed and sat down on my soft, plush mattress. Without another word, I slammed the door shut and clicked the lock into place. I shoved my hands through my hair in frustration. I would never hear the end of this when Cael found out that I had relinquished my bed to a siren.

CHAPTER 9
RHEA

Startled from my sleep by a faint shuffling, my eyes flew open, and I jolted upright. Panic surged through me as I found myself face-to-face with an intense, ebony-skinned man brooding over me.

"Cap'n said to eat this." A tin saucer and a cup were thrust in my face, and I quickly grabbed them before they could tumble to the floor.

I was unable to look away as he loomed nearby. What was it about these humans? Did the salty sea air somehow inflate them beyond the size of an average human being? This man nearly matched the immense stature and build of that detestable Kai. My gaze wandered, taking in the inking on his dark skin—similar to the markings we put on our skin during a celebration—alongside the gleaming metal loops adorning his ear.

Sensing his growing irritation at my stare, I averted my gaze to the plate in front of me. Disgust twisted my lip. What was this stuff? I touched a flaky tan thing that reminded me of a sea sponge; it was crusty and soft. I prodded a heap of red, oblong things, feeling it squish under my touch. I immediately shoved the plate away and gulped the water he handed me, only to recoil as the liquid hit my tongue, involuntarily spewing it across the room.

"What is your problem?" The man groaned as he darted out of the line of fire from the spray of water.

"What's wrong with this water? It's not crisp and salty." I looked down into the cup and smelled the contents.

It didn't really have a scent at all. Humans were strange creatures. I eyed the cup again; my parched tongue felt better just from the liquid touching it, but I did not want to drink this peculiar water. I inhaled deeply, pinched my nose, and downed the cup's contents. My dry throat was instantly relieved, but my taste buds protested loudly. I sat the empty glass beside the plate and then looked back up at the man.

He motioned at the plate. "You're not going to eat?"

"Not that," I said with a sneer.

"Suit yourself." He lifted the plate and moved toward the door, and I rose and trailed behind. He paused, casting an irritated glance in my direction. "Where do you think you're going?"

"I need some air," I stated plainly, crossing my arms over my chest.

"Not going to happen, siren." He growled in my face and leaned over me in a threatening manner.

Did everyone aboard know my true identity? I glanced down at my spindly legs. Well, I used to be a siren.

"I do believe the captain of the ship gives the orders. I require his audience," I said in a lofty voice, showing him that his intimidation tactics did not work on me.

His dark eyes beaded with anger as his pupils shrunk two sizes. Without another word, he marched out the door and slammed it shut. I shrugged at his childish mannerisms and occupied myself with exploring my new surroundings. I didn't have a chance to see the room last night. Once my head hit the bed, sleep had claimed me.

The room sprawled in darkness, its vastness a reflection of the shadowy character who called it home. My steps echoed softly as I moved with measured caution, absorbing the grand atmosphere created by the dark wooden floors and the coordinating furniture. My fingers glided over the intricate carvings adorning the wardrobe door, the craftsmanship exceeding even the most lavish shipwrecks I'd ever explored. This room radiated an unapologetic masculinity, the color palette limited to the deepest shades of blues and grays. Apparently, hunting my kind paid well.

The only thing that softened the room were pieces stolen from the sea. I reached for a conch shell on the desk, running my fingers over the smooth, cool surface. A pang of homesickness tugged at my heart, reminding me of my family and the urgency to save them. I prayed that the Dark Water had not reached my home and that everyone there was safe. Anger erupted within just thinking about the precious time I was wasting relying on this blackhearted pirate, but it was a necessary evil.

I blinked a few times to clear my misty eyes as I let them wander over other objects in the room. Some things I knew the names of, others I did not. On a cluttered desk, I picked up a small metal object with multiple prongs on the end. I turned it in the palm of my hand, trying to understand its purpose. When I caught my reflection in a mirror, I walked up to it. I ran the prongs of the metallic thing through my wild hair that still smelled slightly of vomit.

The grating sound of the door scraping against the

wooden floor had my heart flopping in my chest like a fish on dry land. I tried to snatch the object from my hair but only managed to get it hopelessly tangled in my locks. So much for trying to be inconspicuous. I continued to try to yank the thing from my hair as Kai entered and stalked toward me. I stopped moving altogether, the silver object dangled in my hair as he loomed over me.

He reached up with the ruse of being gentle and ever so lightly grabbed onto the item. "This is a cartographer's compass. You use it to chart maps, not comb your hair," he said in a superior tone, yanking the compass from my hair.

I hissed as he ripped a few strands from my skull. Without thinking of the consequences, I struck him across the face. An eerily calm smile spread across his face, but I could tell he was trying to hide the fact that I had taken him off guard. He was obviously not used to someone fighting back.

"Sea demon," he cursed as he stepped closer.

"You haven't seen a sea demon...yet," I warned and matched his macho display by mimicking his movement and stepping closer.

We were so close our breaths mingled and our noses almost touched. As I breathed deeply, I detected the fresh salty sea air and spices. The pleasant, seductive scent on him angered me, which was mirrored as fury overtook his features. I prepared to fight to the death, but to my surprise, he was the first to step back.

"What else do you want, sea demon? I gave you the nicest cabin aboard my ship, and yet you still antagonize my first mate," he said in frustration, jamming his hand through his wavy brown hair. An act that I wished he hadn't done because now I was hung up on his unruly windblown curls.

I crossed my arms defiantly across my chest. "My name is Rhea," I corrected him again, "and I am not antagonizing anyone. I simply asked to go up on deck. I need some air."

"You're not running around loose on my ship," he spat.

"What harm could I possibly cause? We are working together, are we not? I have no desire to bother you or any of your crew members. I give you my word." Although I teetered on the brink of pleading, such a display was beneath my dignity. I was nearly desperate for a breath of fresh air. The cabin was becoming increasingly stuffy with the rising sun.

"The word of a siren means nothing to me," Kai said.

"The feeling is mutual, but it's going to be a very long trip if we cannot at least agree to play nice," I countered.

He looked down at me and seemed to be considering my words. "Very well, but I do not make idle threats. If you even attempt to use your siren song again, I will turn you into fish chum."

I swallowed past the lump that formed in my throat just from the picture his threat incited. "Fine," I answered and lifted my hands in defeat. I would promise just about anything at this point for a breath of fresh air.

"You'll need some pants." He glanced down at my bare legs.

"What are pants?" My brow wrinkled in confusion.

He threw his head back and laughed. "Here." He rummaged through the fancy wardrobe and threw some black material at me. "You already have on my shirt, might as well wear my pants."

Something rolled in my stomach when he reminded me that I was wearing something that belonged to him. The desire to snatch it off was so great that my fingers itched, but I knew very well that I had nothing on underneath, and I was not going to find myself any more vulnerable in this man's presence than I already was.

He walked toward me smoothly, like a predator, and placed a finger under my chin. When he lifted it, a part of me wanted to pull away, and the other part was enthralled by the sheer manliness that emanated from him.

"Put these on and then join me above." His eyes bore into mine, and I finally found my fleeting senses and tugged away from his grip.

He smiled in a smug way that had me longing to wipe it from his face, and then he turned and walked out the door.

I glanced around the room and then fumbled with the black pair of pants-thingies, finally managing to slip them on. Only to have them slide right back off and pool around my ankles. I walked around the room until I found some rope. With it, I secured the pants in place. The pants were still too long, even with them hitched up to my waist, so I rolled them over a few times and then walked out of the cabin.

The sun was high in the sky by the time I ventured out onto the deck. My skin sang as the salty wind kissed it. I inhaled deeply and walked toward the railing. The vessel surged rapidly through the water, leaving me astonished at the speed humans could travel above the water's surface.

I gazed down at the churning ocean below, and a pang of sorrow caused tears to well in my eyes. Longing swept over me. The desire to immerse myself in the comforting embrace of the water was nearly overwhelming. Yet, Kai's words echoed in my mind—I was no longer a siren, and the consequences of going overboard could be fatal. Reluctantly, I scanned the area until I spotted the captain positioned high on a platform, hands firm on the wheel. His watchful, guarded gaze followed me as I slowly circled the boat's perimeter. The other men parted like a school of fish when I came near. Did they know I was a siren as well? I finally walked up the stairs and stopped behind Kai.

"Who is that man?" I asked, pointing toward the one who had brought me food earlier. The one Kai said I had been badgering.

"That is Cael, my first mate. As you can probably tell just by looking at him, he is not one to mess with," he said dismissively. Signaling the end of the conversation again.

I should have let it be, but something about him drove me to provoke him. "You're not really a morning person, are you?" I walked over to the railing and leaned against it, finally gaining his attention as he turned toward me.

"I have never, nor will I ever have the desire to carry on a conversation with a siren," he said in a grumpy tone. "This is a business arrangement and nothing more."

A snippy comment was on the tip of my tongue, but I didn't have a chance to voice it.

"Capitán! Land ho!" an unfamiliar voice yelled from high above.

I walked to the edge of the stairs. As I looked up, I had to shield my eyes from the blinding sun. Perched amongst the sails was a man in something resembling a wooden nest.

"What is that?" I asked in awe.

"That's a crow's nest... Well, aboard this ship, it is known as Rat's nest," he answered without looking my way.

"Rat! Watch the bow! Coral reefs surround Turronto Port, and the tide is a moody wench!" Kai thundered, and his voice vibrated deep into my bones.

I nearly jumped out of my skin. The captain had come up

alongside me and yelled over my shoulder at the man high up in the air. My skin instantly tingled at his nearness. I immediately retreated a few steps to put some space between us. When his eyes finally met mine, I saw a smugness in them. He was obviously pleased that he had been able to rattle me.

"Perhaps you need a pair of siren eyes. None compare." I straightened my backbone, trying desperately to hide the fact that his nearness unnerved me.

"If you think you can do better, siren, be my guest," he whispered. As his breath brushed against the shell of my ear, a shudder ran down my spine.

"All hands on deck! Lower the mainsail! Ready the capstan and prepare to heave to!"

I didn't get a chance to argue as he jumped down from the pavilion and started yelling orders. I watched for a while, amazed at how fast and fluidly the men moved to his harsh commands. When I glanced up at the "Rat's nest" he referred to, a smile spread across my face.

Nobody was paying any attention to me as I walked over to the rope ladder ascending to the structure high in the air. Tentatively, I gripped the rope and started to climb. I started questioning if this was a good idea about halfway up when the wind started whipping and the rope ladder started swaying. I clung to it tightly until the wind died down and then continued.

"Señorita, what are you doing? You shouldn't be up here!" A hand reached down, gripped my own, and pulled until I was safely inside the structure high in the air.

"I wanted to see what a rat's nest was, and the view..." My mouth fell open as I looked out across the sea.

The scene was breathtaking. I had seen the ocean from

below but never from above. As far as the eye could see, the sea stretched on for miles. The waves rolled in a rhythmic motion as the sun glistened on the water, making it look like a treasure trove. To our right, I could just make out the land as it came into view—the tans and browns of the beach and the greenery of the trees. Several kinds of birds chirped, and seagulls were cawing as they drew closer to the land.

"Si, it is breathtaking, señorita. Allow me to introduce myself. I am Rat."

I pried my gaze from the ocean and looked at the man who had helped me.

He was much smaller and leaner than the other men, with a thick dark mustache above his lip. He shoved his black hair out of his face as the wind tossed it.

"Rhea." I smiled at him as his eyes twinkled with kindness.

He grabbed my hand, brought it to his lips, and kissed my knuckles. "The pleasure is all mine, señorita."

"Rat!"

He tugged away and leaned over the siding as the captain called his name.

"Si, Capitán?" Rat called down.

"How many leagues..." Kai's words died on his lips as I leaned over the railing, and he went stark still.

"What are you doing up there?" he thundered.

I shrugged and glanced back out across the sea. I had no intention of yelling back and forth with him like younglings. Instead, I rested my elbows on the railing, enjoying the view. The captain simmered with anger and started up the rope ladder. He was moving faster and with more precision than I thought possible for someone of his size. I turned toward him as he landed with a loud thump inside the lookout tower.

"Leave now, Rat." Kai's tone was deathly calm and rang with warning.

"Adios, señorita!"

I gasped as Rat jumped over the railing.

My skin tingled with discomfort as I watched him free fall until he grabbed onto a rope, swinging around to land on the deck. I turned back to the captain as he took a menacing step toward me. I retreated until my back collided with the railing.

"Do you have a death wish, sea demon? You barely just learned to walk—you don't have the stamina to climb a mast."

I batted my eyelashes to further enrage him. "Your concern is touching. It almost seems like you care."

"I do care. I care about that treasure on that sunken ship." He snarled as he ventured closer.

I rolled my eyes and crossed my arms defiantly across my chest. It was a pity there wasn't any treasure on that ship. I smiled to myself at the deceit. I couldn't wait until I rubbed that information in his face, pointing out that a siren had outsmarted the dreaded Blackheart Kai. He stepped around me, rested his forearms on the railing, and looked out across the sea.

"So, can you see the reef and the sea's bottom with your wonderful siren eyes?" he mocked, changing the subject.

"No, but the sea tells me everything I need to know. The reef is about ten yards off the starboard." I smiled victoriously when the smug look faded from his face and was replaced with fleeting shock.

"And just what exactly did the sea say?"

"If you stopped long enough to listen, it would speak to you too." I followed his gaze as it danced across the glistening water.

"Why would I do that? That's what you're for." The sarcasm returned as quickly as it had fled. "If you and the sea are correct, we are right on course."

Before I could respond, he blasted another round of ear-piercing orders and then turned to leave. I watched him skeptically as he leaped over the railing, gripped the rope ladder, and started to climb down. The boldness I had felt with him by my side bounded right over the edge with him. Rat had helped me over the railing, and I didn't know if I could make it back over by myself without slipping. As Kai plainly pointed out, I wasn't too good with the use of my legs yet.

"You're not going to help me? It would mean your death if you let the Princess of Aquarius die aboard your ship. Do you really feel like taking that gamble?" I threw the princess bait out, hoping it would persuade him to help me back down. I was way too stubborn to simply ask this brooding man for help.

The longer I looked over the edge, the higher up it seemed. Funny, I didn't have this feeling when climbing up. My vision began to crisscross, so I focused on him instead of the thought of falling to my death.

"It would be my great pleasure to watch you splatter against the deck. Besides, you got yourself up here, Your Highness. You can get yourself back down." His deep laughter rumbled and grated across my nerves.

I inhaled deeply and then slowly straddled the railing. The wind was still whipping, threatening to snatch me to my death. I gripped the railing so hard my knuckles blanched white. I slowly found my footing on the rope ladder. It swayed back and forth under my body's weight. It seemed like an eternity before I summoned enough courage to release the railing. When I did, my foot slipped and went through one of the holes in the rope ladder. A scream ripped from my throat but was cut off instantly as a strong arm snaked around my waist and steadied me.

"I don't want you coming back up here again. Do I make myself clear?"

My heart lodged in my throat from my near-death experience as my body was hopelessly crushed between the rope ladder and the brawny captain's body. "Do I make myself clear?" he growled again.

Still reeling from the situation, I found myself unable to muster a response, especially the typical defiant retorts I would have offered. Instead, I simply nodded in agreement. He reached down, wrapped his meaty hand around my bare ankle, pulled my foot back through the hole, and placed it on the ladder.

"Hold tight and go down slowly. Don't fight the sway of the rope. Just go with it. I'll be directly below you if you slip again," he reassured me before starting down again.

Embarrassment burned through my body as I followed Kai down the rope ladder. I hated to admit that he had been right, and I proved that fact by nearly tumbling to my death. My tense muscles finally relaxed when my feet hit the solid deck. I glanced around, but the captain had already disappeared in the mass of men running around the ship. The urge to duck below and wallow in my shame was tempting, but I refused to return to the stuffy cabin. Leaning against the railing, I found solace in the open space, feeling free and at ease with the wind gently brushing against my skin and the salty sea spray tenderly kissing my face.

The sun began to set, taking with it the warmth. I

marveled at the brilliant colors that were etched across the sky and reflected in the waters below. The sight was breathtaking. I don't know how long I marveled at the view, but I stayed there until the sky darkened and stars started to sprinkle across it. The ship was now anchored a ways from the shore. I turned, realizing that the busy commotion had died down and it was just the captain and me left on deck.

His eyes met mine, and he seemed at complete peace in the silence, leaning against the railing. Hunger and fatigue tugged at me, but I was still not ready to go below. With cautious steps, I made my way up the stairs and stood behind him. I found myself admiring the texture of his silky, curly hair swaying gently in the night breeze. A sudden longing seized me, a desire to reach out and run my fingers through his hair to see if it was as soft as it looked. The fact that the thought even dared to cross my mind appalled me and had me shaking my head to rid myself of the horrid idea.

"A shilling for your thoughts, siren." His deep voice shattered the quiet, and I startled when he finally decided to speak to me.

"What would I do with a shilling? I will take some fish, though. I'm starved."

My response awarded me his attention, not that I really wanted it. He glanced back at me with a slight upturn of his lips that I might even classify as a smile.

"Cael informed me that you have not eaten. I suppose I could rustle you up some fish to please your delicate princess palate," he said with a smugness that I found rather irksome.

I was not being difficult, but I did not intend to eat the strange human food offered this morning. Sloshing in the water pulled my attention from the pirate. I bent over the railing to see a massive school of dolphins splashing around the ship.

"Dolphins!" I said in surprise.

Kai glanced at them and then back at me as I watched their antics.

"Guess they're attracted to you," he said as he focused straight ahead again.

I watched them closely. They were acting strange. They were definitely trying to get someone's attention, but I seriously doubted it was me. No fish or mammals that swam the seas were attracted to sirens. We were predators. They usually swam in the opposite direction, but maybe they couldn't tell what I was in this human body.

He interrupted my musing. "Better get some sleep. We go to shore just as soon as the sun touches the horizon in the morning."

"You're going to let me go on land?" Try as I might, I could not hide the excitement from my voice.

His glance dismissively brushed over me, and the only response I received was a curt shrug. I walked along the railing, watching the dolphins, as I returned to the small cabin in the ship's hull. *Strange indeed.*

CHAPTER 10
KAI

Dawn shattered the darkness all too soon for my liking. My aching muscles protested loudly as I forced my body out of the makeshift hammock I had slept in the last few nights. I would be glad when that siren was out of my hair and I got my bed back. The crew slowly emerged from their barracks below like zombies out of a tomb.

"Look alive, bilge rats! Prepare the dinghies to go ashore." They quickly perked up at my announcement and rushed around, eager for the pleasures of land.

Cael walked up beside me and looked out toward the port. "What are you going to do with the siren?"

"She'll have to go with us." I huffed.

Turronto Port was not the most reputable port around. It was ripping at the seams with cutthroats, bandits, and prostitutes, but I had little choice in the matter. I was not willing to leave her on my ship. There was no telling what kind of havoc she would cause to my ship without me onboard to keep her in check.

"Good luck with that." Cael's laughter rumbled in his chest as he left my side and helped the men ready the boats.

I shook my head and started toward my cabin to collect the little headache. I opened the door slowly without knocking, half expecting her to still be curled up in my bed. Instead, she was pacing back and forth in the room. She was dressed, her face clean, and her long red hair was tied in a braid, swaying back and forth as she paced.

"About time," she sassed and threw her hands on her hips.

"You need to take the excitement down a couple of notches," I warned as I walked up to her. As usual, she held her ground and stared up at me. "The people at this port will skin you alive if they find out you are a siren. You have to blend in."

Rhea pressed her lips into a thin line, and I knew she was holding back a rebuttal, but she just nodded her head in understanding. With her newfound submission, I motioned for her to precede me. We stopped at the edge of the railing, and I watched her as she glanced down.

She hesitated, her gaze lingering on the boats below.

"Don't just stand there." I motioned toward the rope ladder that swayed on the side of the ship.

A sheen overtook her eyes, and I was sure she was thinking about her near-death tumble from the mast. Rhea looked at me, and I simply raised a questioning eyebrow at her. With a huff, she eased her body over the ledge and slowly descended the ladder. She wobbled as her feet hit the boat that bucked in the rough waves.

"Sit here, señorita," Rat practically singsonged as he made room on the bench for her.

She glanced back at me, rewarding me with a smile that was just as deadly as it was sweet, and then she sat beside him. Rat smiled at her, raking his gaze admiringly over her face like a lovesick puppy. The sudden urge to pick Rat up by the nape of his neck and toss him overboard overtook me, but I ignored the feeling.

"Row," I thundered, and the oars slipped into the water, setting the small boats into motion.

I was at the back of the boat with a good vantage point to observe the looming beach, but my eyes kept returning to the siren. She submerged her fingers in the water. The sheer pleasure that overtook her features when her hand dipped below the surface had me momentarily captivated. There was a rosiness to her cheeks that I had not noticed before and a twinkle in her honey-swirled eyes that was bewitching. *Bloody sirens and their hypnosis.* I shook my head and focused back on the beach.

Rhea sat up straighter and pulled her hand from the ocean when we were only a few feet from the beach. The boat scraped against the sandy shore, and the men piled out. Rhea stood up, wobbled, and nearly fell over the edge of the boat. Without thinking, I scooped her up in my arms, walked across the swaying boat, and placed her feet on the sand. With her body pressed so close to mine, her scent assaulted my senses, and I couldn't help but inhale the fragrance of the salty sea mixed with a touch of exotic citrus.

Shock overtook her features as she looked up at me, confusion scrunching her brow.

"You were taking too long." I provided an excuse and brushed past her without another word.

"Head to the merchant and get the supplies we need to mend the boat," I boomed as I trudged through the sand.

The crew immediately grumbled their complaints.

"You heard the captain." Cael sneered.

"You'll have plenty of time to hit the taverns, but you will get my supplies before you drink yourselves into a stupor."

Without any further protests, the men trekked off in the direction of the town. I started after them, only to be stopped by Cael's voice. "Are you forgetting something...?"

I glanced back around and noticed that the siren had not moved from her spot on the beach. She was staring down at her bare feet, sloshing them in the damp sand. I withheld a curse that threatened to leak from my lips as I stomped back down the beach toward her. I opened my mouth with the intention of yelling at her.

"It's so soft and warm," she blurted, kicking my brain off track.

Delight shone on her facial features, making her brighter than the still-rising sun.

"You've never touched sand before?" I came up alongside her, entirely forfeiting the idea of scolding her for delaying me.

"Just what is on the ocean floor. This is different somehow. We're not allowed anywhere near land. After my sister's dea —" Her eyes rounded, and she quickly stepped out of the little sand hole she had dug with her bare feet.

She stood stark straight by my side as if waiting for me to move. It didn't matter to me what she was trying to hide, but I'd be lying if I said my curiosity wasn't piqued. I stomped back through the sand with her close on my heels as I followed my crew.

I gripped her upper arm and pulled her closer to my side when we ventured into the market area of the port. When I glanced in her direction, she took in the sights of the market through rounded, awe-filled eyes. It was a small market stationed on a single road with vendors on each side, nothing spectacular or even worth my time, but by the look on her face, it was the grandest bazaar ever seen.

"Fresh fish!" a grungy-looking man with holes in his shirt announced and threw the fish in front of Rhea's face.

She instantly stopped, and her little nose twitched as she inhaled the fish. Without warning, she grabbed the fish from the merchant's hands and ripped into its flesh with her teeth.

"What the…" The man with the salt and pepper hair sputtered as he reached for Rhea.

I casually stepped in front of her, blocked the man, and tossed him a small silver coin. He fumbled to catch it and then looked at me in awe at the amount I had given him. The harshness of my gaze dared him to press the matter further.

He walked away from us without another word. "Fresh fish! Get your fresh fish!"

I turned, and Rhea's eyes beheld mine, but I couldn't blame her, really. The man had shoved it in her face. I gripped her wrist and continued pulling her along beside me as I tried to ignore her inhaling the raw fish fillet. Once she finished her breakfast, I pulled out a bandanna from my pocket and handed it to her.

"You have fish on your cheek," I said when she looked at the rag like she didn't know what I wanted her to do with it.

She took it from me and wiped her face, but the fish particles still remained on her skin. I took the bandanna from her hand and stepped toward her, wiping the fish from her face. She blinked up at me a few times. I realized how close I was to her, but for some reason, I could not make my feet move to put distance between us.

"Cap, we have a problem with the supplies!" Cael yelled from up the road, snapping me from the trance.

I continued up the path with the siren close in tow and did not miss the looks of unadulterated lust that the men were throwing her way as we ventured up the narrowing street. I had hoped the baggy men's clothing she wore would downplay her sensual, lithe body, but obviously, I was wrong. The desire to slit every man's throat that looked at her threatened to overtake me, but that was stupid. Why would I care if they ogled the sea demon? I squared my shoulders and picked up my pace, trying to put distance between me and my murderous thoughts. I stopped only when I reached the building with a broken sign that read Turronto's Tavern.

"The owner of the lumber shack is inside," Cael confirmed, clearly aggravated with the man. "He said he was going to charge us double for the supplies we needed. Something about payment due from the last time…"

"That filthy bilge rat," I cursed under my breath. "He lost those supplies fair and square last time in a card game." I booted the door open, and it crashed against the wall, causing all attention to turn to me as I entered.

The people inside parted as I made a beeline for the rear of the tavern where that leech liked to hide in the shadows.

"Captain Kai, it is a pleasure." Dante's words dripped with sarcasm as I stopped in front of the table where he was sitting.

"You seem to be causing my men some hardship. The fact that they have not run you through yet really astounds me," I answered and sat down in the chair next to him.

My crew would not dare lay a finger on him in reality. Dante ran this hovel of a port, and anyone who raised a hand to him would not likely make it back to their ship in one piece before his men fed on them like a school of barracuda.

I felt Rhea's presence behind me, and when Dante's eyes lifted from mine and took on a sheen of desire, it was confirmation that she was at my back.

"What is this nonsense about charging us double? You know bloody well you lost that game of cards for the last supplies we purchased." The anger I forced behind my words drew Dante's attention away from Rhea and back toward me.

"It wasn't a fair game," Dante whined, banging his tankard of beer against the table. I watched in mock fascination as the contents spilled over the lip of the cup and splattered onto the table.

"You do realize you were playing with a pirate. Fair isn't exactly in my vocabulary." I scoffed. "Besides, I didn't make the bet, and I didn't make you drink. It was your own fault that you were so drunk that you couldn't even read the symbols on the cards." A wicked, cocky grin graced my lips, and Dante's face reddened with anger.

He opened his mouth to speak, closed it, and stood up. I instinctively placed my hand on the hilt of my sword as he walked beside me, but I was not his target.

"I'll let bygones be bygones if you allow me a romp with your redheaded lass here." His voice dripped with libido as he gripped Rhea by the wrist and wrenched her toward him.

Rhea's body collided with his, and the contact sent a bolt of angry electricity up my spine. Rhea hissed and raised her hand to strike him, but before she could retaliate, I latched onto his wrist and squeezed.

One of his bones snapped under the pressure, but the sound could not be heard over his high-pitched screaming.

91

Before I could think better of my actions, I slammed his palm against the table, pulled out my dagger, and stabbed it through the back of his hand, anchoring him to the table.

He continued to wail, and my men drew their swords as his goons stood and attempted to save their worthless leader.

"Look what you did to my hand!" Dante sputtered the words as he desperately tried to suck in air in between his bouts of panic. Satisfaction oozed through my being as the table became stained with the miscreant's blood.

I leaned toward him and growled in his ear. "Touch her again, and you won't have to worry about your hand because I will cleave you to the brisket, savvy?"

My gaze traveled to Rhea, who stood at the ready. If she was shaken at all from the encounter with Dante or the gory display, I couldn't tell from her demeanor.

With my hand still on the hilt of my knife, I sat back down in the chair. "Tell your men to stand down," I threatened, slightly shifting the blade.

Dante screamed so loud I thought it would shatter the glass in the room.

"Now," I threatened, giving the dagger another little jerk.

"Take your seats!" Dante whimpered through his pain, and his men immediately sat down.

"My men are going to load the supplies we need into our boats...at cost," I added for good measure, "and then we are going to pretend like this little unfortunate incident never happened." I smiled at the tears that ran down Dante's wrinkled, worn face.

"Whatever you say," Dante gritted out between clenched teeth.

I slowly stood, snatching the knife from his hand as I rose

from the seat. Dante yelled and clutched his maimed hand to his chest. With a quick swipe of my eyes, I motioned for my men to move out. They began to slowly back their way out of the tavern. I placed my hand on the small of Rhea's back and ushered her toward the door, knowing that any second now, this whole thing had the potential of turning into a bloodbath.

"Nice doing business with you." I mockingly saluted Dante, putting the final nail in the coffin as I pushed Rhea out the door.

CHAPTER II
RHEA

Kai pushed me toward Cael, who caught me and shoved me protectively behind him. I braced myself for all hell to break loose. Seconds turned into minutes as they stood there with their swords raised, ready for battle, but nothing happened. Cael glanced around with uneasy eyes, obviously as perplexed as I was that the man inside had not instantly retaliated.

I pulled away from Cael's grip and walked back over to the captain. "I think it's best if we stop standing around and take the supplies to the ship as quickly as possible."

Kai motioned for his men to move out and grabbed me by the arm, pulling me along with him. I didn't protest as he dragged me around like a wayward piece of seaweed. Honestly, I was still too shocked to do much more than put one foot in front of the other. The amount of violence I had just witnessed from the captain was frightening. Had his cool demeanor snapped in a matter of seconds just because he was arguing over supplies, or did it have something to do with the man touching me? I shook my head. That couldn't be it. I was sure that Kai would have allowed that man to do whatever he wanted with me to get his supplies, so the thought was absurd.

Kai finally released me when we came to a rundown large wooden shack. I peeked inside and saw a massive amount of lumber and other supplies I did not recognize.

"Shuffle your feet and keep your eyes peeled. Dante could retaliate any second," Kai reminded his crew while assigning four men to keep watch.

With the men carrying as many supplies as they could handle, we trudged back to the beach.

I slowed again when my feet hit the fluffy light-colored sand, still marveling at its warmth and the sensation it sent through me each time I touched it. Kai barked orders like an angry seal and sent the men back for another load. I glanced at his back and then at the water as it leisurely kissed the shoreline with its gentle waves. My heart called to the ocean like a lover lost at sea. I desperately needed to feel the coolness of the sea against my skin.

Once I walked to the edge, I dipped my toes in the water. I immersed my feet in the shorefront, and happiness flooded my body. I sat in the sand, not caring at all that my clothes were getting wet, and allowed the water to wash over my feet and legs. Then I closed my eyes. For the first time in several days, I was at peace.

The nagging feeling of someone looking at me had me opening my eyes and turning toward the ship. Kai watched me carefully but never moved to stop me. When my gaze met his, a strange pang gripped my chest. He seemed to be in a peaceful state, just as I was.

"Kai! Is that you?" The enchantment between us broke

when a strange female voice rose above the sound of the crashing waves.

My muscles instantly tensed, not knowing if this stranger was a friend or foe. The female, whose hair color matched the sand I was sitting on, threw her arms around Kai's neck, pulling him in for a kiss. My teeth gnashed on their own accord. *Obviously, a friend.* She finally released him and beamed up at him like he was a lighthouse in the midst of a storm. I watched them from my spot on the shoreline, unable to make out what they were saying. I didn't miss the fact that his hands were still resting on her waist.

Suddenly, they both turned toward me. My cheeks grew hot with embarrassment when I realized I had been caught staring at them. Slight panic curled down my spine as they began to walk up the beach toward me.

Kai motioned to me with a slight shift of his head. "Penelope, this is Rhea."

"Hello." Penelope bent toward me, extending her hand in a kind manner that I did not expect.

I returned her smile and gripped her hand.

"Penelope has taken pity on you and your filthy state and has offered to take you to her cabin to get cleaned up." Kai's eyes bored into mine, something hidden beneath his expression that I could not decipher. "Might as well go. You smell worse than that fish you crammed down your throat earlier. It will probably take us another hour to load all these supplies." Kai cleared his throat, lifting a questioning eyebrow at me.

I slowly stood, my baggy clothes dripping with salty water and sand.

Penelope smiled at me and latched onto my arm. "Come!"

We turned to leave, only to be stopped by Kai's voice. "I'll be there to collect you shortly." There was a warning in his voice that I was sure Penelope missed, but I heard it loud and clear.

I threw a devious smile in his direction and followed Penelope as she led me off the beach and up a winding path.

"Do you know the captain well?" I asked between puffs of breath as the incline steepened.

"Sure, he stays with me every time he's in Port Turronto." Penelope threw the words over her shoulder, clearly not as out of breath as I was.

My heart tensed like someone had reached into my rib cage and given it a little squeeze. I tried to blame it on my spindly legs and the trek up the mountainside, not on her revealing that Kai stayed with her. Why was I even surprised? I'm sure he had women in every port. I snorted to myself at the irony.

"Here we are," Penelope announced as the ground leveled out, revealing a small but well-fashioned hut tucked neatly into the mountainside.

My pulse thundered in my ears, and my lungs screamed for air as I leaned against a boulder, taking a much-needed rest. I finally sucked in enough air to ease the ache of my lungs. I sat up straighter, my eyes absorbing my surroundings.

To my left was a severe drop-off that would mean instantaneous death for anyone who walked off the edge, but that was not what caught my attention. I stood and walked carefully to the ledge to get a better look at the view. The ocean stretched for miles, the sight similar to what I saw up in Rat's lookout tower on the ship.

My eyes and heart tugged toward Aquarius, flooding me with sorrow. Dark Water grew closer to them with each passing day. The thought of my mother, father, younger sister, my people, and maybe even Orm suffering the wrath of the Dark Hydra was suffocating. I still had time, fleeting though it may be. Dark Water churned through the ocean slowly, and the cold waters around Aquarius would work in our favor, slowing the evil even more, but eventually, it would reach my home.

"You love the ocean? I can tell." Penelope interrupted my thoughts of doom, drawing my attention back to her.

"With my entire being," I answered with a bit of sadness lining my tone.

"So does Kai. I used to think he stuck around for me when he was in port, but let's be real, it's all about the ocean. The sea's his one true love, no doubt about it."

When I turned to Penelope, she looked at me with sorrowful eyes. I smiled, trying to rid myself of the doom-filled thoughts that constantly plagued my mind. "I know the feeling."

Glancing sidelong at Penelope, I finally mustered up the courage to ask her about Kai. I certainly wasn't going to gain anything from my short, snarky conversations with him. "How much do you know about Kai? Do you know anything about his family?"

Penelope seemed taken aback by my question, and I feared I had crossed a line, but I desperately needed to know more about the man I was putting hope in to help me save the Seven Seas.

"Not much is known about Kai other than the rumors that spread around about him, and believe me, most of those are true," she said with a look of wariness. "No one really knows about his family. He doesn't talk much, least of all about his past. Let's just say I don't think you become a pirate if you had a good upbringing. Know what I mean?" The sadness in Penelope's eyes instantly disappeared as she led me into her home. "Come on, let's get you cleaned up. It will make you feel better."

The small hut she led me into was nothing like the finery in Kai's cabin. The floors and walls were made of some sort of dried mud that had hardened to a rock-solid consistency, and there were few pieces of furniture, but it was nice and tidy. She motioned at a metal tub that looked barely big enough for me to fit in, filled to the brim with water.

"I was getting ready to wash myself before I heard the commotion on the beach." She shrugged. "I had already filled it full of water. It's probably cold by now, but you're welcome to it."

I stared at the water, bent, and dipped my hands in like I had done with the wooden bucket I used in Kai's cabin.

"Give me those dirty clothes. I'll find you something clean to wear." She held her hand out to me in an impatient manner. "Better hurry. Kai will be back soon, and I promise he does not knock before entering a woman's room." Penelope smiled.

"I've already found that out," I answered and quickly undressed.

"Hurry up and get in," she scolded before venturing outside with my clothes.

I quickly immersed myself in the frigid water, ducking under the surface to wet my hair. By the time I came back up for air, I already felt better.

Penelope walked back through the door. "There's a bar of soap next to you. Nothing fancy, but it gets the job done." She pointed to a rectangular white object, and I grabbed it and held it up to my nose.

It didn't have much of a smell and looked awful. I tentatively bit into it, instantly regretting the decision.

"What are you doing? Don't you know what soap is?" Penelope fussed, throwing both of her hands to her hips.

I shook my head because, honestly, I didn't know.

"Where did Kai find you?" Penelope asked. She extracted the soap from my hands and lathered it on a cloth.

"Here, now wash." She pushed the rag toward me, and I did as she instructed, scrubbing every inch of my body.

"Now your hair." She rubbed the soap against my scalp. The uneasy feeling of a human touching my hair quickly vanished as I watched bubbles form from the soap.

After she finished scrubbing my hair, I ducked back under the water to rinse off the bubbles. When I surfaced, I felt like myself again.

"Come on, dry off with this, and try these clothes on." Penelope handed me a large cloth, and I quickly wrapped it around my nakedness.

Penelope helped me into the new clothes and finished by tying the front of the dress. "Even in one of my oldest dresses, you still outshine me." Penelope huffed and motioned toward a broken mirror she had sitting up against the wall.

Penelope had chosen an emerald-green dress that was short and flowy and came just above my knees with long flounce sleeves that hung off my shoulders. The bodice was ruched at my bust and had a tie front. My hair was still soaking wet and dripped onto the dress, deepening the color.

"Sit here." Penelope motioned to a chair. She used the cloth to dry my hair and then ran an object with bristles through it, pulling out all of the tangles. "Now you're ready. I probably just shot myself in the foot for helping you. Once Kai sees you, he'll likely drool all over you." A touch of anger lined her tone.

"You don't have to worry about that. He hates me, and I assure you the feeling is mutual," I vowed.

"Mm-hmm, that's not what I witnessed on the beach when I came down. He couldn't take his eyes off of you, and you him," Penelope said, causing a strange flutter in my chest.

I chewed on the bottom of my lip. "I'm just trying to figure him out." The conversation made me uncomfortable.

"Let's go! Time's wastin' and the tide is shifting."

Just as Penelope predicted, Kai burst through the door without so much as knocking. We both jumped at the sudden intrusion. Kai stopped in the doorway, his eyes swallowing me whole. "Damn it, Penelope. Did you have to put her in that? I'm trying to keep the men away from her." His voice rumbled with anger and annoyance.

"I didn't do it on purpose! That's the ugliest dress I own. I can't help it that she looks like that," Penelope spat.

Kai's gaze brushed over me again, leaving a cold trail wherever it traveled. I swallowed hard and stood, facing him.

"For your troubles." Kai tossed Penelope a gold coin. She easily caught it and placed it on the table before her.

"I'd rather you stay the night." She batted her eyelashes in a way that made me long to pluck them from her lids.

"Can't," Kai answered sternly. "Let's go." He stepped closer and gripped my upper arm.

"You have dragged me around this entire port all day today. I am capable of walking on my own." I yanked my arm from his death grip and marched toward the door. "Thank you for your kindness, Penelope. It is something that I have not been accustomed to since encountering Kai." I scowled as I paused at the door.

Penelope's only response was a widening of her eyes, like she was shocked that I would speak to Kai in such a manner. With a shrug, I started back down the long trail that led to the beach.

On the way down, I was all too aware of Kai's leering eyes. Every time I turned to look at him, he didn't even attempt to hide the fact that he was watching me. He just shot me a cocky grin and continued to stare. The act caused a rush of adrenaline to flood through my veins.

Finally, I broke through the dense brush and back onto the beach. All eyes instantly turned to me. I swallowed hard and backtracked a few steps, only to collide with the solid body of the captain.

"Is there a problem, sea demon?" he whispered and leaned closer, brushing his beard along the shell of my ear.

"No." I shoved away from him and tried to make my captain-induced limp legs cooperate.

I marched toward the small boat and awkwardly climbed inside. It burned me up inside as Kai watched me struggle, still smirking at my flustered antics. I tore my gaze from his and scanned the boat, feeling increasingly uneasy under the scrutinizing stares of the crew.

I fumbled nervously, clenching the dress I wore between my sweaty palms.

Kai cleared his throat loudly, his glare roaming over all the men, and one by one, they reluctantly turned their gazes from me. All except him, of course.

Relief washed over me as we reached the ship, easing the

tension that had gripped my body. The men crowded out the boat and up the rope ladder. I glanced back at Kai, watching him as he watched me. Our bodies swayed in the steady rise and fall of the boat in the waves.

"You going to stand there all day?" he chided.

"You first," I snapped. I no longer wore those pants things and had very little underneath the dress. My cheeks heated with shame, thinking about climbing the ladder with him directly below me.

He straddled the rolling boat as he ventured closer. "You might slip again." He stopped only a few inches from my face. The motion of the waves brought our lips closer with each rise and fall.

"I'm not that helpless," I challenged.

His gaze brushed over my face agonizingly slow. "Suit yourself." He shoved past me and up the ladder with ease and smoothness.

I glanced at the swaying ladder as the boat beneath me bucked in the sea. I swallowed past the lump that had formed in my throat. Now all I had to do was make it up the ladder without disgracing myself.

It took entirely too much effort and time, but I eventually made it up the ladder and onto the deck of the ship. I was half expecting the crew to be watching my every move and waiting for my head to break over the railing, but no one paid me any mind as I clumsily hoisted my body over the edge.

"Get those dinghies secured and the rest of those supplies unloaded. I want to be ready to sail within the next hour," Kai thundered from behind the wheel.

"What about repairing the boat?" Cael asked as I slowly

walked up to the helm to stand out of the way of the men who rushed about.

"We will prepare the ship in open waters. I don't want to stay in this port any longer than we have to." Kai lowered his voice, and Cael's eyes widened with understanding.

"I'm surprised that Dante let us leave without so much as a slap on the wrist," Cael added.

"My thought exactly. The sooner we get out of here, the better." Kai's gaze shifted to mine before he continued to bellow orders.

I glanced at the port, an uneasy feeling oozing up in the pit of my stomach. Call it female intuition or the intelligence of a siren, but something was not right about the whole situation, and I could tell by Kai's stiffened posture he felt it too.

The sun slowly sank beneath the horizon, and fatigue tugged harshly at me. My eyes felt like someone was trying to pull them closed. I wove my way through the men that still darted around the ship. We had left port and were out of danger, so I returned to my cabin.

Candles cast a subtle glow throughout the room, providing enough light for me to wash off the lingering salt spray from my face. In the gentle light, I changed into one of the captain's oversized shirts. I slunk into the bed, pulled the covers over my body, and closed my eyes.

The cabin door flung open and banged loudly against the cabin wall, and I shot straight up, my head buzzing as my heart lodged in my throat.

Kai's boots echoed across the floor as he approached me. "Slide over, sea demon. I refuse to sleep in that hammock another night."

"I'm not sleeping beside a heathen," I hissed, bunching the covers tightly to my chest.

To my horror, he never stopped until he was by the bed. The tension in the room heightened as he stood there, his presence looming over me, challenging the unspoken boundaries keeping us apart.

"You don't have much choice," he countered, pulling the edge of the covers back. "It's either this or I can throw you back in the cell you're so fond of." The weight of his words hung in the air, leaving me with an impossible decision to make.

The image of him sleeping next to me did unspeakable things to my insides, stirring an uproar of conflicting emotions. Yet the thought of returning to that dark hole below filled my head with panic. Reluctantly, I scooted over, creating just enough space for Kai to join me on the bed.

"If you try anything, I will slit your throat," Kai declared with a stern gaze. He emphasized the point by placing the dagger, previously concealed in the top of his pants, on the small wooden nightstand. The sharp gleam of the blade seemed to highlight his threat.

"Don't worry, I won't try to take advantage of you," I retorted with a forced laugh. The uneasy humor died to a deafening silence as Kai peeled off his shirt, tossing it casually to the floor.

The bed yielded to his weight, threatening to edge me closer to him. With a decisive roll, he turned over, presenting his back to me. The ship rocked gently, and the moon cast a soft glow through the small cabin window. I stared into the darkness, unable to get comfortable knowing that Kai lay so close to me. As a princess, I had never shared my seaweed bed with another male, although I had plenty of offers. I had been certain that Orm would have been the first to lie beside me and not Blackheart Kai, the sworn enemy of my people.

My eyes burned like someone had poured sand into them, begging me to close them and get the rest my body demanded. We had been like this for a while, and it seemed as if the pirate captain truly only had sleep on his mind. I blinked a few more times, trying to keep my eyes from closing, but eventually, exhaustion won the battle.

CHAPTER 12
RHEA

A loud crash and the splintering of wood that shook the entire ship woke me from my slumber. I screeched and tumbled to the floor in a mass of blankets. My heart threatened to burst from my ribcage as I sat motionless, trying to make sense of what was happening. I glanced at the bed, noting that my sleeping partner was no longer there. *Barnacles!* I had slept more soundly than intended with the enemy at my side.

I threw on my dress from yesterday and rushed outside. Another loud boom, followed by more splintering wood, met me as I reached the deck. My mouth dropped open when I saw two large wooden beams protruding out of the deck of the ship.

"Stop knocking holes in my ship!" The captain's voice rang out loud and angry. "If you drop one more beam from up there, I will hang you by your cojones. Look what you've done to my deck!" Fury rolled off him like a tidal wave, so I steered clear of him and the men who obviously were having difficulties securing the beams above.

I watched in fascination as the men scaled the mast,

swinging from pole to pole as they worked vigorously to repair the rigging and mast.

"Tie that tighter," Kai growled then, in seconds, leaped onto the rope ladder and climbed up to the men.

There was nothing I could do to help them. I would be more hindrance than aid if I got in their way, so I found a nice shaded spot and made myself comfortable.

"Here." Cael invaded my secluded spot, handing me a plate of food and a cup. I tentatively took it. I picked at the food, Cael's watchful eyes following my every move.

My mind wandered back to the delicious food of my kingdom—seaweed wraps filled with succulent sea berries, kelp salads with a hint of salty ocean freshness, and my favorite pearl-like orbs that burst with savory liquid when bitten into. The memories of those flavors only intensified the disappointment of the bland and strange textured food before me.

"Cael, bring me that extra rope," Kai yelled.

Despite myself, I smiled at Cael, who released a frustrated huff as he lugged the rope up the mast.

The sun rose higher in the sky, bringing with it a suffocating heat. The men continued to work, and despite my efforts not to do so, I kept glancing at the captain. Kai had pulled his hair back, tying it out of his face, and had shed his shirt long ago. As he lifted the large wooden beams to repair the mast, his body glistened with perspiration. I glanced down, berating myself for finding pleasure in the way the captain looked. Masking such deadliness in an appealing outward package was a cruel ploy.

"Rat, throw me that rope!" Kai bellowed, causing me to glance back up.

Rat worked tirelessly right alongside the other men. I glanced at his Rat's nest, noting that no one was in the lookout tower. I stood and faced the wide-open sea. We were far from port, as we had traveled all night to distance ourselves, but we were also very vulnerable without any sails and a half-deconstructed mast and rigging.

My gaze swept across the horizon to ensure that no one was prowling around out there. Both my eyes and heart stumbled as a ship no more than a league away came into view. I eased closer to the front of the ship and squinted against the bright sun to see it better. It could be anything. Ships probably traveled through there often, I rationalized, trying to calm myself as panic clawed its way up my throat. I blinked a few times. This ship was bearing down on us, heading right in our direction at top speed.

My limbs began to shake as I turned. "Kai!" My voice trembled with anxiety as I tried to gain his attention to warn him of the impending danger.

"That's Captain to you," he yelled, never turning to me or taking his eyes off his work.

"Kai!" I yelled louder, completely ignoring his command to call him Captain.

Anger radiated off him as he looked down at me with dwindling patience. His gaze followed mine as I turned back toward the oncoming ship. A slew of curses left his lips as he scrambled down from above. "All hands on deck! Prepare for battle."

I never moved, my hands deadlocked on the railing and my eyes on the ship that grew closer with each passing second. The scraping of metal against wood caught my attention, and I looked down at the hull of the ship. At least a half dozen cannons emerged from the inner hull, aimed toward the oncoming vessel.

"It's one of Dante's ships," Rat yelled from above, and the blood drained from my face.

"I knew he let us leave port way too easily," Cael barked before he echoed Kai's orders.

We were vulnerable, like starfish clinging to a rock with no way to flee and no way to turn the ship to avoid a broadside hit.

"Get below!" Kai harshly ripped me from the railing, my body colliding roughly with his.

"No." Hot tears stung my eyes. "I will not die in that hole. I'd rather throw myself overboard and drown."

Kai stopped his mad dash and glanced at me with a hint of respect in his eyes. "Then get up to the helm and stay behind me."

I didn't argue and rushed to do exactly what he said as he continued to ready his men for the fight that was nearly upon us.

Kai joined me at the helm, snatching the wheel in a desperate attempt to get the ship to turn with the tide.

"Their cannons have greater reach than our own," Cael whispered.

"I know," Kai ground out between clenched teeth.

As if on perfect cue, the entire atmosphere shook as Dante's cannons exploded. My heart slid down to my stomach as Kai threw me to the ground, covering my body protectively with his.

Something splattered across my face and the other exposed appendages of my body. When my brain registered that the substance was blood, I screamed. A wretched, rotting smell assaulted my nostrils.

"What the hell is this?" Kai's chest rumbled against my back as he stood, pulling me with him. He was drenched in blood and guts.

I glanced around the ship, and my legs nearly buckled in upon themselves at the carnage all over the deck. The men stood, staring blankly at one another, each covered with the same blood and gore. It was peculiar that I did not see any human body parts. I reached down and picked up what looked like an iridescent tentacle.

The cannons exploded again, and Kai slammed my body against his, wrapping an arm around my waist and using the other to force my head onto his chest. *I guess there were worse ways to die.*

Debris rained down all around us. I carefully pushed myself from Kai's embrace and looked up at him. Inky black blood dripped down his face, with guts and slime in his hair. I wanted to laugh, but the look on his face forbade me from doing so.

"They're leaving, Cap'n!" someone yelled, prying his attention from mine.

"What was the point of that?" Cael thundered as he came alongside Kai. "We got out of that easy, other than we'll all have to soak for a week to get rid of this awful stench." Cael reached up, plucked a tentacle from his shoulder, and threw it to the deck in disgust.

Leaning down, I picked up the discarded tentacle. I turned it in my hands again, trying to determine what it was. Suddenly, it hit me like a typhoon.

I bit my lip and glanced around the ship, putting pieces of

the mutilated animal back together like a puzzle in my mind. "Kai, I'm pretty sure this is a cirrata." I was certain that was what Dante shot at us out of his cannon.

"I don't care what it is," he snarled, combing his fingers through his wavy hair to remove the waste.

"Kai," I repeated. "Cirratas are nearly extinct. That's why it took me a minute to figure out what it was. I haven't seen one in years. They were nearly wiped out by—"

"Leviathans," Kai interrupted.

"Good thing there aren't any around. If a leviathan scented just a drop of a cirrata's blood in the water, it would travel miles to get to it," I said, tossing the slimy tentacle to the deck.

An explosion of salty water rained down on us, followed by the ship bucking wildly in the sea. Water beaded and dripped from its body as the dragon-like creature with tentacles emerged from the depths of the ocean.

I looked up at the creature that had to be at least four times longer than the massive ship and gasped. "A leviathan."

"Sink me," Kai spat as the beast opened its mighty jaws and roared so loudly I was sure the pain in my ears was from busted eardrums.

"Fire!" Kai thundered, reminding me that the weapons were already loaded and prepared for the other ship's attack.

The cannons exploded in unison with a deafening blow. I reached up to cover my ringing ears, not that it did any good. The massive leviathan flinched as the cannonballs ripped into its flesh, but it was no more than a mere nuisance to a being that large. The men rushed about the deck as the beast bellowed again, flinging its tentacles at anything that moved.

"Cael, the blades!" Kai flipped and ducked as the beast swiped at him.

Cael rushed to a lever I had not noticed before, grunting and straining his muscles as he flipped the wooden switch. The ringing of steel against wood and metal echoed in the air. I looked down the side of the boat as massive jagged blades protruded from all angles along the ship.

Kai grappled with the wheel, causing everyone to tumble to the deck. The beast screeched as the blades dug into its skin, slicing off at least two of its eight tentacles.

"That's it, my beauty! Raise the harpoons!" Kai's malicious laughter echoed, the sinister tone sending a chill through me and setting my nerves on edge.

I jumped out of the way as more than a dozen wooden contraptions that looked like giant slingshots rose from beneath the ship's deck, all armed with sharp-tipped harpoons. The size of the spears would quickly end the sea creature much easier than the cannonballs.

I stood there in momentary shock. I was on a floating death trap. How had I forgotten that this was Blackheart Kai's monster-hunting ship? Everything about it now was deadly, the perfect killing machine. When the leviathan rose from the depths, I'd thought we were all goners, but as the ship shifted into a weapon, I was confident the leviathan was the one who didn't stand a chance.

"Fire!" Kai boomed.

A dreadful feeling sank to the pit of my stomach as a few of the harpoons were launched, sinking deep into the leviathan's flesh. It screeched, eyes widening, and looked for an escape.

"Rope that devil," Kai ordered.

Nets attached to ropes anchored to the boat shot out from below the ship's hull, trapping the creature and preventing its escape. The leviathan struck out with its one free tentacle. I was moving, but I was not quick enough. The tentacle struck me, pulling my legs from under me and swiping me over the railing of the ship.

I screamed as I fell into the ocean. The billowing water consumed me immediately. I gasped for air but only swallowed a mouthful of salty water. I kicked and pulled with my arms, but these stupid legs of mine would not tread the water like my beautiful tail. My fight was useless, the current caused by the thrashing leviathan too strong. I was pulled deeper into the abyss.

CHAPTER 13
RHEA

My body convulsed in its desperate need for air. It felt like my chest would explode if I did not take a breath. My lungs spasmed, causing my mouth to open spontaneously. Water rushed down my airway, filling my lungs. I screamed, bubbles escaping from my mouth as the last bit of air was ripped from me.

Pain radiated from my lower half, then my legs melded together. Just when I thought my time was through, I gasped, and water passed through my gills, allowing me to breathe underwater. I looked down in stunned silence. My siren body was fully restored.

I flipped my powerful tail to distance myself from the massive leviathan that thrashed in the sea. My head broke through the surface of the water, my eyes searching for the ship. Kai gripped the railing, staring directly at me. I was too far away to make out his facial features, but I could have sworn that his shoulders slumped with relief upon seeing me.

He yelled something incoherent over the thundering waves and battle aboard the ship, then disappeared from sight.

I searched for the sea creature as its fear vibrated through the water. It was hopelessly trapped. The leviathan would have already returned to the depths of the sea after discovering that the cirrata was not there for his dining pleasures, but the heathens aboard the ship were determined to kill it.

Another explosion shook the skies as Kai commanded more harpoons to be released upon the creature. Its cries tore at my resolve. This was heartless and cruel.

The leviathan fought against the ropes and nets and dove underwater. I gasped when the front end of the ship dipped below the surface. Ducking under the water, I watched as the leviathan's scales shifted from midnight black to the palest of blues. The camouflage was self-defense to ward off the threat, but it would do him little good. The ship was too buoyant and popped back up out of the water like a cork, bringing the leviathan with it.

Blood seeped through the water, staining the crystal blue sea. I had seen enough. This was going to end now. I fought against the swirling current and came up alongside the ship. For a fleeting second, I remembered the captain's words about what he said he would do to me if I ever tried to use my song on him or his crew again, but in this instance, I didn't care.

My song was mighty, and I could put the entire crew under my spell with just a few notes. The melodious song tingled in my voice box as it came forward. Instant relief washed over me as my tune filled the air. The attackers stopped dead, and all eyes turned to me.

Kai gnashed his teeth at me and threw a slur of curses my way, but I ignored him. He couldn't reach me this far out in the water, not unless, of course, he shot me with a harpoon. Judging by the look on his face, that was not entirely out of the question.

I continued to sing, forcing the men to lower their weapons and cut the ties that bound the leviathan.

Kai gripped the railing, simmering with anger, utterly helpless in stopping his men from doing my bidding. When the final rope snapped and the leviathan was free, it bellowed and turned toward the ship, but I focused my song on it, releasing the men I had captivated.

Yells and curses brought my head back around as the men slowly started to come out of my trance, but I was too focused on the massive beast that thrashed in the water with me to pay them much mind.

My song calmed the creature, and it dipped into the water with just its head visible on the surface. I stopped singing, reaching up to brush my hand along the slick scales on its nose. It was severely injured, but it would survive. It blinked at me a few times as I released it from my bewitchment. I never felt I was in danger, even though the creature could easily open its mouth and swallow me whole if it wanted to. It snorted in the water, spraying my face with a salty mist.

I smiled at it. "Thanks for that."

It ducked beneath the surface, and just as suddenly as it had appeared, it returned to the depths to which it belonged.

As I turned to the ship, I swallowed the lump in my throat. I was sure I had doomed myself by singing. The crew's malicious glares made it clear they had no idea I was a siren. Not until now, anyway.

Scooping up my pride, I swam back toward the ship. Groveling was beneath me, but I would beg Kai to take me to Medusa if I had to. The lives of my people depended on me getting that locket and stopping the Dark Hydra, but all that was now questionable.

. . .

Kai

WHAT THE HELL had just happened? One minute, we had the leviathan trapped and at our mercy, and the next, it was gone like a fleeting memory. I could taste the victory on my tongue like a fine rum until that little sea demon snatched it away from me. I gritted my teeth so hard that cracking them was a definite possibility.

She slowly made her way back over to the ship. Her honey-swirled eyes reflected a mixture of anger and fear as she glared in my direction.

I would be lying if I said I did not find her spunk enthralling. When I looked down at her, I could not keep the smug grin from my face. It took a lot of guts to defy me and then gather her pride and return. I had the unyielding urge to forgo the punishment she deserved for costing me a monster kill, but the thought soured in my stomach as quickly as it had appeared.

When she had started weaving her trance through the air, I considered shooting her—until I was distracted by her ginger hair blowing in the wind. Her ability to commandeer the attention of my entire crew and a leviathan with just her song astounded me. I had never seen anything like it before. Usually, it took a school of sirens to take down an entire crew. This siren may be deadlier than I realized. *Was that why the sea witch wanted her dead?*

Her song had not influenced me, but I still found myself captivated by it. Her voice was like that of an angel, so calm and dripping with pure honey.

"Cap'n! That sea devil is climbing up the side of the ship," Flynt thundered, leaning over the edge and pointing a pistol at her. "Want me to put a bullet between those pretty eyes?" He cocked the trigger.

Sink me. I had not yet prepared myself to explain to the crew why a siren was aboard the ship, but it looked like it was now or never. I needed to calm them before they slaughtered her and hung her head on the bow of the ship.

"Stand down," I ordered as I shoved my way through the masses of men crowded around the side of the ship she was clawing her way up.

Shocked faces turned my way, but I ignored them as I lazily leaned against the railing, waiting for her to make an appearance.

"The Cap'n's bewitched by the demon," Flynt accused, and several rewarded him with grunts of agreement.

"I am bewitched." I smiled at the crew. "Bewitched by the hoard of treasure the siren promised me in return for taking her to Medusa." A hush fell over the crowd. Medusa was a name not lightly spoken of among monster hunters. None were as deadly as she. "The siren has promised the entirety of the treasures of a sunken ship if we take her to Medusa." I raked my hands through my hair as I ensnared their greed with the promise of treasure.

"How do you know you can trust her?" a voice rang out from the back.

Good question. In truth, it didn't matter one way or the other about the treasure she promised because she would be dead long before she had a chance to fulfill that bargain, but that was not something I was willing to confide in the crew.

They would mutiny for sure if I told them I had made a deal with a sea witch.

"It's real," I promised.

Rhea's hands latched onto the railing, and she hoisted herself over the side. The thought of being cordial and helping her skipped across my mind, but I booted it away. Especially with my crew watching.

She landed on the deck with a thud, pulling her long pink iridescent tail over the side. It landed with a flop in front of me. My gaze traveled over the length of her tail. It should have disgusted me, but for some reason, I could not take my eyes off the shimmering scales that seemed to explode with a different color every time the sun hit it.

"Sea devil."

"Scourge of the sea."

"You'll get what's coming to you, siren."

The crew threw hate-filled remarks and slurs her way as she pulled her tail protectively closer to her body and tried to cover her bare chest with her long scarlet hair. She flinched as a few men stepped closer to her, the act igniting my anger.

I stepped in front of her, placing my hand idly on the hilt of my blade. The crew stopped moving. "Here are your options," I stated plainly. "You can get back to work readying the ship to sail to Libya. You can pack your things if this task is too daunting for you, and you will be dropped off at the next port...or you can keep coming at the siren, and I will be forced to spill your guts onto the deck. The decision is yours."

Their eyes shifted from me to my sword. Cael stepped next to me in front of the siren, sword drawn and ready as an added incentive. One by one, they slowly dispersed and resumed the work they'd been doing before Dante and the sea creature interrupted our task at hand.

"I hope you know what you're doing." Cael huffed and walked off to join the men.

I glanced down at Rhea, whose face was pinched with nerves and fury. I could tell by the sheer anger rolling off her that picking her up was a bad idea, but I couldn't leave her sprawled out on the deck with murder in my crew's eyes.

Against my better judgment, I bent down and lifted her. Her tail fin slapped against my thigh, soaking through my pants. She made the entire act all the more difficult by not wrapping her arms around my neck, but I could easily lift her dead weight without her aid.

I carried her below to my cabin, neither of us uttering a word to the other or allowing our eyes to meet. I sat her down in a chair near my desk. She adjusted herself and flicked her tail in what appeared to be annoyance. I turned to leave.

"You have the nerve to call us monsters? Monsters are not born. They are made by their acts," her voice broke through the strained silence.

I stopped in the doorway, glancing back at her. A lone tear glistened on her cheek, and she quickly wiped it away.

"You're calling me a monster?" I questioned.

"You are a monster." Her voice rose an octave, and her gaze brushed across the floor planks, as if she refused to look at me.

I considered her accusative words, realizing she may not be completely wrong. "I never claimed not to be," I answered honestly.

"That leviathan was just hungry. It had no desire to hurt

us, not until it was provoked." She blinked a few times up at me.

"That *leviathan* was the one we were tasked to kill. It has sunk over a dozen ships. You dare to say that it meant no harm?" I growled.

"If Dante used the cirrata to lead the leviathan to us, don't you think he was probably guilty of doing the same to the other ships? A leviathan would never attack a ship without cause," she bit out.

I opened my mouth to argue when realization stood and slapped me across the face. Was it possible that Dante used a bloody leviathan to end his enemies? It required more brains than I would ever credit him for, but it was not out of the question.

I searched her face, tracing every soft angle. "It still deserved to die."

"Why do you hate us so much?" She lifted her eyes, and it was my turn to look away. For some reason, I could not face those rounded, puffy, tear-stained eyes.

"That's none of your business," I gritted out, my anger swirling just thinking about my past.

I gripped the door's edge, intending to slam it, when her voice stopped me again. "I can't stay here like this." She motioned down at her tail. "I'll die if I don't get back in the water."

Her voice already sounded scratchy. Was it from holding back tears or her body drying out?

"Good." I huffed. "Then I won't have to deal with you and your suicidal quest any longer." I slammed the door and waited just outside as I collected my anger and shoved it back down deep where it belonged, along with my memories.

A scream ripped from the siren, the sound grating at my last resolve and sending my pulse skyward. I threw the door open to find her writhing on the floor, her tail turning back into human legs. To allow her some privacy, I silently closed the door. I wouldn't want anyone to see me if I was in that much pain, so I afforded her the same courtesy.

I made my way back on deck. My crew watched me with careful eyes as I walked up to the helm. Cael instantly relinquished the wheel to me. I caressed the smooth wood with my fingertips, and the salty air whipped at my hair, dousing the last bit of my rage. Nothing, not even a fine bottle of rum, soothed me like the sea.

"Did you kill her?" Cael asked seriously, and it took me a second to comprehend why he asked.

"No, she is changing back into a human. Apparently, it is a painful process," I explained.

"Are you truly ready to face Medusa again?" Cael glanced around, and I assumed it was to ensure no one was listening in on our conversation.

"I have no intention of facing her again. My task is to deliver the siren, steal the necklace from her—if she can get it —and then kill her." I shrugged.

"I know you better than that, Kai," Cael whispered. "I think you are becoming attached to that which you are meant to kill." Cael spoke with the voice of a wise man but the words of a fool.

"You've been out in the sun too long, my friend, and it has fried your brain. I care not for that sea demon, and nothing will keep me from getting my hands on the Wraith," I declared in an unyielding tone. Yet, beneath the surface of my words, a storm of turmoil had begun to rage within me.

CHAPTER 14
RHEA

D ays slowly melded into weeks with the sluggish speed of a sea snail. I was losing my mind trapped on this awful ship with that dreadful pirate captain. I spent my days doing nothing more than sleeping, eating, going on deck, and repeating the process the next day.

We'd stopped at another port a few days ago, but Kai had refused to let me go ashore. He said I had caused enough trouble at the last port. A few of his crew members had deserted ship, apparently too frightened to continue on to Medusa's lair. At least we had fresh food. Kai had bought me a few pieces of clothes to wear instead of his clothing, which thrilled me because I was tired of his salty, rugged scent invading my senses.

I glanced down at the clothing he had chosen for me. I was still shocked that I preferred what he had picked out over the dress Penelope had given me. I brushed my hands along the flowy black pants, marveling at how silky they felt against my skin. They rose high on my waist, complementing the white, cropped shirt with delicate buttons running down the bodice. He had bought me a pair of shoes too, but I refused to wear them. I couldn't stand to have my feet so confined.

I inhaled deeply, filling my lungs with salty sea air. My gaze darted to the rushing waters as the ship pounded over the waves. What I wouldn't give to jump overboard, to feel the cool ocean water against my skin and wash away some of the sweat caused by the suffering heat.

"How much longer?" I tried not to whine, but it came out that way anyway. I angled my body toward Kai, who leisurely stood behind the wheel.

I had tried to avoid him over the past few weeks, but I would go stir-crazy if I didn't speak to someone, and I secretly prayed that he would say that we were nearly there.

"We are under full sail. I can do no more. The ship can only travel as fast as the wind allows," Kai answered without glancing my way.

"Seems to me you have more patience when it comes to the prospect of death," Cael's deep voice rumbled as he leaned against the railing beside me.

"I have no intention of dying… I can't." I exhaled, staring helplessly toward Aquarius. "The fate of my people depends upon me."

Cael crossed his arms over his chest, seemingly intending to stay for a while. "Tell me about your home and people."

Kai glanced at Cael with evident annoyance written across his pinched face.

"Aquarius is a beautiful kingdom. One of the largest siren kingdoms around." I paused mid-sentence as I was about to reveal the location of Aquarius. Sea monster hunters did not need to know the whereabouts of my home. Kai glanced back at me when I paused but then focused back on the horizon.

"My father is there, and my mother, and I have a younger sister. I had an older sister, but she was killed by humans." That last part came out lined with venom, and I was surprised that neither man flinched or even seemed at all concerned about my sister's death, but why should they? "When she died, it became my duty to carry on our legacy." My voice deepened with sadness, gaining me a quick glance from Kai over his shoulder.

"And then there is my fiancé, Orm." I swear Kai's shoulders stiffened, and an evil thought blossomed in my mind. "He's so handsome and strong. Captain of the siren army." I forced my voice to become loving and dreamy sounding.

"A fine specimen, I'm sure." When Cael joined in, I was shocked. Stranger still was the smile that spread across his face and the anticipation in his eyes as he watched Kai.

"Quiet, both of you," Kai scolded. "I'm trying to focus on our bearings."

Cael doubled over with laughter. "Since when does talking disturb your navigation?"

"Since now," Kai grumbled.

Cael walked off, still laughing. I scrunched my brow in confusion as I watched Kai.

His gaze finally sought mine. "Tell me, sea demon, how do you plan on defeating Medusa? Anything of flesh is affected by her stare. You may have a better chance as a siren, but I wouldn't rely on that if I were you."

I paused. The thought hadn't crossed my mind. I honestly didn't think I would make it this far, but as the prospect loomed before me, a sinking feeling settled in my stomach.

Kai cocked a dark eyebrow at me. "And don't say your

siren song. Medusa is a gorgon. It may not work on her. Do you even know how to defend yourself?"

A lump swelled in my throat, and I swallowed. "No. Princesses are not exactly trained in self-defense..." I bit my lip when he motioned for another man to take the wheel, and then Kai walked toward me.

His presence was suffocating. He was so close I could feel his body heat warm against my skin.

The hiss of metal rang through the air as he pulled his sword from the scabbard, and I cringed.

"Take it." He handed me the hilt, and I wrapped my fingers around it.

I had never held a sword before, and its weight astounded me. How did this man parade around with this and several other weapons strapped to his body at all times?

"Your stance is important. Spread your legs apart and bend your knees slightly." Using his booted foot, he maneuvered my feet until he was satisfied with my posture. "This way, if someone or something throws their body weight against you, they will be less likely to knock you over. Medusa will use her serpent tail to try to knock you off your feet. If she does, you will be dead."

I couldn't believe he was offering to help me, but I absorbed his words like a sea sponge.

"Hold the blade before your face. You have to protect your upper body at all costs. You have to watch your opponent and use all of your senses. Hear her muscles coil. Smell her skin and the musk it gives off when she is getting ready to strike." He repositioned my arm when the sword started to droop. "Even something as simple as a quiver of her muscles could give away where she intends to strike next." Kai positioned my arms and gripped my chin, forcing me to look up at him. "No matter what, do not take your eyes off your opponent."

I shook my head in understanding as my nerves began to break through the surface of my emotions. I angled my head toward his voice. "How did you survive?"

"I didn't." He breathed in my ear. "Some wounds are not visible to the naked eye."

My fingertips tingled as I tried to process his words. What wound did he speak of?

"Cael, help the sea demon out, will you?" he added before I had a chance to ask him anything further.

My stare shifted to Cael, who had stopped what he was doing to watch the show, along with several of the other men.

"My pleasure, Captain," Cael answered in a voice that was all too eager.

Cael pulled his sword from his waist, the shiny metal of the blade reflecting in my face. I hesitated as the massive man approached me. He struck out as quickly as an eel, striking my sword with such force that it flew from my hands and landed with a loud clang against the floorboards. Cael raised his blade, lightly brushing the tip along the hollow of my throat.

"He that wavers is like a wave of the sea, blown and tossed by the wind." Kai's voice made me jump as he came up behind me, his warm breath caressing my neck.

"You're a poet now?" I asked as he picked up the blade, handed it to me, and repositioned my body.

"No, just speaking words of wisdom." Kai pressed his solid body to my back and placed his rough hand on top of mine, gripping the sword's hilt.

His scent engulfed me, flooding my senses and distracting

me from the man with the blade in front of me. Cael struck out again. I would have been too late again, but Kai was in charge of this dance now. He parried and blocked Cael's attack, the blades echoing when steel met steel. The force of the swords coming together sent a vibrating tingle down my arm, but that was nothing compared to what Kai's closeness was doing to my body.

I tried to focus on Cael as he circled, waiting for the opportune moment to strike. When he did, I blocked it. Kai's hand was still on top of mine, but he was letting me make the decisions now.

"Good." His voice slithered through my ear and all the way down to my toes. "Again."

I could not keep the smile within when Cael attacked again, and I successfully blocked him. Cael's eyes sparkled, and his face shone with amusement.

"Watch his body language. See how his muscles just tensed," Kai whispered.

On cue, Cael's blade sliced through the air, aiming for my midsection. My reflexes were sluggish, and the blow would have cut through my skin, but Kai's arm snaked around my stomach and pulled me backward, just out of reach of the tip of the blade. My body slammed against his, knocking the wind from my lungs. My mind told me to push away from him, but my body had other intentions. My back and shoulders were flush against his rigid torso, my frame melding perfectly with his. I glanced over my shoulder, blinking up at him as his deep blue eyes consumed me and swallowed me whole.

"Land ho, Capitán." Rat's voice echoed from above, knocking me from my trance.

I wet my lips, which had suddenly gone dry. Kai's pupils dilated as he glanced down at my mouth.

Kai cleared his throat, pushing me at arm's length. "That's enough for today."

My back stiffened, and I was frozen in place as Kai walked off and started thundering orders.

"I'll take that." Cael reached down and plucked the sword from my hand. "Cap'n obviously got lost in his little training exercise and forgot where we were. He's going to need this." Cael motioned to the sword in his hand.

"Where exactly are we?"

"The island of Sarpedon, home of Medusa," Cael said without another glance in my direction.

I rushed to the bow of the boat, watching intently as a speck of land way off in the distance came into view. My nerves increased tenfold the closer we sailed to land. Kai instructed the men to adjust the sails, causing the ship to slow as we approached the island.

My eyes traced the side of a steep, jagged cliff, and my mouth fell open in disbelief. The sheer extent of the obstacle before us was intimidating, and doubt crept into my mind. There was no way we were making it up that cliff. A sense of isolation washed over me as I turned to survey the landscape. To the left and right, the treacherous cliff stretched as far as the eyes could see.

I walked over to Kai, who scanned the perimeter like a predator, muscles tensed, ready for anything.

"I take it she does not like company." I tried to sound light-hearted but could not seem to hide the tremor in my voice.

"That's an understatement," Kai muttered.

"Is it like this all the way around the island?" I held my breath, hoping there was nice beach access somewhere.

Kai's gaze shifted forward, and he motioned with his head. "Only way in is through that cove."

I followed the direction he indicated to a crack in the cliff. I would assume this would be good news, but something about Kai's stance and how his eyes contemplated every inch of the area had my fear blossoming.

"Lower the sails and get the quant poles!" Kai's voice echoed off the cliffs in the distance, making him sound even more menacing.

With the sails lowered, the ship came to a complete stop, and the heat from the sun instantly became suffering without the gentle breeze. We were nearly at the entrance of the crevice in the cliff, and I could see why Kai ordered the sails to be lowered. It was a tight fit, and the boat would have never fit through with the sails raised. The men hauled up long, skinny poles and used them to push the boat forward.

They expertly navigated the ship down the long, winding passageway with great ease and precision, but as the close quarters surrounded us, a sense of trepidation crept up my chest. A potent combination of anticipation, excitement, and fear heightened the intensity of the moment. I should have been scared stiff, but this was why I had left my home.

As daunting as the obstacle before us was, it also carried the promise of hope. The narrow passageway, though confining, represented a gateway to end the turmoil caused by the Dark Hydra.

The boat creaked and whined, wood scraping the rocks the further we ventured in. No one spoke; I wasn't sure if anyone was breathing at the moment. A gasp caught in my throat as the ship snared on a protruding boulder.

"Easy," Kai warned barely above a whisper. "The tide is low today. Push off the starboard."

The crew shifted to the right side of the boat, all the men pushing with the quant poles simultaneously. Finally, the ship squeezed by and continued down the narrowing slit in the island.

I eased toward the ship's bow, carefully watching for any signs of danger. Anticipation fluttered in my chest.

"Breathe." I sensed Kai's presence behind me. His thick baritone voice calmed my tattered nerves.

I sucked in a ragged breath and walked closer to the railing. Just ahead, the passageway widened, and with it came a glimmering current of hope.

The ship easily passed through the end of the cliff, giving way to a massive lagoon. My mouth tumbled open at the enchanting scene. A giant waterfall cascaded over the cliff, pouring into the deep aquamarine lagoon, providing perfect, peaceful harmony. Flowers and plants of greens, purples, and blues lined the edge of the water, painting a serene scene against the otherwise jade forest. Rocks broke through the surface of the lulling water covered with a velvety-looking green moss.

"It's beautiful," I whispered as elegant white birds sang, brushing past us and landing on the low-hanging branch of a tree.

I turned, eyes wide, when I heard the metal of Kai's blade hiss as he drew it from his scabbard. "Looks can be deceiving."

CHAPTER 15
KAI

I scanned the smooth surface of the water, my gaze snaring on each ripple. My muscles tensed, stretching taut across my chest and shoulder blades, ready for anything the Blood Cay had to offer.

The birds took to the air, and the melody of wild noises reverberating through the air died to a deafening silence. My grip on the hilt of my sword tightened.

"What is it?" Rhea whispered, squeezing my forearm with urgency.

The answer to her question broke through the surface of the water, adjusting her body on a rock in a tantalizing manner. Her eyes slithered to mine, batting unusually dark lashes at me. She flipped her long golden hair over her shoulder, exposing her chest with a deadly smile.

"Sirens," Rhea mouthed, barely audible in astonishment.

"Bloody hell," I cursed as the siren flipped her aquamarine tail back and forth in a captivating motion through the water.

She licked her sun-kissed lips, opened her mouth, and started singing a song that echoed throughout the lagoon.

"Humph, you call that a song?" Rhea mocked.

"Cover your ears! Drown out her song. Don't let that sea

nymph hypnotize you." My voice rang out, and my crew hurried to follow my command.

"I thought we were sea demons?" Rhea contended, arms crossed angrily over her chest.

"No, that title is for you alone." I rushed past her, heading for the ship's bow with the intention of lopping off the siren's head to stop her song once and for all.

"Kai," Rhea warned, stopping my mad murderous dash.

I froze in place as about a dozen more heads broke through the shimmering water's surface. They bobbed up and down in the water, smiling and flirting with the men. As if on cue, they all opened their mouths, mingling their songs in perfect harmony with the one perched on the rock.

The men may have had a chance against one, but a chorus of sirens singing was too powerful to drown out.

"Secure the deck!" I bellowed, snatching rope from the rigging.

The men rushed to the sides of the ship, hellbent on a suicidal leap over the edge. I grabbed anything I could—shirts, arms, hair—shoving them back with all my might, but they kept coming, lured to the depths of the sea by the singing.

Rhea screamed, sending a jolt of adrenaline down my spine. I focused on her as she attempted to block Cael from diving overboard. Cael dragged Rhea to the railing like a rag doll, her efforts no match for his determination and strength.

Rhea threw herself in front of him to block him, but he was a man possessed. I could not reach him in time, even if I tried. Desperation clawed at my throat as I shoved the rest of my men back and hopelessly watched as my friend neared his death. In a swift motion, Rhea lifted her knee, nailing him in the groin. "Sorry," she muttered apologetically.

Relief washed over me as Cael went down on his knees.

"Rat!" Rhea cried, and I followed her horror-struck gaze up to the mast.

Rat leaped off the mast, rope in hand, swinging like a marsupial as he made his way down to the water.

"The grappling hook!" I yelled to Rhea as she finished tying a rope around Cael, anchoring him in place.

Rhea's head swiveled until she spotted the grappling hook attached to a long rope. She snatched it from the deck and tossed it to me.

Rat dove for the water, releasing the rope that kept him airborne. I watched him free fall, his hands in front of him in a perfect dive formation. I slung the grappling hook, praying my aim and timing were perfect. Rat screeched when the hook scraped across his back, catching his vest. I quickly tied the rope off, leaving him dangling above the water like fish bait.

Rhea's hands flew to her mouth as she cut off a scream. Blood sprinkled on the deck, the grappling hook obviously coming in contact with more than just Rat's vest.

I rushed to Rhea's side as a few more of my men bounded to the edge. "It's better than him going in the water," I ground out as I shoved my men back.

I glanced around, ready to stop any more of them who bounded toward the railing, but none came. Rhea bent over, gasping for air.

My heart raced, and I spun around as the sound of sloshing water reached my ears, followed by a resounding thud on the deck. A siren had breached the ship's edge, dragging her body toward one of the men tied to the main mast. I rushed to his side. She screeched and slashed at me with her razor claws, but I was too quick for her. I stabbed my blade through her torso. She shrieked and sputtered as my sword anchored her to the deck, preventing her escape. She fell over dead, her head slamming against the wooden planks.

"Kai!"

The hiss of more sirens as they climbed over the edge of the ship nearly drowned Rhea's voice. I cut another one down that was closest to me and threw a dagger at another one that teetered on the railing. The blade sank deep into her chest, and her wail almost shattered my eardrums before her lifeless body fell back into the sea.

Rhea's stare caught my attention, and I lifted my eyes to meet hers. She glanced sidelong at the men who were slowly but surely breaking the ropes that bound them, then to the sirens that continued to climb up the side of the ship.

I saw it in her eyes before she started shedding her clothes and discarding them on the ship's deck.

"Rhea, no!" It was more of a plea than a command, and the anguish in my tone caught me off guard.

She glanced at me one last time with sorrow in her eyes before she plummeted over the edge of the ship. The sirens climbing up the boat abandoned their tasks and dove after Rhea into the abyss.

Rhea

MY LUNGS FELT like they folded in on themselves as I hit the water. I kicked and fought my way back to the surface, gasping for air when my head popped above the water.

"Rhea!" My salt-stung eyes blinked a few times, trying to

clear my vision as Kai's voice rang out over the water. I glanced toward the ship but saw no sirens and heard none singing. The men returned to their senses and shed the ropes tethering them to the mast. Kai hit the railing hard, and it looked like he intended to jump in after me. Fear clenched my chest but instantly released its hold when Cael tackled Kai to the deck, the two of them disappearing from sight.

I spun in the water, disturbed by the eerie silence. Where were the sirens?

Claws ripped through the skin of my ankle. As I opened my mouth to scream, a sudden force yanked me beneath the surface, forcing me to gulp down a mouthful of the briny sea. I kicked and fought against the bone-crushing grip, but two more sirens swam up, seized my arms, and forcefully pulled me deeper into the abyss, overpowering me. My lungs screamed for relief as air bubbled from my nose the deeper they dragged me.

I smiled when the familiar excruciating pain shot down my legs. My transformations were unpredictable, seemingly triggered only when I immersed myself fully in seawater. However, when I leaped off the boat, there remained the possibility that I would retain my human form—a gamble I willingly embraced.

I breathed deeply, the water finally flowing through my gills. The thick muscles in my tail ached, but my anger outweighed the pain. With a mighty swoop of my fins, I knocked the two sirens still clinging to my arms away. The water instantly turned crimson with their blood.

Two more came at me, teeth bared and claws extended, seeking my blood. Kai's words rang in my ears, and I studied their every movement. When one attacked, I saw it coming. I flipped in the water, using my tail as a weapon. As I struck her in the head, the pop of bones snapping echoed throughout the water. Her body went limp and floated lifelessly to the bottom of the lagoon.

A sinister smile brushed my lips as the other sirens paused in the water, their pupils dilated with hate as they watched me. "Not so simple when you're pitted against one of your own kind," I spat, bracing for another attack.

"Traitor," one hissed. "You will die for this."

She struck out at me, but I easily evaded her assault, sending her spiraling through the current.

A cry ripped from my lungs as another siren snuck up behind me, slashing her nails through the delicate skin along my spine. The open wounds felt like they were on fire as the salt in the water licked them. I slammed my fins into her perfect face, blood gushing from her nose and mouth. My breath hitched when more of them ascended from the depths, surrounding me on all sides.

"Enough!" The golden-haired siren that was serenading from the rock slowly eased from the shadowy depths, stopping a few feet in front of me.

I held my head higher despite the searing pain in my back as her gaze ventured up and down my body. With a flick of her tail fin, she pushed herself closer. "Who are you?"

I returned her leer, my eyes traveling over her form. "Rhea, Princess of Aquarius."

The surrounding area echoed with gasps.

"Liar," one with dark hair retorted.

"Why would I lie?" I countered.

She swam closer to me, her eyes boring a hole in my face. "To save your skin," she mused.

"Quiet!" the blond siren thundered.

I held perfectly still, refusing to shrink back as she ran her slender fingers through my hair, her sharp nails lightly brushing across my cheek.

She released my hair, and the crimson strand floated back toward me. "She speaks the truth. I have never seen the Princess, but everyone knows only she has such attributes." She pointed to my scarlet locks floating in the water around my face and then motioned to the iridescent pink scales lining my tail.

For once, I rejoiced in my unusual coloring. I often cursed the ruby-red hair inherited from my father and my mother's lustrous coral-pink tail, but not today.

The siren paused as if still considering me. "I am Genevien, Queen of the northern sirens, and these," she swept her hand through the water, "are my people."

The darker-haired one came closer to me with a flip of her tail. "Why is a siren princess traveling with cutthroat pirates?"

"Noethia, I will ask the questions," Genevien said with an air of authority. "But I would like to know the answer to that one myself."

I watched them with careful eyes, unsure if I should tell them anything about my death quest. "The pirate captain Kai helped me get here. I hired him to help me find Medusa."

"Kai." Genevien spat his name like it left a bitter taste in her mouth. I couldn't blame her. I had a similar reaction when the sea witch told me I had to associate with him. Genevien flicked her long golden hair out of her face. "Why do you seek Medusa? It is our responsibility to keep intruders out. Even though you are a princess, I cannot let you pass."

I was afraid she was going to say that.

"It is our only chance to stop the Dark Hydra and put an end to Dark Water spreading throughout the oceans."

Noethia's stare flicked to mine, the hate finally fading from her eyes. "Dark Water is real?"

"I've seen it with my own eyes," I assured her.

The gravity of my tone made Genevien pause. Her body language indicated she was carefully considering my words. "Let them pass," she finally ordered.

"You can't be serious. Do you know what will happen to us if we let them pass?" Noethia argued.

Genevien sighed. "Do you know what will happen to us if we don't?" She paused. "Besides, I doubt very seriously that any of them will survive the encounter with Medusa."

Noethia opened her mouth like a puffer fish but then closed it when the sound of something hitting the water with a splash interrupted her.

Kai. I bit my bottom lip as the water encompassed him, and he started swimming toward me.

"Let's go," Genevien ordered, and they all dove into the shadowy depths of the deep lagoon.

Kai was on me in seconds, looping his arm under mine and dragging me to the surface. He sucked in a breath of air when his head was above water. His eyes bored into mine, but he didn't say a word as he pulled me toward the shoreline. Once we were in knee-deep water, Kai bent down and lifted me in his arms.

I hissed in pain when his arm brushed against my lacerated back. Kai's face pinched with anger as his stare swallowed me whole. His bare feet crunched through multicolored pebbles that lined the shore as he carefully sat me down on a moss-covered boulder.

He bent toward me, concern flashing across his face. My heart ground to a halt as he pressed his sizable palm against the flank of my tail, his fingertips delicately tracing my scales, igniting a tingling sensation that coursed all the way down to my fins.

"Why did you do that?" he asked barely above a whisper.

I swallowed past the emotional lump that formed in my throat. A lie was on the tip of my tongue, but that wasn't what tumbled from my lips. "I had no intention of standing by and watching my kind slaughter the crew."

Kai stood, towering over me. His blue eyes that rivaled the color of the lagoon washed over me as he gripped my chin, forcing me to meet his stare. "Don't do it again."

It was not a question but a demand. He released my chin and walked around the boulder to see the damage inflicted on my back.

I focused on the sunlight glittering across the water instead of the big, burly pirate at my backside. I flinched when his fingertips danced along the skin on my back.

"It's deep," he said.

I shrugged, a move I wished I hadn't made when the skin on my back tightened, sending a shooting pain across it. "It will heal soon enough," I said through clenched teeth.

When Kai lifted a pistol in the air, and the weapon exploded with a resounding bang, I nearly jumped from the boulder. In a matter of minutes, the boats were loaded and hit the water, heading in our direction. Kai stepped in front of me as he watched his men.

I tried to ignore the heat simmering in my belly every time my eyes brushed across Kai's physique. Water beaded from his dripping curls, splattering across his sun-kissed skin. The salty water etched a path down his muscular back until it disappeared below his drenched black pants that clung tightly to his brawny thighs.

The scrape of wood against stones broke my trance as the boats reached the shoreline. The crew piled out, grabbed supplies, and walked toward us. I was surprised they approached me at all in my siren form, but they did not hesitate.

Cael handed Kai a shirt, who, in turn, gave it to me. I quickly used the material to cover my chest.

Cael walked behind me when Kai motioned to my back with a quick jerk of his head.

"This is going to need stitches," Cael's voice rumbled from behind me.

My head jerked toward Kai. "What are stitches?"

"They have to sew the skin back together, señorita," Rat cut in with a worried expression on his face.

"That doesn't sound pleasant." I gulped.

Something that resembled a growl left Kai's throat. "It's not."

CHAPTER 16
RHEA

Kai lifted me from the boulder, careful not to press against my mangled back. My emotions waged war with my body as he held me tightly in the rowboat. Although I didn't want to admit it, I liked the feel of his thick, muscled arms around me, and at the moment, I was at peace in his strong silence.

He hoisted both of us up the rope ladder that led to the ship's deck with the greatest of ease, not even breaking a sweat under the rising sun.

Once aboard, he took me below and sat me down gently on his bed. "I'll be back. I'm going to help Cael gather the supplies needed for your operation."

At some point between the time it took Kai and Cael to gather the supplies needed to fix my back, my body transformed back into human form. The pain from the transformation was surprisingly dull compared to the searing agony of my torn back. Sirens typically healed fairly quickly, but the injury must have been more severe than I had originally assumed, given the amount of pain.

I quickly slipped on my pants but had to leave my upper

half exposed until the "operation" was complete. That word sent dread spiraling to the pit of my stomach.

Cael walked into the room with Kai on his heels, arms loaded with supplies. "I'm ready."

I'm not, but I refused to say that out loud and admit my fear in front of these men.

"You'll have to lie on your stomach," Cael instructed.

A tremor shook my body as I obeyed. I snatched a nearby pillow, hugging it close to my breast as I exposed my bare back to him.

"What are you doing here?" Kai's deep voice rumbled.

I turned, angling my head to look toward the door that led into the cabin.

Rat cleared his throat. "Don't make us leave, Capitán. We want to be here for the señorita. We owe her our lives."

Unshed tears gathered in my eyes at Rat's declaration, my throat constricting with emotion. Most of the crew members gathered in the door frame.

Kai turned to me, uncertainty written across his facial expression. "Do you want them here?"

Did I truly desire them to witness the excruciating reweaving of my torn back muscles? Did I want them to see my weakness? *Probably not*. What if I fainted or screeched in pain?

I swallowed past the lump in my throat. "They can stay."

At my words, the crew members crowded in, all with sober expressions on their faces.

"Just stay out of the way," Kai warned them.

The pop of a cork resonated in the room, which was way too quiet with the number of people within. "Take this tequila and dab it on the wounds," Cael said.

From the corner of my eye, I watched Kai take it.

Kai glanced down at me one last time before disappearing from my peripheral vision.

As the liquid touched my skin, a hiss of pain forced its way through my clenched teeth. It felt like Kai was brushing literal fire against my back. Once he was through, the pain slowly subsided.

He held the bottle of clear liquid before my face. "Care for a swig?"

I bit my lower lip, blinking rapidly as I shook my head. Kai corked the bottle and set it on the table.

When a hand brushed against my back, a tremor shot down my body.

"Hold her down," Cael instructed, and two other sets of hands gripped me and pressed my body further into the mattress.

A cry worked its way up my throat. I bit my lip, the taste of copper on my tongue, as I tried to keep the scream within while Cael pushed the needle through my skin.

I had a death grip on the pillow underneath me, and I sank my teeth into the fluffy material as Cael pushed the needle through my skin again and pulled the thread tight. Tears escaped my eyes and splattered on the pillow while Cael continued to work the needle in and out of my skin.

Kai bent before me, his face hovering inches from mine. I quickly buried my tear-stained face in the pillow, but he lightly cupped my cheek in his large palm, prying my face from the pillow.

He brushed his rough thumb over my cheek, dashing away a tear. "I think after what you did for this crew, no one will judge you for showing a little weakness. You cry, scream, hold on to my hand, or whatever else you need to do to get through this."

Kai's words brought even more tears to my eyes. I gripped his hand, hanging on to it for dear life as Cael continued to weave the needle through my skin.

"It's almost over, señorita," Rat encouraged, coming into view with a smile on his whiskered face.

The room started to spin, and I blinked a few times to regain focus. I had made it this far. I wasn't going to lose the battle to unconsciousness.

With one last tug of the thread, followed by a swift yank, Cael declared, "It's finished."

A whoosh of relief left my lungs. The slashes across my back throbbed with pain, but it was over.

Kai stood and gently lifted me to allow Cael room to wrap bandages around my wounds. After they completed their work, I cradled my pillow close, finally feeling the tension release from my muscles, the first respite since they had begun.

"She should heal fine now. We have to watch out for infection," Cael whispered to Kai. I heard the warning, but I did not have the energy to care.

Rat crouched before me. "Rest, señorita. When you wake up, we will have a meal fit for a queen ready for you."

I smiled at him then closed my eyes as exhaustion overwhelmed me. I heard the scuff of their boots against the wooden plank floor as they left the room.

Kai rose from the bed, but not before placing his calloused hand upon my brow.

I kept my eyes closed as Cael's concerned voice reached

my ears from the vicinity of the doorway. "She won't be able to face Medusa in this condition. She'll die."

"She had no chance of surviving Medusa anyway," Kai answered barely above a whisper.

"What are you going to do?" Cael raised his voice slightly, causing my pulse to drum louder.

"Don't wake her," Kai grumbled. His voice faded as he walked out and closed the cabin door.

Sleep claimed me the instant he was gone.

I DIDN'T KNOW how long I'd slept, but I awoke to the cabin door opening at some point during the night. Squinting my eyes, I tried to adjust to the darkness of the room.

The bed gave way to Kai's weight as he crawled in beside me. His scent engulfed my senses, and I inhaled, drawing comfort from it. He trailed his fingers as gentle as the ocean breeze over my cheek before turning over and settling.

I rested beside him and waited until his breathing deepened, signaling he was asleep, before slowly sitting up and easing from the bed.

After grabbing a few pieces of my discarded clothes, I clutched them to my chest and sneaked out of the cabin. Leaving the room practically nude was not my most brilliant move, but I couldn't risk waking Kai. I quickly fumbled in the dark, pulling on my pants. When my shoulders stretched in an effort to pull my shirt over my head, I hissed as my wounded skin pulled taut.

Once somewhat composed, I crept on deck. I glanced over the railing. Fortunately, the rowboats remained afloat in the water. I let out a relieved breath, well aware of the risk involved in lowering them myself and potentially rousing the entire crew from their slumber.

I threw one leg over the railing before a deep voice boomed from behind. "Where do you think you are going, sea devil?"

I rolled my eyes, glancing over my shoulder to see the helmsman Flynt leering at me. After slowly lowering my leg back on deck, I turned to face him. "I have a pressing engagement with Medusa," I answered through clenched teeth.

"The Cap'n said nothing about you leaving." He sneered.

Something about his slimy demeanor and the way his eyes traveled up and down my body raised the hairs on the back of my neck.

His elongated fingers clamped around my upper arm with a viselike grip, wrenching me forward. I tried to catch myself, but he was too strong. My body collided roughly with his. My skin crawled as he wrapped an arm around my waist with the strength of an octopus tentacle, anchoring my body to his. When he pressed against the lesions on my back, tears flooded my eyes.

"Now be a good sea devil and join me up by the helm. I'll make you forget all about that pain in your back." His hot, rank breath blew across my face, causing bile to burn up the back of my throat. "But you can't be too loud, no matter how difficult it is. Don't want to wake Cap'n," he warned, sliding a dagger from his sheath and pressing the tip to the hollow of my neck.

He tried to drag me forward, but I planted my feet, halting his attempt. His face pinched with anger, and he pressed the blade tip further into my throat. A wet substance dripped down my breastbone, indicating he'd punctured the skin.

"Don't play coy. I don't want to mess up that pretty face until after we've had some fun," Flynt grunted.

A wicked smile brushed across my lips as I looked up at him. "Foolish human. It's not the captain you need to be concerned about."

Before he could comprehend the gravity of his mistake, I parted my lips, and my siren song wafted through the air, its gentle melody ensnaring his thoughts like a seaweed in a tide. His pupils dilated, and the hand clutching the dagger went limp, causing the knife to tumble to the deck.

I circled him like a shark, tracing his movements with predatory precision. "I should make you jump overboard and drown yourself." I cursed in his face. "But that would make too much noise and would foil my plans. Instead, you'll return to the helm and keep your mouth shut."

He nodded his head, wholly dumbfounded under the enchantment of my song. My eyes traveled down to the sword that hung on his hips. I grabbed the hilt, pulling the sword from its scabbard. *I might need this if my song fails to work against Medusa.*

I closed my lips, and my song died in the air. Flynt blinked a few times and then headed back toward the helm.

I quickly glanced around to ensure no one else was on deck and then bounded over the railing into the small wooden boat below. It took me longer than planned to figure out how to use the oars. I had never steered a rowboat before. The men made it look so easy, but it was not, especially with my injured back. Finally, I found my rhythm, and the boat glided across the water's surface toward the shoreline.

Moonlight danced across the ripples of the deep lagoon, bringing me some measure of peace in the tense moment. I glanced back at Kai's ship, unease settling in my stomach. Kai would probably be furious when he awoke to realize that I had snuck out in the night, but I had come this far, and I refused to let my people down now. A surprising realization halted my efforts. In that moment, I found myself shocked to realize that I wanted the dreaded Blackheart Kai by my side.

CHAPTER 17
RHEA

Anxiety crawled up my throat, threatening to cut off my air supply as my feet touched the shoreline. I gathered up my fleeting courage and stepped into the dense forest. Everything within me beckoned me to return to the safety and warmth of Kai's bed, but I stomped that overwhelming feeling down and continued deeper.

Moon-dappled leaves created flickering shadows on the ground, causing my heart to falter in my chest with each step. I turned around, my shoulders tight with tension as the wind rustled through the leaves, my mind conjuring up nonexistent monsters. Inhaling deeply, I willed myself to calm down. I would never make it if I died of a panic attack before I reached my intended target.

My gaze snagged upon a small footpath that cut a nearly invisible trail up the hillside. I bent down, my hands brushing against a massive, slithered pattern etched through the sandy sod. Clear evidence that Medusa's serpent body used this area as a pathway to the lagoon. *Had she witnessed our fight with the sirens?* The thought had my leg muscles tightening as my body prepared for flight or fight, but I forced them to loosen as I continued up the trail.

The walk felt like an eternity, or maybe my trepidation made it feel that way. I paused as the path gave way to a small clearing with a cave entrance jutting out the side of the hill.

As I stepped out of the shadows of the forest, I expected something to pounce on me. I stood unmoving at the entrance of the cave, my grip tightening on the hilt of the sword.

I glanced back only once, taking comfort in the fluorescent moon that hung above me before stepping into the shadowy cave.

It took my eyes a moment to adjust to the cave's darkness, but when they did, I focused on the bumpy stone walls with fingerlings of tree roots pushing through. With each hesitant step I took, my legs quivered, but I willed them to carry me deeper into the cave.

Something wet dripped on my face, brushing down my cheek, and I stifled a gasp. I glanced up, only to find water trickling from cracks in the ceiling, and exhaled. It could have been much worse, like Medusa's venom dripping on me. The moonlight at the entrance waned as I ventured further inside, gradually extinguishing what little light there was until I was enveloped in inky darkness.

Kai's words rang in my ears. I needed to use my other senses. I shuffled my feet through the darkness and extended my arm, sword in hand, as I picked my way through the dark. My ears pricked at the slightest sounds, and I paused until I was certain it was nothing more than a small creature skittering away.

My blood ran cold when I saw a light shining up ahead. I gripped the sword before me, protecting my upper body just as Kai had instructed while I slowly maneuvered around the bend in the cave. It opened up to a sizable cavern nestled deep in the hillside. My eyes absorbed everything at once, and I calmed somewhat when I did not see Medusa within. I quickly glanced back toward the cave's entrance, my skin tingling at the thought of her coming up behind me. Her blocking my escape route stirred greater anxiety within me than the thought of confronting her directly.

I kept my back to the cavern wall as I ventured deeper into the darkness. The pools of water within seemed ablaze, casting a fiery light. Curious, I dipped my fingertips into the water and rubbed them together. They glistened with an oily substance, offering an explanation for the remarkable fire. I raised my fingers to my nose and inhaled, a distinct chemical scent filling my nostrils. I wiped the grease on my pant leg before taking another cautious step forward.

Hissing resounded through the cave, and I spun around. The echo made it seem like the noise was coming from all directions. *It was her.* I felt it in my gut.

Her large body slithered and her wicked laugh echoed off the cold, damp walls. "Well, well. What do we have here?"

My body flinched at her voice. It was melodious and sweet, yet held a promise of death.

"A female warrior? How unusual. It is normally a man who comes for the head of Medusa."

My sweaty palms tightened around the hilt of the sword. "I don't want your head…"

My attempt at reasoning with her took a quick leap out of the cave as her tail struck from the shadows, knocking the sword from my grip. The clang of the metal striking the rocky ground reverberated in my ears. I threw my back flush against a boulder that protruded from the cavern floor. The lesions on my back screamed in protest, but they were the least of my worries. My eyes desperately searched the ground, any hope sinking when I saw the sword was more than ten feet away.

Her muscles coiled just like Kai said they would. I knew she was lying in wait for me to go for the weapon.

I parted my lips, preparing to use my siren song, when I spotted a pile of bones in the corner of the cavern. How had I not noticed it before? I tried to swallow past my parched throat. I gripped the boulder tighter, the rocky surface biting into my fingertips when I realized the bones belonged to sirens. The unmistakable features of a human torso fused with the skeletal remains of a fish's lower half met my gaze, and I couldn't overlook the telltale signs of teeth marks marring the ivory bones. Apparently, sirens were her dining preference. Something broke inside of me at that moment. I was utterly alone, with no defenses against this monster.

A shiver worked its way down my spine as her hisses echoed throughout the cavern. A single tear of desperation slipped down my cheek as my gaze shifted toward the cave entrance. What I wouldn't give to see Kai storming through the opening right now.

Defeated, I leaned my head against the rough surface of the boulder and started singing. I was positive that my song would have no effect on her, but it brought me comfort. It was low, sorrowful, melodious. Filled with defeat of letting my people down.

"A siren?" Medusa purred.

I didn't respond. It was useless. I continued my tune even as she ventured from the shadows. A note snagged on my tongue as she slithered forward, her massive serpent tail marked with lovely hues of green and black that melded together to form a distinct pattern.

She wasn't what I expected. Medusa was horrifyingly beautiful. Her serpentine hair hissed and struck at me as she ventured closer, stopping just out of reach. Her diamond-shaped golden eyes drifted down my form and then rested on my face as I continued to sing.

Her blood-red lips parted, fangs scraping across her lower lip. "I've never heard a song quite like yours."

I was afraid to stop singing. She wasn't under my trance, but my song seemed to soothe the beast in her. She closed her eyes, letting her head loll from side to side.

"I'm not here to hurt you," I promised, stopping my song.

Medusa pried her eyes open. "I can see that. What is that you want?"

My gaze ventured to the object of my desire, tucked against the cleavage of her pale, viridescent skin.

One of Medusa's eyebrows shot up. "You came for treasures, I see." She started to turn away from me.

I stepped closer to her, prying my body away from the boulder. "No, I came for redemption."

My words stopped her, and she turned to me, her posture suddenly stiffening. "What kind of redemption?"

Her forked tongue protruded from her lips, but I took another bold step toward her. "Is it true that inside that locket is a piece of Poseidon's heart?"

Her jaw clenched, and her pupils dilated as she reached up, running her fingers across the silver locket. Her eyes bored into mine. My mind screamed for me to step back, but my stubbornness demanded I stay put. Medusa carefully opened the locket. A radiant, glowing essence emanated from within, casting an ethereal light upon her flawless, high cheekbones and delicate, pert nose. I bit my bottom lip to keep my mouth from dropping open in awe.

Medusa slammed the locket closed. "Does that answer your question? Now you answer mine. Why has a siren ventured into my lair in search of my locket?"

The fact that she had ceased her murderous intent and was now conversing with me like a civilized being encouraged me to speak further.

"I need it to stop the Dark Hydra." I shifted pleading eyes to her. "Rumors are that only Poseidon could stop the Dark Hydra, and that is the only piece of him left in this world."

"Poseidon," she spat. "Do you know how I got this?" She pulled on the chain, the pendant dangling before my face. Medusa's nostrils flared, causing goosebumps to erupt across my flesh. I shook my head.

She angled her body away from me. "I was beautiful once, so much so that my allure tempted Poseidon himself." Medusa's voice cracked with emotion, and so did my heart. She inhaled deeply, as if she were immersing herself in her memories. "He professed his love to me, but I refused his advances, enticing his anger." She paused, her eyes searching my face. "He came for me one night... I screamed for help, but no one came."

She trembled, and I reached a comforting hand toward her, but she pulled away. I eased my hand back to my side.

"He took me on the cold stone floor of Athena's temple." She shifted her teary eyes to me. "When he was through, he reached into his chest, plucked out a piece of his heart, and gave it to me."

"Why?" I asked, barely above a breath.

She smiled as salty tears dripped down her chin. "He said that he knew Athena would seek revenge on me, but with his heart tucked close to my breast, I would be protected from her wrath."

My gaze glided over her body, stopping on the hair of snakes, which seemed just as distraught as Medusa was.

"His heart protected me from death, but not from her vengeance. She turned me into this monster, ensuring no man would ever desire me again. One look from me will turn any human to stone," Medusa explained, her voice heavy with sorrow as she slithered further into the shadows. "I wish I had died instead."

"That's why I am not affected. Because I am not human?" I asked.

Medusa responded with a single nod, confirming my suspicion. Tears welled in my eyes. Medusa was not the monster that legend made her out to be. She was merely a woman severely wronged by some detestable god of the seas.

I stepped into the shadows alongside her. "I would think you'd long to get rid of that locket. I don't know why you haven't tossed it into the sea by now. I know I would have."

Medusa retracted, coiling her tail around her body. "It's not that simple. If I take off this necklace, I will fall victim to my own curse and turn to stone. For you see, despite my gorgon appearance, I am still human."

My blood turned to ice water in my veins as my gaze drifted back to the locket. It wasn't right for me to ask a woman so severely wronged to forgo her life to save a world that so easily disregarded her.

Medusa interrupted my thoughts. "Tell me about this Dark Hydra."

My pulse drummed a little harder as I lifted my eyes to meet hers. "The Dark Hydra is an evil being created by Hades to destroy everything in the oceans. Poseidon was the only one who could defeat the monster. He locked it away, but now, with his death, the Dark Hydra has been released, and its poisonous Dark Water is spreading throughout the oceans, killing anything in its path. If it's not stopped, everything of the sea will perish."

Medusa's eyes narrowed as she absorbed the gravity of my words. The faint hiss of her serpentine hair seemed to echo the tension in the room. "Everything..." Medusa echoed.

There was a sheen in her eyes, a far-off look that hinted at her depth of thought. She absentmindedly reached up and ran her fingers across the delicate silver chain. I watched her, unmoving.

She finally focused her attention back on me. "You will be sure to spread the word that I, Medusa, was not the monster everyone proclaimed me to be and that I willingly sacrificed myself to save those of the oceans."

It felt like someone dumped a handful of sand down my throat as I tried to swallow past my emotions. The word *don't* was on the tip of my tongue, but I bit down until I tasted my blood. This was her right, her decision to make, and if Medusa sacrificed herself to save the lives of thousands, I would ensure the entire oceanic realm named her a hero.

My muscles tightened as I stood up straighter. "I promise everyone will know what you have done."

A tear dripped down Medusa's face, splattering across the green-tinted skin of her chest just below the locket. Medusa reached up with shaky hands and unclasped the locket.

A sad smile tugged her lips. "I forgave Poseidon for what

he did to me. Sometimes, the bad things that happen in our lives turn into the best things that could have ever happened to us." Medusa handed me the locket, and just as soon as she released it, her body began to slowly turn to stone. "Finally, I will be at peace and alone no more."

My vision blurred with unshed tears as her life dwindled and her body morphed into solid rock. I stepped back as the snakes on her head dropped from her body and slithered out of the cave. I marveled at her face, now clear of serpents. She truly was lovely.

With a trembling hand, I reached up to brush away the liquid tear trailing down her stony cheek. She stood there, a beautiful statue, one that should be remembered.

I glanced down at the silver locket tightly clenched in my hands. It pulsated with power against my flesh. Up close, I observed the finely crafted locket, its shiny metal etched with an intricate wave pattern. Against my better judgment, I fastened the clasp around my neck for safekeeping and looked back at the statue of Medusa one last time.

"Rhea!" A voice boomed down the cave, bouncing off the walls with such force that debris and dust fell from above.

In a matter of seconds, Kai was at the cavern's entrance. Something within me snapped upon seeing him. I once hated him with every fiber of my being and all he stood for, but overtime, he had slowly melded into something more than just a slayer of my kind. His gaze swallowed me whole as I slowly approached him. He stepped forward, his eyebrows drawn together, betraying his concern. I threw myself into his arms, burying my face in his chest, and soaked his shirt with tears of sorrow I had bravely withheld from Medusa.

CHAPTER 18
RHEA

Kai reached up, brushing the palm of his hand against my cheek while his other hand kept a death grip on his sword. I wanted to stay buried in his embrace longer, but he lifted my face from his chest.

His gaze brushed down the length of my body and then settled back on my mine. "Are you hurt?"

"No." I exhaled.

His fingers slid to the back of my neck, urging me to return to the safe cocoon of his strong arms. I pressed the side of my face to the hollow of his neck and felt his Adam's apple bob in his throat. I lifted my gaze and followed his to the statue of Medusa. Something flashed across his eyes. Anger? Hate? I couldn't tell, it was gone as quickly as it appeared. He glanced down at me, his gaze snaring on the locket around my neck.

Kai lifted his hand like he intended to touch it but then dropped his hand to his side. "Let's get out of here."

I nodded and went to collect my discarded sword.

"Where did you get this?" Kai's deep voice rumbled, shaking me to my core as he motioned at my *borrowed* sword.

My run-in with Flynt replayed in my head like a dirty nightmare.

"I found it on deck," I lied.

Kai reached across me, plucking the sword from my hand. "Flynt would never leave his sword on deck."

"Who says it's Flynt's sword?" I countered. It looked like any other blade to me. How could Kai possibly know it belonged to Flynt?

Kai flipped the sword upside down, pointing the hilt in my direction. My stomach knotted when I saw the scribbled markings on the handle that clearly spelled FLYNT.

Kai stepped toward me, brushing the hilt of the sword against my collarbone in a threatening but tantalizing manner. "Now I ask again, sea demon. How did you get his sword?"

I breathed deeply, remembering his threat of what he would do to me if I used my siren song on him or his crew. I bit my bottom lip but stopped the second Kai's pupils dilated, focusing on my mouth. My blood turned to liquid fire as he stepped into my personal space.

"Don't lie to me," he warned.

I stood up straighter, refusing to back down to him. "I will not take the blame for his actions. I would have never used my song on him if he had kept his hands to himself."

When Kai's upper lip curled into a snarl, I stepped back. He latched onto my wrist, tugging my body to his. My body quaked at his nearness, but I wasn't sure if it was out of fear or his proximity.

"What…did…he…do?" Kai gritted out each word like it was poison on his tongue.

Without thinking, I raised my hand, brushing my fingertips across the small cut at my throat caused by Flynt's blade. "He…" I paused, unsure what to tell Kai to keep his anger at bay and, most importantly, keep him from punishing me.

Kai's attention zeroed in on my neck, and he ripped my hand away. His rough fingertips danced across my skin with such gentleness that it broke out in goosebumps.

"He did this?" Kai seethed.

I swallowed past the lump forming in my throat as I caught the almost unnoticeable twitch in Kai's jaw. "Yes."

"Flynt will pay dearly for this. I promise you that," Kai said through clenched teeth.

I stood there, too stunned to speak, blinking up at him. Was Kai directing his anger at Flynt for his trespass, not at me?

Kai stepped closer, making my head dizzy with his tantalizing scent of salty sea air and masculine spice. His swirling blue irises bored into mine, threatening to drown me in those deep pools.

He reached up, wrapping his hand around the back of my neck, urging me forward until our breaths mingled. "Do not ever do that again…" The pressure on my neck increased, but not painfully so. In truth, the deadly grip enthralled me. "In the future, if you leave my ship without my permission, the punishment will be severe."

My heart threatened to take flight from my chest as Kai lowered his face to mine. I didn't move. I couldn't. He was going to kiss me, and the bad thing was I desperately wanted him to. When he pressed his lips to mine, my world exploded. He was gentle and caressing at first, like he was savoring my taste, but the longer we stayed locked together, the more passionate he became.

An electric shock coursed its way through my body, and I went weak in the knees. Kai tightened his grip on me to keep me from sliding to the cavern floor in a puddle of mixed emotions. If this were my punishment, I would jump ship again at my next chance.

Kai pulled away, combing his fingers through his dark hair as he looked anywhere other than at me. "We need to get back to the ship."

I stood in stunned silence as he walked out of the cave. I don't know what hurt more. The fact that I had allowed Captain Blackheart Kai to kiss me or the fact that he so quickly dismissed me afterward. I swallowed my bruised pride and slowly followed him out of the cave. Thankfully, he was a few paces ahead of me, so I did not have to face him at the moment.

We followed the winding foot trail through the lush forest back to the lagoon. The closer we got to the water, the stronger the necklace pulsated with power. I reached up, clenching the locket in my fist. Having something this powerful against my flesh made my skin crawl. I had no idea what this thing was capable of or what it might do to me.

My heart came screeching to a halt when something hissed in my ear. With sluggish movements, I turned my head to see one of Medusa's wicked snakes hanging from the branch of a nearby tree. It was so close that I swore its forked tongue brushed against my cheek.

I gasped as a blade flew toward my face, slicing the head of the serpent from its body before it had a chance to strike.

"Keep moving," Kai snapped, disappearing through the foliage as quickly as he appeared.

Something warm and wet slid down my face. With shaky

hands, I reached up and wiped at the substance. My fingertips were stained crimson. A tremor ran down my spine just thinking of the blood splattered across my face. I picked up my pace and did not stop until I reached the lagoon.

Kai stood with his back to me in front of a dinghy. He turned toward me, and the expression on his face betrayed his impatience, so I quickly stepped into the small boat and sat down. Kai pushed off the shore and began to row us back to the ship.

I leaned over the side of the boat, dipping my fingers in the cool water, and then splashed my face to remove the offending blood that had started to dry on my skin.

I squirmed as Kai watched my every movement with calculating eyes. "How did you defeat that beast?"

I nearly jumped out of my skin at Kai's harsh tone.

My gaze flicked to him. "She's not a beast, and I didn't defeat her. She gave me the necklace."

"Gave?" Kai scoffed.

"Yes, gave. She sacrificed herself to save the inhabitants of the Seven Seas." I watched Kai for any hint of emotion, but as usual, he was unreadable. "Does that surprise you?" I pressed the subject.

"No," he said, barely above a whisper. "She spared my life once."

A heavy sensation settled in my stomach, and unspoken questions scorched my tongue, yet Kai turned his back to me as he rowed against the tide. His actions left no room for doubt—he was done with the conversation. I bit my lip to keep the words within that jumbled on my tongue.

As we approached the ship, someone threw down the rope ladder. Kai seized it and signaled for me to go ahead, while he steadied the swaying boat. I quickly brushed past him and scurried up the ladder. I swung one leg over the ship's railing, and Cael promptly lifted me, setting me down gently on the ship's deck.

Cael's eyes rounded as he stared at the locket around my neck. "You did it."

I gripped the locket, feeling self-conscious as all eyes turned to me. "In a manner of speaking."

Kai bounded over the railing, and I watched as he scoured the ship, searching for something—or someone—in particular. His muscles tensed under his flowing, half-opened white shirt when his gaze landed on Flynt.

"I have something that belongs to you." A clear threat rang in the hollowed edges of Kai's statement. Flynt retreated a step as Kai pulled Flynt's sword from his belt.

I reached out, brushing the fabric of Kai's shirt. "It's over."

Kai glanced down at me, and I saw a chasm as empty as the depths of the sea. I took a step back. The anger swirling in his irises was paralyzing, unlike anything I had ever witnessed.

Flynt's gaze shifted to me, and his lip curled into a snarl. "It's the siren's fault, Cap'n! She bewitched me with her song and stole my sword." Flynt's eyes were wild with hysteria as he laid all the blame at my feet.

I kept my mouth shut. I had already said too much, which unknowingly landed us in our situation.

Kai tossed Flynt's sword to the deck. The metal blade hissed as it scraped across the wood. "Pick it up," he said through clenched teeth.

Flynt glanced at the sword and then back to Kai. His face turned ashen, and beads of sweat gathered on his brow. Flynt snatched a sword from another crew member's scabbard and held it protectively before him. I didn't miss how the blade trembled in his hand.

Kai began to circle Flynt with calculated precision. "I believe my instructions were clear. I said not to touch the woman."

Flynt's movements were quick and jerky as he shifted to keep eye contact with Kai. "She's no woman. She's a sea demon." Flynt spat in disgust.

Kai's lip curled upward in a threatening and unsettling way, revealing his pearly white teeth. "No one gets to call her that but me."

The dark rasp of his voice sent goosebumps spiraling down my arms. *Kai was out for blood*. He struck out with such speed and agility my mind could hardly process his movements. Flynt barely had enough time to raise his sword to ward off Kai's blow. Cael shoved me protectively behind him as the two opponents shuffled across the deck, locked in a deadly dance.

Kai was cunning, swift, and ruthless with his attacks. Everything about him was perfectly orchestrated to deliver lethal doses of fear into his enemy's bloodstream. If Kai's blade didn't kill Flynt, I was sure he would fall over dead from sheer fright.

The clanging of sword against sword reverberated deep into my bones until I feared I could stand no more. A gasp was wrenched from my lungs as Flynt landed a lucky blow, slicing into Kai's forearm. Kai's blood splattered across the wooden deck as he deflected the next attack. The urge to jump in between the two men was nearly suffocating. I took a step forward, trying to wriggle my way around Cael's broad form, and then froze in fear when realization dawned on me.

I fell back, gripping the railing of the ship to keep upright as the weight of shame pressed heavily against my shoulders. What drove me to put myself in harm's way by using my body as a barricade between the two warring males was the same thing that had driven me into Kai's arms after Medusa's death. *I cared for him.* Kai was like a phantom crab. He had easily passed through the walls I built around my heart and had burrowed deep within.

A tear slipped from my eye, caressing my cheek as it fell to the deck. How could I betray my family and my people by caring for the one human determined to end all of us?

Kai parried Flynt's blow, and my heart leaped to my throat, lodging itself there when Kai ran Flynt through. Flynt sputtered and swayed before his lifeless body landed against the deck with a loud thud.

"Clean this mess up," Kai growled, wiping the blood from his sword on his black pants.

He turned to face me, and Cael quickly stepped out of Kai's way as he moved in my direction like a predator. Kai gripped my arm, pulling me along behind him in the direction of the stairwell that led to the lower deck. Everything within me cried to escape his grip, but I shoved that part of me into the recesses of my mind and allowed him to pull me below. I could still feel the anger rolling off him like waves in a squall.

Kai opened his cabin door and gently pushed me inside. I stared at him as he stalled in the doorway, unable to say or do anything as more tears gathered in my eyes. Kai reached up, lightly brushing his knuckles across my cheek. His tender touch enticed more tears until they dripped from my eyes and onto Kai's fingers.

"You're safe now. Go lie down and get some rest." Kai's baritone was firm but laced with concern.

He ever so slowly pulled his hand away from my face and shut the door behind him. Once the door was closed, I heard the unmistakable sound of the scuff of his boots as he walked back up the stairs. I flung myself onto the bed, burying my face in the pillow, using it to stifle the sounds of my heart tearing apart.

As I lay on the bed, the weight of guilt settled over me like a suffocating fog. The image of Kai shutting the door and the echo of boots fading away stirred a haunting realization. He had killed one of his own crew members with disturbing ease, a reminder of the darkness that clung to him—a darkness I found myself drawn to.

Horror clawed at my insides, not just for the life he had so easily taken, but for the countless others he had ended as the feared Blackheart Kai, killer of sea creatures. The allure of his strength and the chilling reality of his deeds collided, leaving me torn between the attraction that drew me to him and the horror of the blood on his hands.

CHAPTER 19
KAI

Anger still simmered under my surface, threatening to consume me in a blazing fire. I stopped once I reached the upper deck. The only evidence remaining that Flynt was ever aboard my ship was the blood that seeped into the wood of the deck. Henry, my cabin boy, fell to all fours and vigorously scrubbed the offending stain, creating a sudsy mess that turned an obnoxious shade of pink. Before long, the blood would vanish, much like Flynt's life. Regrettably, my fury would not be so easily extinguished.

"I don't understand what it is with you and our helmsman. We can never keep one longer than a year." Cael's voice slithered in my ear, his humor an attempt to calm the raging beast within me, but I was past the point of no return.

My chest still burned in the aftermath of waking up and not finding Rhea by my side. I had turned this cursed ship upside down, looking for her, until I realized she had gone after Medusa alone. That may have been the original plan. I had no intention of tangling with Medusa again or putting my men's lives at risk, but plans changed, and so had my concern for the brave little sea demon.

I walked up to the helm, Cael flanking my heels as I resumed control of my ship. "We don't need him."

Cael eyed me with concern, but I blatantly ignored him, hoping he would vanish. "What's our heading, Cap'n?"

I almost scoffed out loud as Cael prodded at the tender wound of my emotions. I had no idea where we were going or what my next move would be, and he bloody well knew it.

When I didn't answer, he motioned to my arm. "You want me to look at that?"

I glanced down at my arm, forgetting that Flynt had inflicted a wound. "It'll be fine. I'll have Rhea bandage it later."

A sly smile brushed across Cael's lips. "So, it's Rhea now, and you trust her enough to tend to your wounds?"

"Why don't you piss off?" I boomed, gripping the wheel so hard my sun-kissed knuckles blanched white.

Cael's smile widened. "Aye, aye, Cap'n."

The sun slipped into the ocean, taking with it the light and all the brilliant colors it left behind. I stood behind the helm, legs slightly spread apart to keep my knees from buckling in fatigue. My gaze kept drifting to the hull of the ship, causing my thoughts to go adrift. Whenever I thought about Rhea nestled in my sheets, my skin broke out in a cold sweat. Common sense and self-loathing rattled against the cage of my mind, trying to make me understand how stupid it was to react that way toward a siren. I shook my head as sleep weighed heavily on my eyelids. We had left Medusa's island hours ago, and I had been in this position since then. My body and foggy brain demanded a few hours of rest.

"Go below, Kai, before you run us aground." Cael's voice jolted me awake, jump-starting my lazed pulse.

Without another word, I released the death grip I had on the wheel, allowing Cael to take control, and dragged my exhausted, tightly wound body below. I stopped in front of the cabin door, arguing with myself, telling myself not to go in after that kiss I planted on her, but my hand lifted and turned the knob of its own accord. I quietly pushed the door open. To my surprise, Rhea had left a candle burning. My gaze snagged on the tiny dancing flame and the drips of wax as they ran down the length of the candle.

When I looked at the bed, my stomach hit the floor. Rhea was face down on the mattress, and red stains seeped through the pristine white sheets. I was by her side in a matter of seconds, pulling back the covers to find the source of blood. Rhea moaned into the pillow, hugging it tighter in her sleep. I moved as quickly and quietly as possible to keep from waking her. She wore one of my white shirts, now saturated in blood. I cursed under my breath for not noticing it before. She'd probably torn her stitches when she confronted Medusa.

I put my arms on either side of her, leaning down. "Rhea," I whispered in her ear.

She shifted and turned her head, batting her ebony lashes as she stared up at me, confusion twisting her brow.

I tugged at the hem of the shirt. "I need you to take this shirt off. Your back is bleeding. I think you tore your stitches."

Rhea gasped and sat up. She reached around to her back. Horror danced across her eyes as she looked down at the blood that stained her fingertips and then at the tainted sheets.

She bounded from the bed. "I'm sorry." Her gaze darted from me to the bed as she chewed her bottom lip.

"No need to be. Sheets are easily cleaned." I didn't know why, but it pissed me off that she was apologizing about the sheets. "I'm going to have some hot water brought down so you can bathe and clean your wounds."

"Thank you," she said, barely above a whisper.

I reached up to touch her face again, but I shoved my hand in my pocket instead. I walked over to the door, slung it open, and bellowed for Henry. He appeared in the doorway, hair sticking up in all directions and sleep stuck in the corners of his eyes. At sixteen, he wasn't a boy any longer, but I kept him on my ship to ensure he was cared for until he could fend for himself.

"Fill the tub with bath water," I instructed.

He threw his hand to his brow in a salute. "Aye, Cap'n." Then rushed off to do my bidding.

I stood outside the cabin door as Henry toted bucket after bucket of steaming hot water. "It's full, Cap'n."

"Back to bed with you then."

Henry nodded to me. "Aye, Cap'n."

I glanced inside the cabin as Rhea looked at me and then at the copper tub. "Be quick about it," I instructed and closed the door.

I stood guard outside the door, arms crossed over my chest as I waited for her to get in the tub. The sloshing of water indicated that she did as I asked. I stalled a few more minutes before pushing the door open and going inside.

Rhea watched me with careful precision. I half expected her to scream at me to get out, but she surprised me yet again as a smirk flickered across her face. "Isn't it improper in the human world for a man to watch a woman bathe?"

There was something in her tone that was as wicked as it

was lovely. It enticed me to step forward. "You'd have to be a human first for that to apply." I stopped only a foot away from the tub. Against my rakish behavior, I kept my eyes above the waterline. Why I would show such respect to a siren baffled me.

She shrugged and continued to lather the soap on her smooth skin like my presence was little cause for concern.

I knelt beside the tub, dipped my hand in the warm water, and extracted a cloth. "Turn over, and let me take a look at your back."

She paused, mistrust evident by the way her shoulders pulled taut. She tossed me a warning glare before she flipped over, folding her arms across the edge of the tub and resting her chin on top.

As expected, a few of the stitches had torn. The lesions on her back were red and angry-looking, with dried blood caked across the surface. I dipped the rag into the water and gently scrubbed around the wounds to remove the dried particles.

"Something is warring within you. I see it in your eyes." Her melodious voice broke my concentration.

My attention had been so hyper-focused on her back that I missed that she had turned her head and was observing me. I refused to look her in the eyes or acknowledge that she had so easily read me. There was a war going on inside of me. The almost nonexistent part of me that felt bad for having to kill this siren was arguing with my all-consuming evil that always got what it wanted ahead of anything else. I knew which one would win this war, and it wasn't mercy. I didn't get the nick-name Blackheart Kai for showing compassion, and at this point, I wasn't sure I had a heart at all.

Once Rhea must have realized I wouldn't share anything

with her, she turned away, flipping her auburn hair over her shoulder, and I returned to cleaning her cuts. The thought of running my blade through her back leaked into my mind like poison. It would almost seem fitting to end her life while she was submerged in the water. Maybe I was showing a shred of compassion. To make her death quick and as painless as possible. I dropped the cloth in the water as I eased my hand toward the small blade I had tucked into the top of my boot.

Something tightened in my chest as my fingertips brushed against the metal hilt of the blade. My hand stilled when Rhea started to sing. It was low, barely above a whisper, and wove through the air. Her voice reached into my chest, past the evil that resided there, and latched onto my heart. She wasn't using her siren song. No, this was just her melodic voice, and something about it calmed the raging, vindictive beast that resided within me.

I abandoned my futile attempt to kill her as I knelt before her. Our eyes locked as she continued to sing. She reached out, threading her fingers through my hair. An electric shock, like lightning when it hit the sea, shot through me when she brushed her fingers against my scalp. Her voice, her eyes, her very being, everything about her enchanted me. Rhea had done what no one else had ever been able to do—calm the raging storm that constantly billowed inside of me.

She stopped singing and smiled at me as her hands ventured from my hair and brushed across my beard. "There, that's better. Your sea-blue eyes are clear again. They darken when you are angry or upset. Did you know that?"

Something inside me snapped at her words, and I shot to my feet. Rhea watched me as I retreated a few steps. I had never been scared of anything in this world, be it beast or man, but this siren frightened the hell out of me. She had the potential to make me a better man, and that was not something I would ever yield to. I flung the door open and bolted out of the cabin before Rhea could transform me into something I wasn't—a decent human being.

CHAPTER 20
RHEA

Something was wrong. I could feel it deep within my bones, yet I kept my eyes closed. The nagging feeling continued to pester me until I pried them open. I blinked a few times to adjust my vision to the gentle glow in the room. I glanced at the window. The sun was just peeking above the ocean, pouring rays of warm sunlight through the pane. Then it hit me. The putrid scent of decay curled in the air, lodging in my nose. Fear snaked through my veins as I leaped from the bed, threw open the cabin door, and rushed up to the deck.

A gasp tore from my lungs as my eyes confirmed what my mind had already grasped—*Dark Water*. Panic seized me as I spun around. The inky evil enveloped us from all directions. My knuckles whitened as I clutched the railing, my knees trembling in fear.

A hand grasped my upper arm, wrenching me toward a solid body. "Rhea, is there a reason you are prancing aboard my deck in nothing but a shirt?" Kai reprimanded.

I glanced down at the white shirt as the wind whipped at the hem, blowing it against my mid-thighs. At that moment, I couldn't care less about my half-dressed state, but it was evident that Kai did. I could see the muted fury behind his indigo eyes as he used his body as a barricade between prying onlookers and me.

I reached up, gripping Kai's shirt collar in desperation. "Kai...Dark Water has spread further than I imagined..." Tears leaked from my eyes as I turned and watched the black water dance in victory with the rotting corpses of sea animals riding the waves.

Kai surprised me by wrapping his arms around my waist from behind, hugging me tightly to his chest.

"It will be fine," he whispered in my ear.

I tugged away from the solidness of his chest. "Fine? How can you possibly say this will be fine? We're trapped! How are we going to make it to the Dark Hydra? How am I going to save my family?" I was on the brink of a panic attack. My lungs tightened with each syllable I spoke, making inhaling difficult.

Kai cupped my face between his rough palms, forcing me to focus on him. "I need you to breathe."

"But..."

"Breathe," he demanded.

I inhaled a shaky breath, and he used his thumbs to wipe away the tears running down my cheeks.

Kai pulled me back toward the railing. "Look down."

I followed his command, glancing at the water below, and went still.

Dark Water closed in from all directions, yet there remained a small six-foot diameter expanse of crystal-clear ocean surrounding the ship. Dark Water swirled almost angrily, like it was desperate to reach us, but no matter how hard it tried, it could not break through the invisible barrier.

I turned to Kai in awe. "What is this?"

Kai's gaze traced the V of my shirt. He reached up, running a finger seductively down my throat, venturing lower until his aching, sweet touch finally stopped when he reached the locket. "This."

Realization dawned on me, dousing the fear that had nearly consumed me. I undid the clasp and slowly removed the locket from around my neck. The metal twinkled in the sunlight as I marveled at its power. I extended my hand over the railing of the ship, the locket dangling over the water. Dark Water made an evil hissing sound as it scurried further away from the locket.

My mouth hung open as I clasped the necklace back around my throat. "It works."

"I would hope so, after you risked your life for it." Kai seethed.

Something flashed across his steely face, something dangerous and foreboding. I took a tentative step back, reminding myself that even the most stunning of blades were lethal, and Kai was just as deadly as he was handsome.

Kai stepped toward me in a manner that made me want to shrink away, but I held my ground. "Go below and put some clothes on before I am forced to gouge my own men's eyes out."

I swallowed past my dry, scratchy throat as I looked around the ship. Sure enough, all eyes were on me, and they were particularly interested in my bare legs. Without another word, I rushed down the stairs, threw my clothes on, and returned back on deck.

Kai had resumed his position at the helm. His gaze met mine, and something warm and tingly ran down the length of my spine, reminding me of getting stung by a sea anemone, but in a good way. I crammed that feeling deep down, focusing my attention on the rise and fall of the black waves that seemed to be screaming of our impending doom.

I demanded that my shaky legs cooperate as I climbed the stairs to the helm. Cael stood by the Captain, both men strong, unmoving towers with unreadable expressions. Their serenity stood in stark contrast to my escalating terror. I chewed on my bottom lip as I gripped the railing and continued scrutinizing the monstrosity known as Dark Water. Each carcass of a sea mammal or fish that littered the water carved a notch in my heart. I couldn't help but feel guilty for each of their forfeited lives. If only I had moved faster, done more…

"Enough," Cael interrupted my musing with a stern expression etched across his face. "Stop worrying about things you have no control over."

Hot tears burned behind my eyes at his words, but I refused to shed them in front of him. He spoke words of wisdom, just like my father, and I knew my fear would defeat me if I gave in now.

The ship glided seamlessly through the water, the darkness never coming closer to us.

I aimed my nervous demeanor at Kai. He stood tall and strong, unmoving like the mountainside. His eyes focused on the horizon. His expression almost seemed to dare Dark Water to try him.

"How long until we reach the Dark Hydra?" My voice trembled, betraying my fear.

"Soon enough," Kai's strong baritone drummed through the air, reaching into my chest and squeezing my heart.

I inhaled a shaky breath as I focused on the horizon. Gone was the beautiful casting of the sun against the crystal-clear water. Now, all we faced was darkness. Nothing dared to touch the inky black depths.

"Can I go up to Rat's nest?" I held my breath as my eyes pleaded with his. Kai turned toward me, a look of refusal written across his features. "Please. I have to see the stretch of its destruction. I have to know."

Kai's eyes met mine, and I swore I saw a crack in his rough expression. With a swift nod of his head, he permitted me to go above.

"Rat!" Kai bellowed. "Help the sea demon." There was a twinkle of mischief in his eyes that caused the heavy burden of the day to lighten ever so slightly.

Rat swooped down from the watchtower, dangling before me. "Si, Capitán."

My lips ticked up in a smile I could not contain as Rat offered me his hand. Rat helped me maneuver each placement of my foot to ensure that I did not have a repeat of the last time I had been in his domain. With slow precision, I made my way to the top. Once in Rat's nest, I glanced down at Kai. His gaze remained fixed on me, and I could have sworn I saw his manly chest heave as though he'd been holding his breath, but it was likely my imagination.

I mustered up my courage and looked out across the expanse of the sea. My hand flew to my chest. It felt like someone had lodged a knife there and twisted it. I expected patches of Dark Water scattered across pristine blue, but I saw a never-ending siege of death and destruction. As far as I could see, there was nothing but Dark Water.

"Oh, Rat." I gasped.

Rat smiled, but it did not reach his eyes. "I know, Señorita." His voice broke with emotion.

My eyes met his, and a thought skipped across my mind. Not only were the inhabitants of the oceans losing their lives and homes, but also those who sailed the seas. Everyone was suffering because of the Dark Hydra.

Rat stood behind me in silent support as I stared out into the bleakness until the sun sank below the onyx waves. The sight was so disturbing I wondered if the sun would ever rise again.

"Come, Señorita. It's late," Rat said as he lightly touched my elbow.

I slowly pried my hands from the railing. They cramped in protest from being in the same position for so long. Even with Rat's insisting, I was still hesitant. I felt like a beacon in the darkness with the heart of Poseidon glowing around my neck and had the unrealistic feeling that if I took my eyes off the Dark Water, it would swallow us whole.

I wiped my sweaty palms on my pants legs before slowly descending the rope ladder. So overwhelmed by terror, I failed to notice Kai waiting at the bottom until his arms encircled my middle. He quickly lifted me from the ladder, hesitating before setting my feet back on the deck.

The salty wind whipped my fiery locks across my face, and Kai lifted his hand, tucking my hair behind my ears. The gesture was so simple, yet it struck a chord in my heart.

Kai cleared his throat. "You should get some sleep." He dropped the hand that had reached for me to his side like he had touched literal fire. The sting of his rejection and disgust cut deeper than the claws of the siren that had ripped into my back.

I shoved my feelings and all the disappointments of the day deep into my inner chest of emotions and slammed the lid shut. After turning away from him, I walked absentmindedly toward Kai's cabin. I reached the door and turned the knob. The lush bed called to me like a lover. I couldn't wait to fall into the fluffy sheets, but something was nagging me. When I had asked Kai how much longer it would take to reach the Dark Hydra, his response was vague. How much longer I would have to endure this heartache? I needed, no, demanded, to know the number of days.

I walked back out of the cabin. My hand brushed against the wood rail that led up the stairs, but I stalled there. Deep, husky voices that sounded like Cael and Kai were coming from below. My brow scrunched in confusion. Since killing Flynt, one or the other was always behind the wheel, so why were they below? I turned toward the voices but stalled before going lower. I had not been to lower decks since my first day aboard the ship. Not since Kai had locked me behind those bars. Just thinking about the rank darkness had panic swelling in my breast.

I took a brave step forward and then another, determined not to let my fear overwhelm me. Kai wasn't the same man he had been before. He wouldn't throw me back into that cell. I stepped onto the stairs, hissing in aggravation when the wood squeaked under my feet. I froze, looking around to see if anyone heard the noise, but after a few precious seconds passed and no one came after me, I continued my descent.

The voices grew louder the deeper I went, but the words remained muffled. I came upon a room with soft lantern light glowing under the doorframe. The door was slightly ajar, so I peeked inside. It was a simple bedroom, and I immediately assumed it belonged to Cael since he was the one sitting on the meager bed in the middle of the room. Kai stood off to the side. I could barely make out his silhouette in the shadows, but there was no mistaking that voice—the one that hummed in my bloodstream every time he spoke.

"We're going to wait here for her to show up," Kai confirmed.

Cael's body tensed at Kai's words as I quietly shuffled closer. What she was he talking about, and why were we waiting on whoever she was? With Dark Water spreading further than I imagined, we did not have the luxury of waiting on anyone. The thought of opening the door and telling him just that crossed my mind, but my curiosity held me in place.

Cael stood, his brows knitted so tightly together it looked like they were about to touch. "You can't uphold the sea witch's bargain, and you know it. Who do you think you are fooling?"

Chills shot through my body at the mention of the sea witch. I placed my hand over my heart in an effort to stifle my heartbeat, afraid that it would alert them to my presence. It drummed in my ears so loudly that it almost drowned out the voices of the men in the room.

Kai took an intimidating step toward Cael, bringing his body into view. "I told you that nothing or no one would keep me from getting the Wraith."

Cael shook his head, brushing his gaze to the floorboards. "You love her," he whispered.

"I don't love anyone. I never have, and I never will," Kai growled.

"You're actually going to stand there in front of me, of all people, and tell me that you still plan on killing that siren?" Cael scoffed.

My knees buckled, and I sank to the wooden floor. *Kai was going to kill me.* I gasped for air, finding it increasingly difficult to breathe. It felt like someone had reached inside my chest and squeezed the organ that resided there— someone was squeezing my heart, and that black heart's name was Kai.

Kai stood taller, making himself all the more threatening. "Make no mistake, nothing has changed. I will kill that sea demon, take that locket, and hand it over to the sea witch just like she asked me to."

Sea demon. Tears spilled over my eyelids at the spite in his words. I had become all too familiar with him calling me that, and it was starting to resemble a term of endearment when he spoke it, but now…

I reached up and touched the locket around my neck with trembling hands. This had been Morgana's plan all along. She wanted me to find Kai for a reason. She wove that plan so perfectly I was now confident it was her who had washed me up on the beach that day. She wanted me dead, and she wanted this locket. Who better to do it than Blackheart Kai, the sea monster slayer?

Desperation clawed against my skull as I took a tentative step back. I turned with the intention of running but bumped into a barrel. I watched in horror as the empty barrel teetered and then crashed to the floor. Boots scuffed against the wooden planks, and I heard the squeak of the door opening, but I did not wait around for them to find me. I raced up the stairs to the deck.

When I hit the railing of the deck, air burst from my lungs.

I looked across the inky water. I couldn't jump, and I couldn't stay here. Either way, I was doomed.

"Get away from that railing."

I spun around as Kai and Cael slowly approached me. Their movements were slow, like I was a timid seal about to flee, and I was.

My eyes brushed against the Dark Water that sloshed below the ship. Would I survive if I jumped in? I gripped the locket that seemed to glow brighter in my palm. I would be safe as long as I had this.

"Rhea." Kai's voice held a subtle warning, and something flashed across his expression that I could not read in the moonlight.

I was about to jump when Rat slung down from his watchtower above. Concern danced across his features as he reached a hand toward me. I had come to care for many of the crew members aboard this ship. Most of all for the captain, who had reached into my chest and yanked out my heart, crushing it beneath his shiny black boot.

I hesitated for another moment, wondering what would happen to them if I jumped in and took Poseidon's heart with me. I had seen the destruction Dark Water caused. With it gone, Dark Water would likely swallow this ship like it was nothing more than a wayward shrimp. I mustered up enough strength to stare Kai in the eyes. He stood there like a statue, cold and uncaring, like he hadn't tricked me or ripped my heart in two. I was startled to realize that I wanted him to say something, to deny the words I'd heard, but he couldn't. They were true.

I didn't want Cael, Rat, or any of the other crew members to die, but what were the lives of a few pirates worth when it came to everyone and everything that resided in the ocean? If the sea witch or Kai got their hands on this necklace, all would be lost, and the Seven Seas would cease to exist.

Kai stepped toward me, and that was all the incentive I needed to throw myself over the edge of the ship and into the swirling Dark Water.

CHAPTER 21
RHEA

My dive from the ship was far from graceful. I hit the water hard, the impact stealing the air from my lungs. I fell into a never-ending pool of darkness. Dark Water hissed and bubbled away from me as I fought my way back to the surface. I broke through the water, gasping for air and blinking to clear the salt water from my eyes. Dark Water was all around me, reaching out for me like the monstrosity it was. The locket glowed brightly against my breastbone, and the evil blackness shrank away. I gulped away my rising fear. I would be fine as long as I had the locket.

When I glanced around, I couldn't see the ship in the dark, moonless night. A tightness squeezed my chest once I realized they could already be dead. I could not shake the vision of Dark Water, slithering up the side of the ship and pulling it beneath its poisonous waves.

"Rhea!" Kai's voice broke through the whip of the wind and the angry hiss of the dark waves. Relief flooded through me, even though I knew I shouldn't care that he was still alive. He likely wouldn't be for long, and I had to live with the fact that I could do nothing about it. He brought this travesty upon himself by making a deal with the sea witch. Maybe she would spare their lives if he cried out to her instead of me. It was doubtful, though.

The familiar pain that I had come to welcome rendered my lower body. In a matter of minutes, I had my beautiful tail back and dove deep beneath the ebony waves. I tried to ignore the pain that continued to build in my chest. The farther I swam away from the ship, the more my heart cleaved in two. If I were entirely honest with myself, it was not the act of leaving the ship that induced this feeling, but Kai. My eyes stung, and it wasn't because of the salt in the water but the tears pouring from them.

I increased my speed as my anger gave way to fury. Kai wasn't worth my time or my tears. It was my fault that I had fallen for his treachery. All the glimpses of kindness and tenderness he had shown me were to bend me to his will. Anger snaked through my veins, causing my internal temperature to rise several degrees. If Dark Water didn't kill Blackheart Kai, I would. If it were the last thing I ever did, I would find him, reach into his chest, and crush his black heart with my bare hands.

Kai

I SEIZED the railing so hard my knuckles blanched white. When Rhea leaped into the swirling black abyss, I was sure that what remained of my heart jumped right in after her. My emotions were warring with themselves. Should I follow the little sea demon who was swimming away with my tattered heart, or should I uphold my duty to my crew?

A strong hand gripped my shoulder and squeezed. I didn't

need to turn around to know it was Cael. He stood behind me in silent support, and that was all I needed to decide. Rhea had Poseidon's heart around her neck. She would be safe from Dark Water, or so I hoped, but my crew needed me, needed their captain.

"What are we going to do?" The panicked voice of one of my crew members rose above the hiss of the Dark Water.

I turned in their direction. All eyes were on me, awaiting my orders. I opened my mouth, unsure what I would say to alleviate their fears as Dark Water drew nearer.

"Capitán! Off the starboard!"

I turned around, looking to the right of the ship as inky black tentacles latched onto the railing. Every muscle in my body tightened as my men picked up spears and others drew swords.

"Stand down," I ordered, and they all looked at me, confusion written across their features. "This particular sea monster is an expected guest."

I stepped closer, noticing how Cael's dark brows drew together and his hand danced above the hilt of his sword.

The sea witch pulled her massive body over the railing, landing with a thud. She shook her pearly white hair like a wet dog, sending the deadly water flying in all directions. Dark Water splattered across my ship, eating holes in the places where it fell. My anger increased a notch at the way she disrespected my vessel. Finally, she looked up, her soulless black eyes meeting mine. She smiled at me insincerely, displaying her fangs.

Her gaze brushed over my men and then back to me. "It seems a certain siren is missing."

"Leave us," I boomed, leaving no room for argument.

Questioning glares were thrown my way, but my men heeded my instructions and went below. Rat scurried down from his lookout tower and followed the rest of the crew below, closing the door behind him.

"Where is she?" the sea witch questioned, drawing closer to me.

I leaned against the railing, hoping my indifferent attitude would annoy her as much as her presence did me. It seemed to work. Her lips pulled tighter into a flat line, betraying her aggravation.

I turned, motioning to the water. "She jumped ship mere minutes before you arrived."

The sea witch's eyes followed mine and rounded in horror at my words. "You lie, she would have died. Unless…"

"Unless she had the locket of Poseidon around her neck," I completed her sentence.

"You insolent fool!" she hissed, striking out at me with one of her ebony tentacles.

She was swift with her strike, but I was faster. I pulled my sword from its scabbard as I avoided her blow. The tip of her tentacle was inches from my face. With one quick swipe of my blade, I amputated it. She squealed in pain as the tentacle flopped against my deck like a decapitated snake. Her dark-blue blood showered my deck as she pulled the nub protectively to her body. I watched in mock amusement as the tentacle quickly grew back like nothing had ever happened.

Sink me.

She glared at me. "Your speed is impressive." She seemed to be changing tactics, but I wasn't sure why. "Tell me how a mere siren escaped the mighty Blackheart Kai's grasp?"

And there it was. She was fishing for information, but she was going to come up empty-handed.

"Just a mild setback," I assured her as I wiped her tainted blood off of my sword with a bandanna I had shoved in my pocket. I let the fabric fall to the deck with a sneer of disgust. No doubt the sea witch's blood was deadlier than Dark Water itself.

Her tongue shot out of her mouth, licking the seam of her blood-red lips. "According to your reputation, I expected her head to be handed to me on a silver platter, and instead, you have had a mild setback." The sea witch eased closer to me, her eyes scrutinizing me for any telltale sign of what actually happened.

I returned my sword to its sheath. "You will have the sea demon and locket in due time." A spark of anger ignited in my chest when I spoke the nickname I had given Rhea. I hoped that the sea witch had not noticed the change in my tone, but by the look of victory that rendered her face, my normally schooled demeanor had faltered, and it just cost me dearly.

"I see," she said in a voice that dripped with poison. "That little princess got to you."

My whole body went rigid with anger, and the sea witch smiled in triumph, having put a dent in the otherwise flawless emotional armor I wore.

"No one got to me." I plastered on a solemn expression in a desperate attempt to gain some of the ground I just lost. "But there is something that you can do to help us get to the siren before she reaches the Dark Hydra."

One of the sea witch's white brows shot up in question. "Me aiding you wasn't part of the deal." Her tentacles snaked closer to me, but I held my ground. "What exactly is it that you want?"

"We are at a standstill. You can clearly see Dark Water surrounds us and what it can do to my ship." I motioned to the holes in the deck that Dark Water had eaten away. "I need another ship. Preferably one made out of the impenetrable bones of a leviathan."

Now it was my turn to smile as her face fell.

"You think me stupid enough to give you the Wraith? It's my only leverage to ensure you do my bidding."

I walked up to her, towering over her massive form, and I swore I saw a faint spark of fear in her eyes. "Quite the opposite, but I seriously doubt you want to do your own dirty work." I leaned over her. "And I doubt very seriously that you are willing to go anywhere near the Dark Hydra."

Fear skipped across her facial features, and I knew she would not deny my request. She may be a witch, but not even she could control the Dark Hydra.

She struck out, latching onto one of my arms with her tentacle. The suckers underneath her tentacles bored into my skin, but I did not so much as flinch. "How do I know you will uphold our deal after I give you the ship?" She tightened her grip on my arm, and my fingers started to tingle from lack of blood flow.

I smirked at her. "You don't, but what other option do you have?"

She released my arm with a growl. "If you betray me, I will trap you and your precious Wraith inside one of my magic bubbles and take pleasure in each passing day as you wither away to nothing but bones."

Maybe I was demented, but for some reason, that did not

sound as bad as some of the death threats I'd received in the past.

"Then stop stalling and get me my ship." I snarled in her face.

Her gaze angrily brushed down my body before she moved away from me. She held out her hand, and in a puff of purple smoke, a bubble appeared, the Wraith within it. My skin broke out in goosebumps with anticipation. I had waited my entire life for a ship like that and was finally about to receive it.

With an impressive arm, the sea witch threw the bubble into the swirling black sea. Knots of tension formed in my shoulders as I watched the bubble explode. Once the smoke cleared, there sat the Wraith in all its glory. It was massive and at least twice as big as my current ship. They had cut the bones of the leviathan into perfectly proportioned planks, which had an ivory color that contrasted starkly with the pitch-black water.

Dark Water slithered toward the ship, and I stepped near the railing to get a better view. It attempted to crawl up the side of the Wraith, but as soon as it touched the leviathan bones, it instantly disintegrated into powdery sea foam. Even with the sea witch scrutinizing me, I could not keep the victorious, hungry gleam from my eyes.

"I see that you are satisfied," she mocked.

I crossed my arms over my chest, leaning against the railing. "Ecstatic."

The sea witch slithered toward the edge of the ship, pulling her tangled mess of tentacles in her wake. "Good. Then get that locket and bring me that siren's pretty little head."

She jumped overboard, landing in the swirling Dark Water below.

I smiled to myself. "It will be my pleasure to go after that sea demon." I turned toward the hull with a sense of anticipation and adventure drumming through me. "Look alive, men! Ready our supplies. We just commandeered a new rig!"

They scurried from below like rats fleeing a sinking ship.

The sun had already started its gradual descent into the ebony sea by the time we moved everything from one ship to the other, and it couldn't have been a moment too soon. Dark Water quickly claimed my first ship, bending and snapping the wood until it sank beneath the deadly waves. A tiny thread of emotion wove its way through my body as I watched the mast slowly sink into oblivion. Where one chapter ended, a new one began.

"Our heading, Cap'n?" Cael's deep voice interrupted the homage I was paying to my old ship.

I turned to face him. He smiled at the helm of our new vessel like the cat who had swallowed a canary.

The salt-laden wind picked up speed, whipping through our sails and dancing across my skin. "To the Mariana Trench."

The home of the Dark Hydra.

Cael's eyes glistened with mischief. "Which route are we taking?"

There were two options. We could go the long way, circling the entire continent of Africa, or take the shortcut through the treacherous passageway between Africa and Asia that would lead us straight into the Indian Ocean. That particular shortcut had claimed the lives of many sailors, and it lived up to its name.

My gaze flitted across the deck of the stunning Wraith, which hummed with power and superiority.

I ran my fingers through my unruly, wind-tousled hair, using a thin piece of leather to bind it out of my face. "Through Hades' Pass."

CHAPTER 22
RHEA

Fatigue weighed heavily on all my extremities, the strain in my muscles surprisingly overriding the ache in my heart. I was nearing the Mariana Islands, which meant the waters were shallower and I could find a safe place to rest. I slowly made my way to the surface, pulling my tired body onto a dead coral reef that jutted above the water. Fragments of the once beautiful species crumbled beneath my fingers, falling to the ocean floor as I hoisted myself up. I hissed as my tail snared on a sharp, jagged piece, slicing through my delicate scales. I glanced down. It was only a minor scratch and nothing to worry about. I applied pressure to staunch the bleeding.

I inhaled a shaky breath. How much more of this could I handle? I had seen enough death and carnage the last few days to damage me for the rest of my life. Every time I closed my eyes for a moment's rest, nightmares of Dark Water plagued my dreams.

The closer I got to the Dark Hydra, the worse the ocean became. This place was a wasteland. Any creature that was able to had fled Dark Water, and its evil devoured anything that couldn't. The stench of death had permanently lodged itself in my nostrils, refusing to budge. I longed for a breath of fresh, salty air, especially if it was laced with masculine spices that smelled like a certain pirate captain.

Kai resurfaced in my thoughts, only enticing my anger. I shoved his tainted memory back into the recesses of my mind where he belonged. He and his crew were probably dead right now and no longer warranted my thoughts or concern.

I was also trying to ignore the fact that the closer I got to the Dark Hydra, the duller the necklace glowed. What had been a nearly blinding luminance was now nothing more than a flickering light that reminded me of a star about to burn out. If the evil here was too great for the small piece of Poseidon's heart, we were all doomed.

A sizable form floating in the current a few feet away captured my attention, distracting me from my despair. What used to be a majestic great white shark was now a massive blob of bones and rotting flesh. I turned away from it, unable to stomach the horrid sight. Goosebumps prickled on my skin. The once notable predator of the sea was no match for the wickedness that seized the ocean.

A disturbance in the water snapped my attention back around, and fear flooded my entire body. The shark's carcass bobbed up and down in the water like a fisherman's cork. Something was trying to yank it underwater. I snatched my tail from the water, drawing it protectively around my body, making myself as small as possible. *What horror could possibly survive in Dark Water?*

With one last powerful tug, the shark's corpse vanished entirely into the depths of the inky black waves. The only evidence that the body was ever there was a slight ripple in the water's surface. The eerie silence that followed was unbearable. The chill of foreboding swept over me, like icy fingers tracing down my spine.

I whirled around, scanning for any trace of what had dragged the body beneath the surface, but my frantic search yielded nothing, not even the faintest hint of bubbles signaling a lurking presence below. My muscles coiled so tight I feared they would snap under the pressure as the silence dragged on. The crimson smear of my blood on the rocky surface caught my attention, and my chest tingled. I had likely summoned whatever monstrosity this was from the depths with my accident. Fresh blood in this dismal water was like ringing a dinner bell to whatever lurked below.

Fear paralyzed me as a jagged fin pierced the water's surface. Four spiky, pointed bones constructed a fin with skin the color of dried blood stretched tautly across. It circled the reef, drawing closer with each pass it made. Whatever this creature was, it was enormous, judging by the size of the fin. Soon, more fins broke through the surface, drawing closer like sharks on a feeding frenzy.

Dread threaded through me when I heard something jump from the water. I slowly angled my body to whatever this horror was. Shock threatened to overwhelm me as a creature with unholy black lifeless eyes and an endless maw of razor-sharp teeth stepped toward me. The beast was nothing but bones covered in sickly gray skin and easily the size of a human man. It opened its mouth, and an ear-piercing screech that signaled my doom reverberated in the air. My eyes snagged on its claws that were at least half a foot in length and razor-sharp. Perfect for ripping through flesh. *My flesh.*

It lashed out, claws swiping in my direction like tiny blades. With my powerful tail, I whipped around, knocking it back in the water. The audible crack of bones and the faint trace of blood mingling in the water assured me that my strike had achieved the desired effect. The creature's lifeless body bobbed face-down in the water. I watched in horror as the masses turned toward one of their own, ripping it to shreds. Flesh and shards of bone flew in all directions. The cannibalistic assault was one of the most gruesome things I had ever seen. In that instant, it dawned on me that my odds of emerging from this ordeal unscathed were next to none.

Once the body had been completely demolished, more creatures surfaced. All their lifeless eyes and expressions turned to me with one clear goal—to devour me. Two more jumped up on the reef. My hands flew to the locket around my neck. I held it out like a beacon, hoping that Poseidon's might was still vibrant inside the shiny metal. It seemed to be working. The necklace was still glowing, barely. The creatures retreated momentarily, only to have three more leap onto the rock. The subtle glow of the locket sputtered like a flickering flame about to burn out until, finally, the light died.

The creatures all stepped toward me in unison. One struck out at my chest, snatching the necklace from around my neck. My skin stung at the contact, and I knew it left claw marks across my chest, but I refused to break eye contact to look at my injury. The thing glanced down at the locket, looked at it strangely, then dropped it, crushing it beneath its jagged, clawed foot. The small piece of Poseidon's heart shattered, turning to dust, and floated away on the wind, taking with it what little hope there was at defeating the Dark Hydra.

I knocked two more from the rock before they could reach me, but my efforts were in vain. They kept coming, multiplying at an alarming rate. I was hopelessly stranded. The thought of out swimming them skipped across my mind, but that would be suicidal without Poseidon's heart. Dark Water was inching closer to my perch on the coral reef. My last defense was my song. I only prayed that it would work against the creatures of pure evil that happily resided in Dark Water.

I poured all that I had into my song, careful to lace each note with death. Hope soared in my chest when they paused their attack. My song lacked its typical lethal impact. It seemed to perplex them, which was evident by the tilting of their heads.

Defeat pressed down on me, as heavy as a beached whale on my chest. Without Poseidon's heart, everything from this point on was just delaying the inevitable. Tears slipped from my eyes as I accepted my failure. Everything that I had been through over the past few months had been for naught. Seeking out the sea witch, drawing a truce with the rogue Blackheart Kai, and sentencing Medusa to death had all been without merit. I should have stayed home and accepted our fate gracefully like my father had asked me to. At least I could have bid my family goodbye and told them that I loved them, but I had been too stubborn, and now I would die alone, being ripped to shreds and feasted upon by these creatures devised of pure evil.

The faces of my family raced through my thoughts—my sister, mother, and father. I could be with them now, snuggled deep in their embrace, accepting our future with grace and going out together, yet my ego drove me to believe in a fairy tale. I thought that I was capable of something more than just being the wife of the next king of Aquarius. *My stubbornness would be my death*. My father had been right.

I halted my song, surrendering to my destiny. Fear lodged

itself in my throat, yet I forced it back down. I was going to die with dignity. I was, after all, the princess of Aquarius. I placed my hands delicately across my lap, waiting for my death from the creatures who swarmed. Kai's face skipped across my mind, reminding me of his features, his cocky smile, and his untamed masculinity. I had been foolish to fall for the manly wiles and danger he emanated. I was getting what I deserved for falling for his treachery and believing he could be something more than a monster.

"What are you waiting for?" I sneered, lifting my chin and exposing my throat. I desperately hoped they would swiftly end my life, sparing me from enduring the agony of them tearing the flesh from my bones.

One of the larger creatures from the group stepped forward, lifting its claws high above its head. I squeezed my eyes shut, anticipating the death blow.

CHAPTER 23
RHEA

Something whizzed by my face, the wind from whatever it was brushing across my cheek. I wasn't foolish enough to believe that the creature had missed due to its proximity. When I heard a screech rip from the creature's throat, I pried my eyes open. It reached up, trying to dislodge the arrow protruding from its forehead. I froze in shock as its eyes rolled back in its head and the creature fell over dead, splashing into the tainted black water.

Hope blossomed in my chest as more arrows soared through the air, burrowing into the creatures' skeletal bodies. I spun around to see a massive ivory-colored ship with masts and rigging reaching toward the heavens. It was ladened with weapons and gliding through Dark Water like a dream, and at the stern, with a bow in hand, was Kai.

I blinked several times, my mind refusing to comprehend what my eyes were witnessing. How had Kai found me, and where did he get this hauntingly beautiful ship? My muscles quivered when I realized that this must be the Wraith and the driving force behind his deceit. Something sinister leaked into my bloodstream. The sea witch had spared her minions' lives and sent them after me in a vessel capable of riding the deadly waves.

Arrows and spears continued to litter the air, and one by one, the creatures fell. Fate was a cruel mistress. I would rather die at the hands of these monsters than at the hands of Blackheart Kai. These creatures were hungry, and my death would only serve as a physical need, but with Kai, I would be another trophy kill to add to his collection.

The creatures circling me in the water quickly abandoned me, focusing all their attention on the more significant threat. They swarmed like barracuda around the ship, trying to claw their way aboard deck.

Kai was shouting, and he and his men were moving as one seamless fighting entity, but I could not understand his words above the boom of battle and the wind that whipped the tears from my eyes.

I sat there in stoic silence, unable to move from my perch on the coral. I was stranded without Poseidon's heart. The vicious creatures may have abandoned me, but Dark Water had not. It eased closer, attempting to slither up the rock to reach me. My eyes shifted from the battle scene to the dark waves surrounding me. The thought of throwing myself in and ending it all before Kai got his hands on me flitted across my mind, but my thirst for vengeance spoke louder than my desire to take the easy way out. If I had the chance to see another day, I would use the very last breath in my lungs to ensure Blackheart Kai met his doom.

I jumped as the boom of a cannon engulfed the surrounding area. The creatures caught in the line of fire combusted, while those that remained unscathed plunged beneath the inky surface. I scoffed to myself. I shouldn't be surprised that Kai had so quickly ended the attack. That was, after all, what he was good at—destroying sea monsters.

The massive ship glided closer to the coral reef I was marooned on.

"Need a lift, sea demon?" A crooked grin pulled at Kai's lips, and my stupid traitorous heart skipped a beat.

"Being swallowed alive by Dark Water sounds more appealing," I hissed, baring my teeth at him.

His smile widened, and mischief danced in his sea-blue eyes. "Perhaps, but I'm not giving you that option."

He tossed down a rope that landed across my tail. I stared at it like it was a sea serpent. If I accepted his help, I would betray myself and my people all over again. I wrapped my tail tighter around my body as Dark Water slithered further up the rock. A tightness squeezed my chest, threatening to crush my lungs. What other option did I have?

I reluctantly picked up the rope and tied it securely around my waist. The air whooshed from my lungs as the rope tightened, hoisting me above the rising Dark Water. My cheeks burned with embarrassment as I swayed through the air like a fish on a fisherman's line. Once I reached the railing, I grabbed on and pulled myself up. Kai stepped toward me in what looked like an effort to help me, but the hiss of warning I threw his way had him halting in his tracks. I slung my tail over, flipping it back and forth in an anger-fueled motion as the crew stared at me. I combed my fingers through my salt-laden hair, ignoring them and their infuriating captain.

Kai's eyes locked on my chest. Sirens seeped lust, but anger like a bolt of lightning shot from his cold oceanic eyes, indicating that was not the reason behind his hard glare. I glanced down. The creature had left jagged claw marks when it ripped the necklace from around my neck. Blood dripped down my torso, mingling with the scales that began at my lower waist.

Kai walked off without a word and returned quickly with a cloth in his hand. "This would have never happened if you'd stayed aboard my ship," he growled as he handed me the fabric.

I grabbed it from his hands, waving it angrily in the air. "No, this would have never happened if you hadn't made a deal with the sea witch. One with a stipulation that included my death." I pressed the cloth to my chest, wiping away the blood.

The crew members who crowded around very wisely chose that moment to busy themselves elsewhere.

Kai stepped toward me. "Rhea…"

I snarled. "Don't you dare say my name. After what you did, you are not fit to speak it."

Kai's eyes bore into me, but that did not stop the anger that oozed from me like ink from an octopus.

"And I see that you received your reward." My gaze skimmed the perimeter of the ship. "But let me guess, the conditions of the agreement have not changed, have they? I'm sure the sea witch still wants me dead."

"She does." Kai didn't even attempt to conceal his ploy, which ignited my anger like whale oil to a flame.

Kai stepped closer, which was the mighty pirate captain's mistake. I snatched a dagger he had strapped to his belt. Anger and hurt pulled a veil over my eyes. All I could see was red. I leaped from the railing, dagger raised, aiming for the black heart that resided in this pirate's chest.

Kai latched onto my wrist, stopping my attack. He banded his other arm around my waist, and my body dangled above the deck as he pressed his muscled torso to mine. He twisted until I was forced to release the dagger. It fell to the deck. The way he held me so gently and intimately, even after I attempted to kill him, confused me, igniting my fury. I used my tail, sweeping his feet from beneath him. We both crashed to the deck. He was on top of me in seconds, subduing my next assault.

"Get off of me," I hissed through clenched teeth.

He pinned both of my arms above my head. "Not until you calm down."

I thrashed violently beneath him, trying desperately to dislodge him. His rigid body was so close to mine, and his masculine scent teased me, further poking at the open wound in my heart. I screamed through my frustration. I couldn't get him off me. Sirens were strong, but this evil being of a man was as solid as a mountain. I went deadly still, stopping all my vain efforts to free myself and hurt him.

"Why did you do this?" My voice cracked with unexpected emotion, and only then did I realize I was crying.

The tears increased as my tail split and I once again had legs. Kai stood, pulling me up with him, but he refused to relinquish his hold. He crushed me to his chest, his eyes swirling with too many emotions for me to read.

He released me, pulled his shirt over his head, and handed it to me. I quickly donned the shirt, cursing its intoxicating scent of fresh salty air and spices. I folded in on myself, hugging my arms across my chest and making myself as small as possible.

Kai took a step toward me. "You were just a means to an end."

I recoiled. I didn't know why I expected him to lie to me to soften the blow. That was not who he was. His blatant truth hurt worse than him reaching into my chest and crushing my heart with his bare hands.

He stepped toward me so quickly that I did not have a chance to evade his touch. His hand reached for my face, his palm brushing my cheek as he anchored me in place by wrapping his fingers around the back of my neck. I tried to ignore the flash of remorse in his eyes, refusing to fall victim to another one of his schemes.

"Then go ahead," I urged. "Kill me."

I stood as tall as possible, laying my vulnerability at his feet.

The pressure of his fingers increased on my neck. "I didn't come here to kill you, Rhea. I came to save you."

I scoffed at his words, allowing my regard to travel up his bare chest and stopping at his eyes. "Do you honestly expect me to believe a word you say?"

He released me, letting his hand fall back to his side. "No, but I hope my actions speak louder than words."

Kai turned away from me. "Cael! Get this ship underway. Let's get out of this godforsaken wasteland."

My bruised heart skipped a beat as the men began preparing the ship to sail. Against all common sense, I stepped toward Kai. "We can't leave." Kai turned to me with a stern expression on his face. "We have to stop the Dark Hydra."

Kai quirked a dark brow at me. "I didn't come to stop the Dark Hydra. I came for you." He closed the distance between us. I desperately wanted to believe his words, but no matter how hard my feelings pulled toward him, I refused to relinquish.

"Why?" The word tumbled off of my tongue before I could

swallow it back down. I didn't want to know why. If I allowed myself to wonder why, I was allowing myself to believe his words were true.

His menacing glare seemed to swallow me whole as he searched my face. I could see the war that was waging in his stormy eyes. "Because you are the only thing in this world that I have ever cared about."

Kai broke me all over again with his words.

Warm tears flooded my eyes, clouding my vision. "I want to believe you." I choked on the words.

Kai reached up, his rough thumb brushing away my tears. "Then you should because I have never spoken truer words."

"Then prove it. Help me stop the Dark Hydra." The words tasted like poison on my tongue, coating my heart in the same vile substance. I couldn't believe after all he had done that I was pleading for his help. "The locket was destroyed." I reached up, idly brushing my fingertips along my collarbone where the necklace used to hang.

Kai's gaze followed my hand, searing my skin wherever his eyes touched. "I don't know what you expect me to do." He turned away, done with the conversation.

"You're Blackheart Kai!" I screamed after him, voice thick with emotion. "Your entire purpose is to kill monsters."

"The Dark Hydra isn't a monster. It's pure evil orchestrated by Hades. Not even the sea witch would risk coming this close to it." He was in front of me again before I could process his quick movements. "How do you think I was able to trick her into giving me this ship before I fulfilled my end of the deal?"

I scanned the ship, covering every inch of the craftsmanship. "Please help me save my family."

My body shook all over in desperation as my cheeks were saturated anew with my tears.

A growl of frustration vibrated in Kai's chest as he angrily shoved his fingers through his unruly hair. "I don't know if I can."

I rushed up to him, gripping his hand and entwining my fingers with his. "All I ask of you is to try. If we die, we die together."

Kai reached up, brushing his knuckles across my wet cheek. "For you, sea demon, I would sacrifice my life."

Kai crushed my body to his as he claimed my lips as his own. Hoots and whistles from his crew members were the only things that kept me from losing myself in him completely. Kai pulled away, determination set in his rugged features.

I chewed on my bottom lip. My emotions were all over the place. I was foolish to trust anything Kai said or anything I felt at the moment, but I could not deny the way my flighty heart beat for his. "How will we get to the Dark Hydra without that fragment of Poseidon's heart?"

Kai walked over to the railing of the ship, a strange, foreboding haze in his eyes. "Why worry about a piece of that bastard's heart when you can have his son?"

My entire body broke out in a cold sweat as Kai hoisted himself onto the railing and dove overboard.

CHAPTER 24
KAI

The frigid water was like a balm to my tattered soul as I dove into the black abyss. This was the second time Rhea had persuaded me to get in the water. Before she came along, it had been years since I had gone into the ocean. I avoided it at all costs. I hated how my blood sang when I was in the sea and how the currents and waves seemed to be in sync with the heartbeat that drummed in my bloodstream.

I harnessed command over the language of the waves and tides, an unbreakable bond that tethered me to the sea's embrace. The ocean coursed through my veins, an unwanted but inseparable companion. I loathed it, yet at the same time found peace in its familiar presence.

I emerged from the depths, combing my hands through my hair to get it out of my face. Rhea's fingers bit into the railing, her entire demeanor betraying her concern. My gaze traveled down the length of the Wraith. All my crew members were staring down at me with looks of confusion and fear. All except Cael, the only living soul that knew my true secret. His eyes shone with a sense of approval.

Rhea looked beyond me, and her knuckles whitened as her

grip on the bone railing intensified. I pivoted in the water to see what demanded her attention. The inky waters retreated swiftly, mimicking a school of fish evading a lurking shark. The tiny fragment of Poseidon's heart had provided a shield merely a few feet wide, standing as the boundary between us and the engulfing Dark Water. As I plunged into the depths, the black water withdrew, shrinking to an almost unseeable point on the distant horizon. I inhaled deeply. *Maybe I could do this.*

A splash brought my attention back around. In the clear, pristine water, I could see Rhea as she swam up to me. She surfaced mere inches from my face. She blinked at me a few times, seemingly still trying to accept my admission. "Why didn't you tell me?"

I swallowed the lump that formed at the base of my throat. "It's been my experience that people don't normally own up to what they are most ashamed of."

Understanding swirled in her honey-colored irises, and she thankfully didn't press the matter further.

Rhea chewed on her bottom lip, a nervous habit that made my blood heat to uncomfortable levels. She stopped when she noticed the intensity of my stare. "Can you do this? Can you defeat the Dark Hydra?"

I could tell by her tone she was hesitant to ask. I didn't blame her for being worried. Hell, I was concerned myself.

"In truth, I don't know what I am capable of," I answered honestly—for once.

I remained ignorant of the boundaries of my abilities, as I had no one to guide me in mastering them. Instead, I suppressed them deep within, burying them in the darkest recesses of my being alongside the painful memories intertwined with those extraordinary powers. I had chosen to deny my heritage and everything that linked me to that tainted bloodline.

Rhea reached a shaky hand toward my face, stopping it in midair. "Then we will find out together."

I plucked her hand from the air, anchoring it to my chest. I didn't want her to go. It was dangerous, and I had no idea what to expect from the monster below, but this was her destiny just as it was mine, and I would not deny her that, no matter how badly I wanted to.

"Cael!" I called over my shoulder before turning to face him.

"Aye, Cap'n."

"If I don't return, take good care of my ship."

A solemn expression overtook his features as an unspoken understanding threaded the air between us. "Safe travels, my friend."

Cael turned away from me, booming orders for the men to prepare the ship for battle. If this whole thing took a turn for the worse, my men would stand ready to place themselves between the Dark Hydra and the rest of the world. A sense of pride bubbled up in my chest.

Rhea gripped my arm, pulling my attention back to her. "I haven't turned back into a siren. I don't know what's wrong."

I smirked at her. "I forgot."

I stretched my palm toward her as she watched me with careful eyes. My power pulsed through the water, turning her back into her original form.

"It was you all this time," she said, barely above a breath. "I thought the sea witch did this to me."

"The sea witch wouldn't lift a finger to help you," I growled.

Rhea looked down at the water. "You saved me more than once by turning me."

I guess I had. If I hadn't transformed her into a human on the beach the first time I encountered her, she would have perished. I repeated the act when she was tossed into the water by the leviathan, dove in to vanquish the sirens threatening my ship, and once more when she unearthed my deception and flung herself overboard. I had been protecting her this whole time and hadn't even realized how deeply I had fallen for her from the very moment I first gazed upon her.

Rhea smiled at me, lightening the dark corners of my heart. "And here I believed you were just a heartless pirate."

I pulled her closer to me, and she came willingly. "Not so loud, you'll ruin my reputation."

Her eyes twinkled with mischief. "Come on, let's go show this Dark Hydra what Blackheart Kai is made of."

She dove underwater, flipping her iridescent pink fins in the air. I glanced back at my ship one last time before sinking below the surface and following her below.

I quickly caught up with Rhea. She was fast for a siren, but nothing compared to my speed when I was in the water. I took a deep breath, the water changing to oxygen as I inhaled. I didn't even know how my own breathing worked. Rhea had gills that allowed her to extract dissolved oxygen from the water, but I did not. I could breathe in the water just as easily as I could on land with no other explanation than I just could.

The farther we descended, the darker and colder the water became. A sense of foreboding washed over me like a tidal wave. I wasn't afraid for myself but for Rhea. The Mariana

Trench was the deepest place in the Seven Seas. I didn't know how much oxygen was in the water that deep nor what other hidden monstrosities might lurk below, but my true concern was that I wasn't sure if I could protect her. On land, brandishing a sword, I feared no one or nothing, but in this submerged realm, I was forced to depend on a strength I had once considered a hindrance.

Rhea's gasp sent a jolt through me, my muscles tensing as I whipped around to see the creatures we had battled above circling us like hungry sharks drawn to chum. I didn't know how these creatures would respond to me. I usually had to fight away the unwanted attention from all the sea creatures when I was in the water. They gravitated toward me like waves to a shoreline. Even aboard my ship, larger animals like sharks, whales, and porpoises would venture to the surface, actively seeking my attention.

I swam in front of Rhea as they drew closer. I held out my palm, allowing my power to pulse in the current. They blinked a few times, staring at me in confusion before lowering their heads and bestowing their honor and respect upon me. We continued toward the bottom with the creatures flanking our sides like royal guards. Rhea's tail fin brushed my leg as she pressed in closer to me, obviously still not trusting the creatures who had nearly torn her in two earlier. I glanced back at her, throwing her a smile that I hoped alleviated her fear.

We both stalled once we reached the ocean floor. The crescent-shaped trench cut a jagged line through the bottom of the ocean, plummeting deeper into the Earth's core. Dark Water shot out from the crevice like lava erupting from a volcano, promising death to anyone who neared it.

Rhea entwined her fingers through mine. I could feel the rapid thread of her pulse as it pumped. "It's worse than I could have possibly imagined."

Her fear did unspeakable things to my insides and invoked a surge of anger to erupt within me. I pulled her close to my side, staring deep into her eyes. "Go back to the ship? I'm not telling. I'm asking you to do this for me."

I was not a man to beg. I issued orders and expected unwavering compliance, but her fear muddled my mind, disrupting all my thoughts and reasoning.

"No." She flat-out refused my beseeching. "I will not desert you. It seems to me that you have had to deal with all of this on your own for long enough. No matter what happens, I will not leave you."

And just like that, this sea demon, the creature I had taught myself to loathe, reached into my big manly chest and squeezed my black heart. She couldn't possibly know how validating her words were nor what they meant to me. My grip on her hand intensified as I schooled my features, refusing to let her see the impact she had on me. "Then let's do this, little sea demon."

Rhea's smile was so bright it had the potential of lighting up the dreary black water, or maybe that was just the effect it had on me.

Hand in hand, we neared the trench. The Dark Water parted, allowing us clear access. The creatures that were impervious to Dark Water went in first, seemingly clearing the way for us to enter. I started after them, but Rhea pulled against me, demanding my attention.

"Kai, no matter what happens, I want you to know that I am proud of you for swallowing your pride and putting the

215

safety of others first. What you have done today, no matter the outcome, is the mark of a true ruler."

"Rhea…"

"Don't interrupt me, please. I have to say this. Even though we were set against each other from the very beginning, I would be doing myself a great injustice if I didn't confess that I've fallen in love with you."

My blood froze, and tension coiled between my shoulders. I didn't know how to embrace her love since no one had ever given it to me. Before I could reply, she plunged into the trench, and the darkness that lurked there engulfed her.

CHAPTER 25
RHEA

I slowed my descent, waiting for Kai to catch up with me. At this point, I was running away from my emotions instead of him. I felt vulnerable and foolish for confessing my feelings to him. I was sure I would take that secret with me to a very near watery grave, but my thoughts pounded so relentlessly in my brain that the words slipped out before I knew what I had done. A small part of me was relieved that I had told him how I felt, but the other part of me still felt like I was betraying who I was and who my father raised me to be.

Dark Water hovered nearby, waiting for me to get too far ahead of Kai. Down here, I was at his mercy. I couldn't get away from him even if I wanted to.

The creatures that attacked me earlier swam close to me, their claws and fins brushing against my skin as they circled close by. Something about their demeanor had changed. They no longer looked like they wanted to rip the flesh from my bones. Instead, they created a barrier around me as if protecting me. *Just how powerful was Kai?* I trembled. I couldn't deny that he was Poseidon's son, given the remarkable power I witnessed from him in such a short time.

My emotions pulled me in all directions until I was physically exhausted. How could he conceal from the world the fact that he was Poseidon's son and had the potential to stop the Dark Hydra all along? He was the true ruler of the Seven Seas. Why hadn't he claimed that role? *People don't normally own up to what they are most ashamed of.* His words from earlier rang in my ears, putting a slight notch of sympathy in my heart. I didn't know what he had been through, but I was sure his circumstances weren't enough to justify sitting by and doing nothing while countless sea dwellers lost their lives.

After what I witnessed with the leviathan, he would probably be elated if all the creatures of the sea perished. As I glided through the currents, a throbbing ache stirred within me, like the relentless pull of the tides against the shore. How could someone who was a part of the sea hate and massacre the creatures he was meant to rule?

Kai quickly caught up with me, bypassing me without a word. His determined expression sent shivers down my already cold skin, causing goosebumps to form. He had that same expression on his face the night he killed Flynt. I would never forget that look in his eyes. With a flick of my tail, I kept up with him as we dove deeper into the never-ending nothingness. I couldn't see Kai any longer. Something touched me. Was it Kai, one of the creatures, or something much worse? The mere thought had me imagining the worst and about to panic.

A gasp of surprise exploded from my lungs when something wrapped around my waist. It pulled me flush against a warm body. I relaxed the moment I realized I was in Kai's arms.

"Easy, sea demon." His wicked laughter echoed through

the water as his lips brushed the shell of my ear. "I'm not going to let anything happen to you."

"Don't make promises you can't keep," I hissed back.

His body stiffened at my words. "You need to relax."

My hand brushed up his amply muscled chest as I looped it around his neck, anchoring myself to him. "I would do much better if I could see what we were swimming toward."

"Let's see what kind of creatures are below," he whispered.

My blood ran cold. "What?

His power seeped through the water. I latched on tighter to him, fearful of what kind of creature he was about to call upon.

Light danced before my eyes, and I had to blink a few times to adjust to the oncoming glow. A scream lodged itself in my throat as several large, bony fish rose from the depths. My focus snared on the massive rows of razor-sharp teeth that protruded from their mouths. Their lower jaws stuck out further than the top, making them all the more terrifying, but nothing compared to the tiny glowing light that hung in front of their faces. It was a strange sort of beauty, glowing a vibrant blue. Something about it made me want to reach out and touch it, but I shoved that thought right back down where it belonged.

"Better?" Kai asked with a smug smirk, tilting his lips.

"No…not really," I answered honestly as I pressed in closer to him. My gaze hopelessly hung on the disturbing creatures that floated nearby.

Kai's arm tightened around my waist. The monstrous-looking fish was nothing compared to the man who held me in his arms. "That's funny," he said. "They seem to have had the desired effect I was hoping for."

I tilted my head up to meet his stare. "What effect?" My brow wrinkled with confusion.

"Getting you closer." His sensual baritone voice caressed my ears, creating a cascading effect that ran down the length of my body.

"Be serious. We're knocking on death's door. How can you possibly think of holding me at a time like this?" I tried to push out of his embrace, but that only made him tighten his hold.

Kai brushed his lips across my forehead. "I couldn't think of a better way to go."

My resolve cracked a little at his words, and I couldn't help but smile. He reached up, gripping my chin between his thumb and pointer finger. "Feel better now?"

A blush heated my cheeks when I realized he was only trying to keep me from having a panic attack, and his ploy worked like a charm.

My smile lingered as he released my chin. "Thank you."

"Don't thank me yet, not until we get through this in one piece," he said as we continued deeper into the abyss.

The strange fish with the lamp heads and the other creatures flanked our sides as we swam down. I was happy I could see what was in front of me, but the elation was short-lived as we reached the bottom of the trench.

I paused, letting my eyes sweep over the desolate wasteland. Nothing met my gaze but sand and scattered rocks below. Not a single creature stirred except those who had ventured down with us, and they appeared fearful. Dark Water seemed thicker down here, reminding me more of sludge than tainted water. I took a deep breath, struggling to inhale amidst the overwhelming filth and pollution.

I ventured a little further out, my reflexes on high alert. "Where is it?"

The muscles in Kai's back seemed to be wound so tight they might snap at any second.

"It's here. I can feel it," Kai cautioned.

I was beyond grateful that I couldn't feel it or see it.

A force of energy pulsated through the water, sending me flying through the current and landing in the slimy black sand.

"Please tell me that was you," I said as I brushed the muck from my scales.

Kai went deathly still. "It wasn't."

The thick Dark Water started to shift, swirling and converging in one spot before Kai. I watched in horror as Dark Water fused together, forming what appeared to be a mountain at the base of the trench. I had to drift back to glimpse the mound's top. It was unbelievably massive. An eerie silence fell over everything once all the Dark Water had gathered together. A shiver of fear coursed its way all the way down to my tailfin.

I was so still I wasn't even sure I was breathing. Kai's fists balled together, and he rolled his head around, loosening up his neck muscles. It was not a good sign, considering he was a murderous pirate always ready for anything.

My heart faltered in my chest, plummeting to the pit of my stomach as a serpentine head suddenly burst out from the mass of Dark Water. The being was entirely composed of Dark Water. Its skin oozed with an evil darkness, and black fangs jutted from its elongated jaw, dripping with the poisonous Dark Water. Its glowing, unholy red eyes scanned over me before fixating on Kai. Fossilized-looking spikes protruded from the seeping black sludge, running down the length of its body. It opened its mouth, releasing a screech that would burrow itself in my memory and haunt my dreams for the rest of my life, as fleeting as that may be.

Kai never wavered. His strength was the only thing holding me together at this point.

The Dark Hydra appeared perplexed that its prey wasn't frantically swimming for their lives. I was sure I had lost my sanity when what looked like a wicked smile crept across the monster's face.

Five more heads emerged from the ooze, each one more terrifying than the last. My mind grew foggy as my body teetered on the verge of shutting down completely. Dark Water continued to melt away until only the monster remained. Its slick, cylindrical snakelike body floated through the water with paralyzing agility, and the six demonic heads all snapped and hissed at Kai. Dark Water spewed from their mouths with each hiss.

I didn't know what I expected the Dark Hydra to look like, but I could not have conjured up a vision so horrible, even in my worst nightmares. It was pure wickedness and precisely what Kai had described. This wasn't just a monster—it was evil incarnate, forged by an even darker force.

Hot tears burned the back of my eyes as I glanced at Kai. Any of those dripping, sharp teeth-lined jaws could swallow us whole. A seed of doubt planted itself in my chest and blossomed into full fear. At the beginning of this seemingly impossible mission, our chances of victory appeared dim, but after witnessing this horror, I was sure our death was inevitable.

CHAPTER 26
KAI

Sink me. The abomination hovering in the water before me was beyond anything I could have ever conceived. One of the heads closest to me lunged, and I narrowly avoided it severing my arm as I surged backward out of its reach.

The beast's long body rippled with Dark Water, creating a holographic effect. It coiled, ready to strike, completely boneless as it effortlessly moved through the water. My power seeped through my fingers, ramming into the Dark Hydra and knocking it back a few feet. That blow should have been enough to knock it clear out of the water. Instead, it rocked backward, like I had merely shoved it.

A scream ripped from Rhea, latching onto my heart like a grappling hook. Four snarling heads held me at bay while the other two attacked Rhea. She flung herself to the side, barely avoiding the monster's bone-crushing jaws. Anger ignited in me like a lit fuse to a cannon. I sent a pulse of power through the water, sending the trench creatures who drifted in the water hurtling toward the Dark Hydra. They were lithe and swift, easily distracting the beast as Rhea collected herself and moved to safety.

My power tugged at my energy, rapidly draining me, but I directed another wave at the malevolent creature. It barely moved this time. Defeat pounded relentlessly in my chest. If my power wasn't enough to defeat the Dark Hydra, our fate was sealed.

Another head struck at me, but I did not move back this time. I veered to the right, using brute strength to slam the beast's mouth shut. All twelve glowing-ember eyes swiveled in my direction, darkening to a deeper shade of red as the monster's fury intensified. It ultimately abandoned its attack on Rhea. I'd just showed it my strength, therefore putting the target on my back. *Good.* I may not know how to control this unpredictable power that flowed through my veins like the surging tide, but I could use my strength. Growing up, concealing my strength and speed had been a challenge, but in this moment, I had no need to hide. I could bask in it.

The Dark Hydra lunged at me, all six jaws wide and open for the kill, but I shot through the water, putting distance between me and the multiple rows of razor-sharp teeth. Then it did something I hadn't anticipated: its mouths opened, spewing a colossal wave of black venomous breath through the water. Power burned through my fingertips as I reached for Rhea. I encased her in a protective bubble as Dark Water tainted the water around her. My skin burned as the Dark Water licked my skin, but I would not relent. I sent another blast of my sea power through the water, clearing away the inky poison that contaminated it.

A head whipped around, latching onto my arm, stopping my power from surrounding Rhea. A growl rumbled in my chest as the beast tore through my flesh, injecting Dark Water into my bloodstream. My eyes misted over in pain, but that did not stop them from seeking out Rhea. She hit the ground hard, and the sound of her body crashing into the sand and the way her head whipped back was like a knife to my chest.

She shot upright, turning eyes filled with terror to me. "Kai!"

Her voice ripped through my soul. Her concern for a wretch like me was undeserving. Rhea shot forward in the water, fear and determination glistening in her eyes.

"Don't!" I managed through gritted teeth.

If this thing tore me limb from limb, I would happily have it do so if it meant sparing her life. I would not allow the one I loved, the light in my darkness, the song in my melancholy heart, to be touched by this evil.

Rhea stopped, for once blessedly listening to me, but I could tell by the defiant spark in her eyes that it would not last long. I used what little there was left of my energy to summon the creatures from the darkness. Rhea screamed in frustration as they gripped her arms, pulling her away from the impending danger.

Another head wrapped around my middle, lifting me from the ocean floor. Air whooshed from my lungs as the constrictor squeezed. I knew it couldn't break my bones. I was too powerful to fall victim to minor human injuries like broken bones. Pain exploded in my shoulder as another set of jaws clamped down. My blood turned to liquid fire as it injected more Dark Water into my body. This would be my doom. Evil begot evil, and it was nothing less than what I deserved.

Throughout my entire life, I had buried the anger and pain inflicted by Poseidon deep within the recesses of my mind, along with any special abilities I possessed. I refused to acknowledge who he was to me and that his blood flowed through my veins. I took my vengeance out on all the sea creatures he created. *Creatures that he cared for.* Tracking and killing them came naturally to me.

Soon, I had melded into something just as wicked as what I was running from. *Blackheart Kai.* I possessed the ability to summon the creatures, the very beasts I hunted, to the surface. They longed to be near me, and I used that vulnerability to massacre them and make a name for myself. I reveled in their deaths, hoping that each one caused just a fraction of the pain for Poseidon that he had caused me and my mother. And then she showed up…

"Kai, please." Rhea whimpered. "Make them let me go so I can help you!"

I learned from that little sea demon that one can overcome hate. She despised me. I was sure of it, and perhaps she still did, but even in the face of her hatred, she helped me and my crew, despite our unworthiness. Her heart was big enough to overpower the black one that pulsed in my chest.

The Dark Hydra squeezed tighter, and another set of teeth sunk into the flesh of my other shoulder. I could not hear my own screams over Rhea's. She thrashed, rearing back and flinging her lustrous tail through the water. I marveled at her strength and her wild beauty that I never imagined I would be attracted to. She fought against the creatures' hold, nearly knocking them over with her might.

I wanted to scream at her and tell her that her concern was wasted on a being as vile as me. I was no better than the Dark Hydra. My vision started to blur, and I could barely make out her form as death rode on a swift ship to collect me. My head lolled backward. It was all I could do to keep it upright.

"Kai, don't you dare give up! You're stronger than this beast…" Rhea begged. She glared at me, and then her composure broke. "Please, don't leave me."

My crippled heart surged at her words, which barely had enough energy to pump blood through my veins. Rhea didn't need me. She would be fine without me. I knew the creatures would carry her to the surface and guarantee her safe return to the Wraith. My selfishness was the only reason I had not ordered them to do so yet. When I died, I wanted her face to be the last thing I saw.

Please don't leave me. Her words sent a jolt of power to all my extremities. Could I ignore such hate that had built inside me like a festering wound my entire life? For her, I believed I could. What would happen if I finally confessed who I was and who my father was? What if I permitted his power, which I had long denied and suppressed, to rise to the surface and consume me completely?

I delved deep, and then I sensed it. Not the minor tricks and water displays I had hurled at the Dark Hydra. Not the faint voice within me that beckoned the sea creatures. No, this power was a tempest, a force so potent that it sent shivers down my spine, instilling fear in me. It was all the forces of the Seven Seas coming together as one, all the might that flooded the oceans, and all the frightening beauty of the forces of nature. If I unleashed it, I may never be myself again or get it back under control. I forced my head up, staring deep into Rhea's eyes. Then a satisfying malice curled within me as I released the dam that held back my power.

CHAPTER 27
RHEA

My tears flowed freely, blending seamlessly with the salty sea. Desperation clawed its way up my throat, threatening to suffocate me. I would never forgive Kai for restraining me and forcing me to watch him die. I thrashed again, but the trench creatures that held me back dug their claws deeper into my skin as I fought against their hold. I didn't care if I perished. I had to do something.

As Kai's head fell backward, a pang shot through my heart, turning my blood into ice water. "Kai, don't you dare give up! You're stronger than this beast…" I swallowed the sob that cracked my voice with emotion. "Please, don't leave me."

I startled myself as the words left me. What would I do without this cocky pirate who made my blood boil? When had the lines between love and hate started to blur? All I knew was that they had, and now I found myself residing in a murky gray area.

A glimmer of hope surged through me as Kai raised his head. His gaze appeared dazed and bewildered, as if he were teetering on the brink of death. Something hardened in his features as his eyes bored into mine.

Power erupted from him like water bursting forth from a dam. The sheer might of him roared through the water, knocking me and the creatures back a few feet. All the Dark Water in the surrounding area dissipated like it was never there, leaving behind fresh, clear water. All that remained was the Dark Hydra itself.

Kai's body radiated from within, his skin gleaming like the sun's rays striking sea glass. My mouth hung open in sheer amazement. His blue eyes appeared electrified, as if lightning itself resided within them. They were both terrifying and hauntingly beautiful, filled with an intense and mesmerizing energy.

The Dark Hydra recoiled, releasing Kai. His power surged through the water, so potent I could almost reach out and touch it. My blood resonated with his energy, drawing me closer to him.

Lightning cracked, and the sea charged with energy as beams shot through the water toward the Dark Hydra. The monster screamed as lightning penetrated its body, leaving holes the size of cannonballs through it.

In that moment, Kai was the most beautiful thing I had ever seen. A halo of power surrounded him, blending his untamed masculinity with all the might of the oceans. His silhouette against the backdrop of the charged water was a mesmerizing dance of power and grace.

Kai extended a palm toward the Dark Hydra, as he had done earlier, but this time, his power gouged a trench through the creature, large enough for a blue whale to pass through.

The battle between Kai and this monstrosity continued to unfold deep beneath the churning waves. The wounded creature writhed in pain, its once intimidating form diminished by the relentless attack of Kai's mighty powers.

Seizing the opportunity, Kai pressed forward, his movements fluid and precise. He navigated the waters with a grace that defied the messy nature of the battle. Each gesture of his hands commanded the elements, directing currents and summoning power that lashed out at the weakened Hydra.

The sea itself seemed to respond to Kai's dominance, becoming an extension of his will. As he circled the wounded creature, his power hummed with the pulse of the ocean. Blow after blow, Kai's power surged through the water, leaving glowing trails in its wake. The wounded beast was now a mere shadow of its former self.

The Dark Hydra, now on the brink of death, retaliated with feeble efforts to regain control. Yet Kai's assault was relentless, unyielding. The Dark Hydra's menacing red eyes widened, betraying its horror. It attempted to escape, but Kai spun in the water, creating a massive whirlpool that enveloped the creature. The vortex tightened, pulling the Hydra into its depths. The monster thrashed and roared in a vain attempt to escape, but Kai's control over the waters was horrifyingly beautiful. The Hydra disintegrated piece by piece until all that was left were murky patches of Dark Water.

A powerful earthquake rocked the ocean floor, and I surged up. My pulse drummed in my ears, overwhelming the deafening roar as the ground fractured in two. Kai swiftly directed his whirlpool toward the chasm. The whirlpool, along with all the remnants of Dark Water and the beast, were drawn into the abyss.

"Back to hell where you belong," Kai ordered, bringing his

palms together until they touched. The chasm sealed, sending a blast of sand through the water as it closed.

I gasped as the grains of sand flew in my direction. Kai moved faster than time, slamming his body to mine, using his physique to shield my body from the debris that hurtled through the water. I squeezed my eyes shut as grit peppered my skin, clinging to Kai as if he were my lifeline. I buried my head against his torso.

"Rhea?" Kai's gruff voice vibrated in his chest, even huskier and more ethereal than I remembered. He reached up, his palm gently grazing my cheek as he pried my face from his torso.

I blinked up at him, astonished by the potency still crashing off of him like waves.

"Are you hurt?" he asked.

I stared up at him, my mind seemingly unable to grasp the words he spoke. He combed his fingers through my hair.

"Rhea? Are you hurt?" he repeated, his grip and the intensity in his glare turning more urgent.

"No," I whispered. I stared at the jagged teeth marks left by the Dark Hydra and the darkness that stained the veins running from his wounds. My heart clenched in my chest as a wave of nausea washed over me, my stomach churning at the sight of him in pain. Despite my inner turmoil, I forced myself to remain calm as my fingertips lightly brushed his skin near the injury, tracing the contours of the damage with a delicate touch. "But you are."

"It will heal," he assured me, pulling my hand away from the lesion like he didn't want me anywhere near it.

My gaze drifted over the open space the Mariana Trench, the pristine water so at odds with the dark evil that was here before. I wrapped my arms around his neck and anchored him to me. "Kai! You did it!" Elation flooded my body.

Kai's debonair smirk heated my blood to uncontrollable levels. "We did it."

A blush tinged my cheeks. "I didn't do anything, Kai."

"Didn't you, my little sea demon?" His voice turned sensual as he pulled me closer. "You believed in me and made me accept who I am. I couldn't have defeated the Dark Hydra without you."

Warmth blossomed in my chest, seeping through my body as I marveled at the glow of his sun-kissed skin.

Kai reached up, gripping my hand in his. "Let's get out of here."

He bent, placing one arm around my back and the other around my tail as he scooped me in his arms.

"Hold on tight," he whispered in my ear.

Adrenaline and excitement coursed through me. I wanted to tell him I wasn't a damsel in need of carrying, but something in the glow on his face made me swallow my words.

Kai shot up with such speed and intensity that I instinctively tightened my grip around his neck to prevent myself from being torn from his arms. Kai smiled down at me. "I'm not going to drop you, sea demon. You're too precious."

I was not the fainting type, but if this hard-core pirate, this killer and commander of the seas continued to say things like that to me, I might just swoon.

Rays of sunlight brushed my skin, heating my frigid blood as we emerged from the trench. As we neared the surface, the shadow of the ship danced above us. Kai shot out of the water like a dolphin, and we landed with ease on the deck of the

Wraith. His grip on me tightened as the crew rushed toward us.

"Cap'n! What happened?"

"Where's the Hydra?"

My head spun, and whiplash threatened my neck muscles as the men all asked questions at once.

"Quiet!" Cael bellowed, and the voices instantly died down. He pushed through the crowd until he was face-to-face with Kai. A grin pulled on his upper lip. "Welcome back, Cap'n."

Kai nodded his head once in gratitude.

My gaze lifted from the crew and swept out across the ocean. Tears pricked my eyes at the scene. The death and darkness that haunted and tainted the waters before we went below were completely gone. Beautiful, vibrant oranges and yellows danced across the crystal-blue water as the sun hunkered down for the night. The cawing of seagulls was music to my ears and something I hadn't realized I'd missed until it was gone.

I glanced at the coral reef where I had been stranded when the creatures attacked me. It was still blackened and charred from the poisonous Dark Water that had stripped it of life, but maybe one day it would be vivacious again.

Kai approached the railing as the trench creatures from below eased above the surface. "Stand down," Kai warned his men as they went for their weapons.

"What will happen to them now that Dark Water is gone?"

Kai's glare never wavered. "They are creatures of the trench. They will be fine as long as they return to the darkness." Kai outstretched a hand toward the creatures, ripples of power washing over them.

I could not hide the smile that brushed across my lips. "Are you thanking them?"

"Shh... I wouldn't want to ruin my sea-monster-hunter persona all in one day."

My smile intensified at his response. "I think King of the Seven Seas has a mightier ring."

Something flashed across Kai's eyes, something I would have missed if I wasn't already staring longingly into them. Dread sank like a boulder in my stomach when I realized I had overstepped my bounds. Kai was still warring with who he was. I didn't understand why, but I could tell he wasn't ready to discuss it, so I dropped the subject.

"Are you going to hold me all day, or will you do your thing and return my legs?" A pleasurable shiver coursed down my spine when the sly gleam in Kai's eyes returned.

Kai's arms tightened around my waist, his fingers putting agonizingly sweet pressure on my skin. "Ask me that again, sea demon."

Heat flooded my body like I had swum through a thermal vent in the ocean. I bit my lower lip, trying to control my raging emotions. "Not in front of the crew."

"Then you better stop torturing me by biting that lip," he growled.

I was sure my cheeks turned every shade of crimson imaginable. Kai smiled, seemingly pleased with the effect he had on me. "Cael, hand the sea demon your shirt, will you? I'd hate for her to bare her backside to everyone."

Cael turned toward us, stripping his shirt from his torso and handing it to me. "Yes, I have a feeling that would be deadly for us all." Cael glanced at Kai, and a knowing look passed between the two.

I slipped my arms through the sleeves as Kai's power pulsated over my body. What used to feel like agonizing pain was featherlight kisses as it washed over me now. Kai sat me on my feet as my brow wrinkled in confusion.

"It didn't hurt that time," I marveled, assuming I was growing accustomed to the change.

"I can be gentle when I want to be," Kai whispered, the stubble on his jaw brushing across the sensitive skin of my cheek.

I reared backward as my mouth opened and closed like a fish and all kinds of words to call him rushed forward at once. "You sea snake! You made me feel that torturous pain on purpose?"

Kai shrugged, a wicked twinkle in his eyes as he turned away from me. I stomped after him, prepared to tear him limb from limb for being so connivingly vile.

A roar ripped from Kai's throat as he gripped his chest and crashed to his knees. It felt like the world stopped spinning, and my legs were moving in slow motion as I made my way to him, then fell to my knees.

Kai's eyes were glassy with pain, and he clawed at his chest like a madman, a person possessed. I latched onto his hands. Terror took root in the pit of my stomach, releasing deadly doses of fear in my bloodstream. The bite marks from the Dark Hydra were blackened and inflamed, as if the skin had been charred, and I could see the black poison coursing through his veins, heading for his heart.

Cael crouched down beside me, fear in his expression. The crew gathered around, all with looks of concern for their captain.

"What do we do?" I breathlessly asked Cael.

Cael's dark brows gathered, betraying his concern. "Get him to bed."

Several men rushed forward, gripping Kai under his arms and lifting him from the deck. I followed them below, fear knotting between my shoulder blades as they laid him in his bed. I crawled in after him, perched beside him on my knees.

"Out!" Cael barked, and the men quickly exited. "What happened down there? What is this?" Cael brushed his hands along the darkened veins, and Kai roared in pain.

I gripped Kai's hand and squeezed as tears flooded my eyes. "Dark Water...it's inside of him. The Dark Hydra was made of Dark Water, and when it bit him..." My voice broke on a whimper.

Kai's eyes shot open, further adding to my concern. His electrifying blue eyes were duller than I had ever seen. So dark that they were nearly black.

My body shook uncontrollably, emotion welling up inside of me. "What are we going to do?"

"I know a lot about doctoring." Cael sighed. "But I don't know anything about this." Hope sank further in my chest when Cael's usually strong, collected demeanor betrayed his fear. "I'm going to get some supplies to clean the wound." Emotion gathering in his eyes, Cael rushed out the door.

I flung myself onto Kai. His body was searing to the touch, but that did not stop me from lying beside him and wrapping my arms and legs around him as if doing so would keep him from slipping away from me.

CHAPTER 28
RHEA

At some point during the night, fatigue had gotten the better of me, and I closed my eyes. The soft lap of waves against the hull of the ship beckoned me awake. I shot upright when I realized that it was morning and I had unwillingly fallen asleep. My gaze snapped to Kai, and all my resolve flew out the window when I saw how deathly still he was.

"Kai," I wailed and threw myself onto his chest.

"Easy, sea demon, wait until I feel better to do that," Kai's gruff voice was a balm to my aching soul. His face pinched with agony, but that did not stop him from teasing me. I smiled as a tear ran down my cheek.

I pulled back the bandages that Cael had applied, but my glimmer of hope failed when I saw that Dark Water was still slowly venturing toward his heart.

I laid my head on his chest as a sob erupted from within. "I don't know what to do, Kai. Tell me what to do."

Kai reached his hand up, brushing it through my hair. "There's nothing you can do. I'm probably getting what I deserve anyway."

I soaked his chest with my salty tears as I hugged him tighter. "Don't say that."

"Your tears are wasted on someone like me, Rhea."

Rhea. At this instant, I hated the use of my name on his lips. That meant he was being entirely too serious and didn't feel like exchanging our familiar banter. I pulled my face from his chest, wiping the tears away with the back of my hand. Folding my hands on top of each other, I placed my chin on them and leaned against his chest. I wanted to see his eyes, see the expression on his brawny, stubble-lined face. If I was going to lose him, I wanted to know everything about him, any detail that would imbed me deeper in his life.

I collected my fleeting courage and asked the question that had been burning on my tongue since I found out he was the son of Poseidon. "Tell me about your father?"

"I don't have a father," he spat. "But if you're talking about the male who contributed to bringing me into this world, I wouldn't know. I never met him."

My brow scrunched with confusion. "Did he not know he had a son?"

"He knew. I made sure he knew by becoming the greatest sea monster hunter that ever lived. No normal man could have accomplished what I have."

My skin broke out in a cold sweat. Kai must have felt my quiver. His hate-clouded eyes became clearer, and the harsh features of his face softened when he looked at me.

I straightened up, my eyes finding a particularly interesting knot in the plank flooring to focus on. "You used your sea powers to hunt and kill sea creatures?"

The words sounded even more awful when I said them out loud. Suddenly, the name Blackheart Kai held an entirely new meaning. He wasn't just a slayer of monsters. He was a murderer with such a devious, spiteful heart that he killed his own kind by luring them to him.

"Yes," Kai confirmed in a solemn voice. "I told you I was getting what I deserved."

"How many have you killed?" I asked, barely a whisper, not sure I wanted to know the answer.

Kai straightened but refused to meet my gaze. "So many that I lost count."

A question hung on the tip of my tongue. If I asked it, it would change everything between us, but I could not go on without knowing the truth.

Anxiety gripped me, and I bit my lower lip. "Have you ever killed a siren that looked like me but had hair the color of a setting sun?" I held my breath, uncertain of how I would react if he confessed to having killed my sister.

Kai's gaze finally lifted to meet mine, and I couldn't help but feel a twinge of discomfort at the raw vulnerability I sensed in myself. It was as though my emotions were laid bare on my face, a fact I begrudgingly acknowledged even as I longed to maintain my composure.

"I've killed many sirens," he admitted, "but never one who resembled you." Kai's voice carried a weight of truth that settled heavily between us.

Something about the way his dull eyes glistened told me he was telling the truth. A whirlwind of emotions swept through me—relief, contentment, and a haunting sense of sorrow.

Kai's eyes glazed over with pain. In that moment, it didn't matter if he was the most wicked being to tread the face of the earth. I loved him, and the thought of losing him filled me with an overwhelming dread. Without hesitation, I fell to my knees beside the bed and gripped his hand in mine.

I brushed my fingers across his knuckles. "Tell me what Poseidon did to invoke such rage and hatred toward my kind?"

Kai gritted his teeth as he tried to sit. I bounded to my feet to help him sit up and adjust the pillow behind his back. "It's not what he did to me. It's what he did to my mother."

I sat on the edge of the bed, pulling his hand in my lap. "Who is she, Kai? Who's your mother?"

Kai looked away like he was too ashamed to make eye contact with me. "Medusa was my mother."

A sick feeling of dread coated my stomach, making me feel like what meager dinner I had consumed last night was about to reappear. "Oh, Kai! I killed your mother!" My hand flew to my mouth, and I bit down hard, stifling the wail trying to escape me.

Kai shot upright, hissing in pain as he gripped my face. "You did not kill her! That bastard killed her by raping her and putting that locket around her neck."

I turned sorrowful eyes to Kai, my heart heavy with understanding. "I realize now why she gave up the locket so easily," I said, the weight of her sacrifice settling within me. "She did it to save you." I paused to recall her stoic sacrifice, then added, "If Poseidon hadn't given her that locket, she would have died years ago."

Kai eased back onto his pillow. "That would have been better for both of us. She wouldn't have been forced to live the life of a monster, and I would have never been born."

I reached my hand to his face. "Kai, you can't believe that."

Kai pulled away from my touch, the act stinging worse than a slap across my cheek. "You have no idea what I believe."

"No, I don't." I stood, glancing down at him. "But the man I have come to know would not say that and would not take his anger and hurt out on innocent sea creatures."

"Then you don't know me at all," Kai stated.

I walked over to the cabin door, then snatched it open. "I guess I don't." Once I slammed the door behind me, I stomped up on deck.

"I take it our patient is in a mood." Cael smiled as I leaned against the railing closest to him and angrily crossed my arms over my chest.

"A mood is putting it lightly," I grumbled.

Cael looked back over the water, watching as the sun began its ascent into the sky. "People tend to be a little touchy when they're dying."

Cael's words doused my anger, throwing a bucket of ice water over it. Guilt racked my brain. How could I be angry at him for his harsh words at a time like this? I blinked as a few tears cascaded down my cheeks.

"Kai doesn't like those," Cael warned, glancing back at me once more. "He had to deal with his mother's tears on a daily basis as a child. He loathes them now."

I sniffled, trying to stop my tears, and stepped closer to Cael. "Medusa actually raised him? Was he not affected by her stone curse?"

Cael's back straightened as if I had touched a nerve. "He told you about her?"

I stepped beside him, watching the sunlight dance in a rhythmic pattern across the water. "Yes. He told me she was his mother but nothing more. Our conversation got a little heated from that point forward."

"Kai has a hole inside of him bigger than this ocean. It's always been there," Cael remarked, his tone tinged with a hint of sadness. "And to answer your question, no, he's the son of Poseidon, he's not affected by her stone curse."

"That's why he's the only man who knew where to find her." I scoffed. "I don't understand how he could have taken me to his own mother when he knew I was after her locket."

Cael's grip tightened on the ship's wheel. "I don't think he ever expected you to succeed, and neither of us knew that removing her locket would make her fall victim to her own curse."

I didn't know how that realization made me feel. Angry at Kai for doubting me or sorry that I had succeeded.

"I didn't," I answered honestly. "Medusa gave me the locket. She sacrificed herself to stop the Dark Hydra."

"He told me," Cael replied, clearing his throat.

I smiled at Cael. "You two have been friends for a long time?"

"We've been friends as long as I can remember." A smile brushed across Cael's lips. "Kai told me that Medusa took care of him until he was old enough to fend for himself, then she put him in a boat with plenty of provisions and sent him away."

I gasped. "How old was he?"

"No one knows for sure. Gorgons don't exactly celebrate birthdays. I suspect he was close to my age when we met on the streets in Cisthene."

I was afraid to ask, but I did it anyway. "How old were you?"

"Ten."

I muffled another gasp by turning away from Cael. Kai had only been a child when his mother put him in a boat and sent him away. That and the fact of what Poseidon had done to his mother—I was starting to understand some of his uncontrollable wrath.

"When we were older and learned how good Kai was at killing sea creatures, we decided to spin a tale, telling people that he was the only man who had ever encountered Medusa and lived to tell about it. It greatly improved our status as monster hunters, and it wasn't a complete lie."

A shiver cascaded down spine. "That's horrid."

"He's not all bad." Cael scrunched his dark brows together. "Not really, anyway. Just a man greatly wronged by circumstances out of his control." Cael glanced at me, but I refused to return his gaze. "I have begun to see a change in him since he found you on that beach. Maybe you're just what he needs to bring him out of the darkness that's plagued him for years."

Cael was wise beyond his years. I had seen a change in Kai as well. Some of his hardness had started to melt away, but I wasn't sure that was enough for him to be the sovereign the Seven Seas needed him to be.

"What about the Dark Water inside of him? What will happen if it reaches his heart?" My voice shook when I asked.

"I don't know. All I know is that Kai is strong and way too stubborn to let something like Dark Water end him," Cael said with a slight smirk tugging on his lips.

His words had the desired effect and slightly lightened my melancholy mood.

Cael held out his hand to me. "Come! Take the wheel.

Everyone deserves to know what it feels like to navigate a ship as magnificent as the Wraith."

A devious smile upturned my lips. "Kai will have a fit if he finds out you let a female steer his precious Wraith." I walked over to the wheel and grabbed on. The current tugged against the rudder, and I was surprised by how much force I had to apply to keep the ship going in the direction Cael indicated.

"Don't fight it so hard. As long as we are going toward the horizon, we're heading in the right direction," Cael said.

I eased my grip on the wheel, allowing the current to help me rather than fight against it. "Where are we going?"

Cael shrugged. "I don't know. The Cap'n hasn't said. Maybe you should go find out when you bring him breakfast."

I smiled to myself as I walked toward the galley. Simon, the ship's cook, usually brought Kai his food, but this was Cael's way of giving me an excuse to go back into Kai's cabin. For a pirate, he was quite the matchmaker.

WITH THE TRAY IN HAND, the contents teetering with each step I took, I walked toward Kai's cabin. I maneuvered the tray without spilling a single drop of the dark concoction in the tin cup. I was pretty sure that whatever was in the cup would likely do more harm than good if ingested, but my palate often did not align with that of land dwellers.

I eased the door open, and my heart immediately shot to my throat when I saw that Kai was no longer in the bed. Every awful thought imaginable bombarded my mind. I shoved the door open with such vigor that it slammed against the wall.

"Still angry, I take it?" Kai's deep, playful voice soothed the raging tempest that was about to surge in me.

Sweat drenched my palms after the momentary scare he'd given me. I carefully sat the tray on his desk before it slipped from my sweaty palms and the contents splattered across the floor.

I inhaled deeply, collecting my emotions as I walked over to him. He was leaning heavily on a nearby washstand with a cream-colored pitcher and basin. My eyes followed his movements as he dipped a cloth in the water and tried to wash his chest. His features twisted with pain as he reached up.

I stepped in front of him, taking the cloth from his hand. "I'm pretty sure you weren't supposed to leave the bed."

"Just because I am destined for Davy Jones's locker doesn't mean I have to smell like death until then," Kai groaned.

Something flashed across his face as I brushed the sudsy cloth over his chest. I tried to ignore the muscles that rippled with tension every time I touched them and the fabric that clung perfectly to his trim hips, enhancing the exquisite V of his abs as they disappeared below his black, flowy pants.

As difficult as it was, I forced my eyes up to meet his. "Please stop saying you're going to die." I was angry with myself that my voice cracked. "I'm going to need you to be optimistic, even if it's just a front." Tears slipped from my eyes.

Kai reached up like he was going to wipe them away. "Rhea..."

I stepped back. "No. I'm asking you to do this for me because every time you mention your death, a piece of my heart shatters."

Kai was in front of me, hands gripping each side of my face before I knew what was happening, forcing me to look up at him. "I can't promise you what will happen to me, Rhea.

This is uncharted water for me. I've never been sick, and I heal in the blink of an eye whenever I get hurt." Kai stared deep into my eyes. "But I promise to fight until my last breath to stay with you. I can't imagine existing anywhere without you."

I latched onto Kai's waist, burying my face in his chest. "That's all I ask of you."

"Am I interrupting something?" I turned to see Cael hovering in the doorway.

"You normally do," Kai growled.

I laughed as I pulled away from Kai. Kai eased back onto the bed, and swiftly, I seized the tray laden with food from the desk and placed it in his lap. To my dismay, he ignored the fare and went straight for the vile liquid in the cup. After downing the cup's contents, he sat it down and pushed the tray away.

I sat on the bed next to him and dipped a spoon in the rich broth with vegetables and meat. I held the spoon before his face, refusing to budge until he took a bite. Kai's glare cut to me, but I just quirked a brow at him. His stubbornness finally relented, and he swallowed the broth down.

"I can see you're being well taken care of." Cael chuckled. When Kai's amusement did not match Cael's, he stepped closer to the end of the bed. "What's our heading, Cap'n?"

"Aquarius," Kai confirmed. "We have to return this sea demon to her kingdom."

My hand stalled midair, and the broth in the spoon sloshed onto the bed. "You're taking me home?" My voice rang with a note of warning, and apparently, Cael heard it because he made a face and rushed out the door without another word.

Kai flipped the soup-stained covers off. "I have to deal with the sea witch, and I have no intention of doing so until you are back in the protective custody of your father."

"You're in no shape to go up against the sea witch!" The pitch of my voice increased with the rise in my emotions.

Kai leaned back against his pillow, placing his hands lazily behind his head. "I don't have much of a choice. We made a deal, and I broke my part." His gaze brushed down my body as if indicating that I was part of the bargain he had broken. "I'm not going to have you anywhere near her," Kai said in a voice that dared me to argue with him.

We shall see about that.

"You don't know where Aquarius is," I continued to argue.

Kai scoffed, leaning back against the headboard. "You'd be surprised by the things I know, little sea demon."

CHAPTER 29
RHEA

I jolted awake as an all too vivid nightmare wreaked havoc on my peaceful sleep. I turned in the bed, desperately needing to see Kai after the night terror took him away from me.

He was sitting upright in the bed, one leg extended and the other bent at the knee, watching me. "That must have been some nightmare."

I stood up from the bed. "Dreaming about home," I lied. The last thing I was going to do was tell Kai about my bad dream where the sea witch was ripping him in two.

The vibrant glow in his eyes and skin had almost completely faded, and huge dark circles stained the skin beneath his eyes. I directed my gaze to his chest. Over the past few days, Kai had lounged shirtless, so it struck me as suspicious that he had put on a fresh shirt this morning before I woke up. I leaned over the bed frame, trying to catch a peek of his chest to see if the Dark Water had spread any further.

Kai smiled, a mischievous glisten in his dull blue eyes. "Looking for something?"

I bolted upright, refusing to say out loud that I was trying to see his chest. If I said that, there was no telling what kind of crude suggestion would come from his lips.

"No," I responded, pulling on my clothes and heading for the door. "I'm going to get your breakfast, and I expect you to eat it all." I slammed the door before he could argue, marching toward the galley.

The heat was already insufferable, and it wasn't even midday yet. Maybe Kai would feel like going on deck after breakfast. The salty fresh sea air would do him some good.

A commotion on deck prompted me to veer and climb the stairs. I quickened my pace as the initial scuffing of boots against wood morphed into what seemed like battle preparations.

The sun beat down harshly upon my skin as I emerged from below. The entire ship was in a state of chaos. The men rushed about with swords drawn and spears at the ready. Weapons gleamed in the sunlight, and a feeling of foreboding settled in my stomach. My gaze swept across the horizon, but all I saw were innumerable waves that glistened like diamonds under the sun's rays.

I wove my way around the crew toward Cael. "What is it?"

The answer to my question latched onto the railing with inky black tentacles. The strength from the force it applied made the ship teeter to the side. I gripped onto Cael's arm as the ship bucked in the water. The air whooshed from my lungs as a familiar sinister laugh echoed from below, chilling me to the bone.

The men rushed to the side, trying to hack at the tentacles that were strong enough to stall the mighty ship, but all they managed to do was enrage her. I watched in horror as more tentacles snaked from the water, wrapping around several of the men. The snapping of bones resounded through the air, causing my stomach to knot. They slumped over, dead, as she dragged them below to a watery grave.

"Cael! Tell them to stop! She'll kill them all!" I pleaded, rushing toward the railing.

Cael yanked me back, baring his teeth. "We never back down from a fight."

"Cael, this isn't any sea monster!" I argued, trying to force myself around his immovable body. "This is the sea witch!" As the words left my mouth, a dark, sooty mist rose from the choppy waves. The magic electrified the air, searing our skin as it swirled around us. The scent of burnt flesh hooked itself in my nostrils.

Cael leaped from the helm, sword drawn. "Hold!"

The men backed up but refused to lower their weapons, not that they would do them much good.

Time seemed to stand still as Morgana hoisted her body over the railing, her eyes probing the crew until they landed on me. Anger overtook her features before she quickly recovered. "I must say, I am disappointed to find you still alive."

"The feeling is mutual," I hissed.

She eased her body toward me, dragging her slick black tentacles behind her. I watched all eight of her legs as she neared me. She caught me off guard once in her cave, her spindly form at odds with her agility and speed. I refused to let myself be caught off guard a second time.

My muscles tensed, and my spine straightened as she stopped mere inches from my face. "Where's my locket?"

"Your locket?" I scoffed, taking a step back. "The owner is whoever possesses it, and that is not you."

"I tire of these games, Princess. Give me the locket, or I

will add this ship, along with all its inhabitants, to the bubble collection on my shelf."

A heaviness settled in my chest as her threat sank in. "The locket is gone...destroyed."

I saw no need to delay the inevitable. She would take this ship apart plank by plank to find what she desired. I was just saving her the trouble and the men unnecessary agony.

Morgana sneered, displaying her sharp, pointed teeth. She lashed out at me, but I was ready for her. I evaded the tentacle that targeted my face. The force was so great that it would have crushed my jaw if she'd landed her blow.

Morgana's face twisted into a bone-grating smile. "I see the captain has taught you well."

The men on deck stepped toward her, faces void of fear, ready to end the monster that threatened them, threatened me. A sense of belonging and pride swelled in my chest.

"Stand down!" Kai's strong voice boomed as he stepped onto the deck.

A mixture of relief and fear swirled in my gut as Kai confidently approached. I knew his swagger was forced. His strength was dwindling, but I couldn't tell by looking at him. He stood tall, carrying himself with pride and dominance. I hoped it would be that easy to fool Morgana. He stopped a few feet away and quirked a cocky brow at her. "To what do we owe this unexpected pleasure?"

Kai baited her, enticing her anger with his words. A skill that he was admittedly good at. I'd never met anyone like him, whose words could penetrate so deep, permanently burrowing under one's skin.

"We had a deal, Captain, and yet I see the siren still alive and my locket supposedly destroyed."

"Oh, it was destroyed," Kai assured her as he stepped protectively in front of me. "Along with the Dark Hydra."

My eyes rounded in horror as every form of evil flashed across Morgana's face. I gripped Kai's forearm, using him as a beacon to douse my mounting fear.

"No one can defeat the Dark Hydra!" Morgana spat as her lip curled.

"Prove me wrong." Kai shrugged his shoulders.

I heard the wicked smile in his voice.

Morgana threw her hand in the air, releasing what looked like black sand. A bubble appeared in a puff of smoke, taking the viewers to a different part of the ocean. I stared at the scene of the Mariana Trench. It was peaceful, calm, and without evidence that the Dark Hydra had ever littered the waters with its evil.

Morgana shook from her head to the tips of her muscled tentacles. The scream that left her lungs would have shattered windows. I threw my hands to my ears to ward off the deafening sound.

"You will die for this! An agonizing death," Morgana threatened.

Kai stood taller, and my skin prickled with goosebumps as the two eminent, vital forces faced off. "Do your worst, witch."

Kai used his body to press me back as Morgana dove over the railing, hurling her body into the water and disappearing beneath the glistening waves.

A swirl of inky darkness polluted the sea where she landed.

"Kai, what have you done?" My voice shook as he faced me.

"There was no delaying this. I broke our deal." He reached

up, cupping my face in his palm. "I just wish I had enough time to return you to your home before she attacks."

Words of argument hovered on the tip of my tongue, but Morgana reappeared, breaking through the surface, and snatched them from my mouth. The world ground to a halt as Morgana transformed into a monstrous figure, ballooning to ten times her original size. Her eyes emitted an eerie, piercing shade of purple, locking onto Kai and me. The ship, at the mercy of her slightest movements in the water, pitched and lurched as though caught in a fierce maelstrom.

"She's a kraken." The words of disbelief barely left my lips before Kai shoved me out of the way as a massive tentacle came crashing down.

CHAPTER 30
KAI

My body protested loudly as it collided with the deck, barely missing the sea witch's fatal blow. My deck, however, was not as lucky. The boards made of the bones of the leviathan cracked under the force.

I was on my feet in seconds, pulling Rhea along behind me as I went for the helm.

"I'll visit worse than death on you for damaging my ship!" I thundered, gripping the wheel in my sweaty palms. "Beat to quarters! Fighting trim! Clew up the main!"

The men scattered, each moving in perfect rhythm to the beat of my commands. Ropes strung through the air, and the sails shifted.

"Harpooners, tie off the darts! Run out the long spears!" I shifted at the helm, and the crew's eyes glistened with a hint of fear and excitement. This was what we lived for. The exhilaration of the chase hummed within me like a fine tune. I wouldn't feel guilty for this sea creature's death. The sea witch was anything but innocent. She wanted Rhea dead. Therefore I would use my last ragged breath ensuring that I sent her to Davy Jones's locker—or I'd die trying.

I glanced back at Rhea, half expecting to see her quaking

in fear. My thunderous heart skidded to a halt when I saw she was no longer behind me. I gripped the wheel until my knuckles blanched white. A flash of auburn caught my attention below, and I breathed a sigh of relief as she dashed across the deck, helping the men prepare the cannons. Pride bubbled in my chest, and I had to shove aside the smirk that tugged at my lips. I shook my head, momentarily breaking the ever-present trance I seemed to be under whenever Rhea was around.

"Heave way!" I bellowed as another tentacle flew through the air, aiming for our main mast. The Wraith was swift, gliding through the water with haunting speed. A massive wave formed beneath the sea witch's arm as it crashed into the water, missing its mark.

"Brace!" Cael yelled as the wave hit us hard, tossing the men about like dice in a gambler's hand. Several of my men gripped Rhea, helping her stay upright. Siren or not, she was now a part of this crew, and my men aimed to prove that.

"Gunners! Make ready! Hit her with plenty of fire and load the carcass shots!" My voice carried swiftly on the wind as the men loaded the cannons with a unique concoction meant to rip holes through the worst of beasts. "Fire!"

The ship jolted beneath our feet as the cannons exploded in unison. Our aim was dead to right, but they barely put a dent in the monstrosity that swarmed in the water. She roared, spewing a heavy rain of seawater across the deck, drenching us all.

"The ocean has sent us its worst, and we're going to send it right back!" I boomed. "Ready the spears!" All eyes turned to me when the weapon was ready. "Fire!"

Massive spears with ropes tied off at the ends thrust forth

from the ship's broadside, sinking deep into the sea witch's hide. She screeched, ducking beneath the water in an attempt to flee.

Rhea bounded up the stairs, eyes wide. I grabbed her and pulled her in front of me, wedging her body between mine and the wheel. The ship jarred and moaned in protest as the sea witch took off, taking us for a rough ride through the water.

"We've got her hooked. Now we'll wear her down," I whispered in Rhea's ear, enticing a twinkle of excitement in her eyes, even amidst the face of danger.

"Full sail!" I roared over the wail of the wind. "We'll make her fight the very wind until she has no more fight left in her."

The sail snapped into place, forcing the sea witch to slow her breakneck speed. I pulled Rhea tighter to my chest as the sea witch fought against our hold, lurching the ship forward. "Not so fun when your prey fights back, is it, witch?"

A shot of agony snaked through my chest, causing me to grit my teeth. The pain was so great it had the potential to bring me to my knees, but I refused to yield to it. Rhea turned in my arms, somehow sensing my hurt. Her gaze swiftly fixed on my bare chest, exposed as the wind violently ripped open my shirt. Her face flooded with concern, and I didn't have to look down to know that Dark Water was mere inches from my heart. Swallowing concern for myself, I instead focused on the imminent threat. I would see this sea witch in hell before I died. I refused to leave my crew and Rhea to face her alone.

The sea witch sharply veered to the right, yanking the ship along like a mere bobber skimming across the water. She began to spin in the water at such speed I feared the ship would lift from the very sea. In seconds, she created a massive whirlpool that swirled with her evil vengeance. The sea witch dove, snapping the line taut as she began to pull us under.

"She's going to drag us to the bottom!" Cael cautioned as he clung onto the mast to keep upright.

Rhea glanced at me over her shoulder, a flicker of fear in her irises. I scanned the condition of the ship. The moan of the boat told me that the pressure was too great and it would be crushed in a matter of minutes if I didn't do something. My crew dangled from ropes they had secured around their waists, swaying like spiders tossed in the wind.

I yelled at Rhea over the commotion. "Keep the rudder straight. If it turns, we will fall bow-first into the center of the whirlpool and be sucked down."

She nodded once in understanding and reached trembling hands to the wheel. Once she had control of the ship, I released the wheel and rushed to the ropes that anchored us to the sea witch. The boat jerked, causing me to nearly lose my footing. I glanced back, picking up speed, when I saw Rhea throwing everything she had into keeping the ship from slipping into the abyss.

Time seemed to move in slow motion as I pulled my sword from the scabbard on my hip. I sliced through the ropes one by one, each line popping and whizzing by my face as the tension released. I reached the last tether, my sword cutting through it like a hot knife through butter. The ship lurched, throwing me and the entire crew to the deck as it popped out of the whirlpool like a cork on a bottle of ale.

My head buzzed as it collided roughly with the deck, sending a jolt of pain through me. I struggled to regain my footing, but the dizzying throb in my skull made everything blur into double vision. The sea witch rose from the depths, a sinister grin pulling on her wicked lips. I forced myself to stand, but the pounding in my head and the pain in my poisoned black heart were nearly too much to bear.

My gaze cut to the helm, desperate for one last glance of Rhea before the sea witch put an end to my miserable life. I needed to see her perfect face, run my fingers through her long copper hair, and press my lips to hers—lips that seemed to be made just for me. Rhea rushed to my side, but she wouldn't make it. The sea witch polluted the salty sea air with her magic. It popped and hissed as it encompassed the ship. The water rose over the sides, entrapping us in a bubble.

The sea witch's magic reached for me, wrapping around me and squeezing. I tried to call on my sea powers, but it was useless. The Dark Water that swirled through my veins weakened me, preventing my ability to rise from the depths.

"No!" Rhea screamed as the rippling magic lifted me from the deck.

"Rhea! Stay back," I roared, thrashing against the sorcery that held me in place as she rushed to the side of the ship closest to the sea witch.

"I'll make a trade," Rhea yelled, demanding the sea witch's attention.

The sea witch threw her head back and laughed, the sound vibrating through my bones. "You have nothing I want."

Rhea stepped closer. "I offer you my father's trident!"

Everything stood still after the words left her mouth. The sea witch ceased her laughing and pinned Rhea with her harsh gaze. I crashed to the deck as the sea witch recalled her magic. Quickly, I regained my footing as Rhea rushed to my side. I plastered her body to mine as the sea witch shrank to her normal size and crawled over the railing. My trepidation rose the closer she stalked.

The sea witch rose taller in an effort to intimate Rhea. "No one can get the trident from Manta."

Rhea stepped out of my arms, closing the distance between her and the sea witch. "Have you so quickly forgotten how I got the information about the locket in the first place and where to find you?"

Something flashed across the sea witch's expression before an eerie smile settled upon her lips. "Maybe you *can* get me the trident."

"Oh, I can get it. The question is, are you powerful enough to meet my part of the bargain?"

The sea witch scoffed. "Your part of the bargain is that I will spare your life."

The mischievous tilt to Rhea's mouth had me momentarily awestruck. "Not for the trident. That trident is the essence of Aquarius. For something that precious, I want more."

The sea witch seemed to be considering Rhea's request. She raked her fingers through her mass of white hair, flipping it over her shoulder. "What is it you want?"

I wanted to hear this myself. Rhea had saved us once again with her quick wit and bravery. Now, I was enthralled, trying to figure out the workings of her devious little mind.

Rhea walked back over to me, placing her hand on my chest. My blood heated as her skin touched mine, but at the moment, it was not from want.

"Rhea…" I warned as my muscles pulled taut.

Rhea ignored me, never meeting my eyes. She gripped my shirt and ripped it open, exposing my black-veined chest.

Suspicion crept into the sea witch's dark eyes, and I knew she was trying to figure out why I was still alive.

Rhea turned back toward the sea witch. "Can you remove the Dark Water?"

"You care for this pirate enough to risk your kingdom's trident?" The sea witch gawked.

Rhea turned to me with unshed tears glistening in her eyes. A calm fierceness settled over her expression as she locked her gaze with mine. "Yes."

For as long as I lived, no matter how short that may be, I would never forget that look in her eyes. It soothed me, beckoning me near and tempting me to dive into those honey pools.

The sea witch smiled. "How intriguing. The siren in love with Blackheart Kai, killer of sea creatures."

The sea witch moved toward me, probing my chest with her gaze. I physically had to stop myself from jerking when she placed her cold, bony hand against my chest. Her black nails scraped against my skin as she ran her hand over my muscles, stopping when she was directly over my heart. The sea witch's black, lifeless eyes rose, boring into mine.

Rhea tensed beside me, and I gripped her hand to keep her from moving against the sea witch.

"Can you remove it, or are you just stalling?" Rhea growled.

The sea witch removed her hand from my chest, turning to face Rhea. "I can remove it." She stepped back. "The extraction spell may very well kill him, but if that's what you want, then it's yours." The sea witch shrugged.

Rhea held out her hand. "You spare the lives of everyone

aboard this ship and remove the Dark Water from Kai's veins, and I will get you my father's trident."

The sea witch eyed Rhea's hand like it was a sea serpent. "Deal." She gripped Rhea's hand and squeezed.

Rhea released her hand. "We have no time to waste. Change me back into a siren, and I will be on my way to Aquarius."

"I do wonder how you ended up with legs?" the sea witch questioned.

My muscles tightened, but Rhea was quick to respond. "I'm not without my wiles, and neither is my father."

"Hmm," the sea witch responded, seemingly accepting of Rhea's lie. "Very well. I will change you back, but you're not going alone. No offense, Princess, but I don't trust you. I'll send one of my minions to escort you."

That did not sit well with me, and neither did this plan. I opened my mouth to say exactly that but was interrupted as the witch turned toward the sea.

I pulled Rhea back to my side as the sea witch's magic sizzled through the air, oozing across the water in a rippling effect. Minutes ticked by until a male siren emerged from the depths. He shook the water from his long white hair, his eyes zeroing in on Rhea. I was already plotting out his demise just from how he looked at her.

Rhea went so still that I stared at her to ensure she was still breathing. Her sun-kissed skin lost its color, paling as the blood drained from her face.

CHAPTER 31
RHEA

My skin heated, not from the suffocating sun but from the anger coursing through me.

"You traitorous eel," I shrieked and bounded toward the railing, intending to leap over the side of the ship and claw Orm's eyes out.

Kai's thickly muscled arm banded around my waist, wrenching me backward until my back collided with his ridged chest. I thrashed in his arms, trying to reach my target.

"Rhea." Kai's voice held a subtle warning. It was warm and deep, pulling a hazy veil over my anger. "Who is this?"

I blinked a few times to clear the rage from my eyes. "Orm, my betrothed."

Kai's muscles tensed, and I couldn't withhold the smile that brushed across my lips as he tightened his hold on me in a possessive manner. He had nothing to worry about. There was no love between Orm and me, and after Morgana had just announced that he was her minion, I certainly had no intention of marrying the betrayer of my kingdom.

"That's right." Morgana moved in front of me, feigned shock on her face. "He was your fiancé... Too bad he is mine now. A deal's a deal."

My eyes flicked to hers. "What deal?"

Morgana's smile widened. "He offered himself to me in exchange for keeping him safe from Dark Water."

I shook my head in disbelief. Orm's betrayal did not surprise me. The bad thing was that there was no longer any Dark Water to protect him from, but he was still bound to their deal. *He's getting exactly what he deserved.*

Orm's glare bored holes into my skin when I glanced in his direction. His eyes ignited in anger, turning a darker shade when he saw the way Kai was holding me. *Good.* I wanted him to squirm like the sea leech he was.

"You're not going anywhere with him," Kai growled in my ear.

I turned in his arms, running my hands up his black-veined chest. "We don't have much of a choice."

Kai's fingers brushed against my hips as he pulled me closer. "This whole idea is foolish." He glanced around, lowering his voice. "I have no idea the amount of power in your father's trident, but judging by the lust in the sea witch's eyes, it's dangerous."

My breath caught in my throat as I stared into Kai's dull blue eyes. "I will not stand by and watch you die. This is the only thing I can think of to save you."

Kai sneered. "I'm not going to allow you to put yourself and the entire ocean at risk to save someone as worthless as me."

His declaration brought a smile to my face and warmed my heart. "I believe that black heart of yours is starting to beat red. The man I met on the beach months ago wouldn't have cared about me, or anyone else, for that matter."

A placid look overtook his features, and he stood up taller.

"No words in the world could encompass all the reasons I am wrong for you." The blood in my veins pumped louder as his grip on my waist intensified. "I am a terrible person and have made all the wrong choices, but being with you, knowing you, has made me want to be a better person."

Tears etched a path down my cheeks, and Kai reached up to wipe them away. "I'm not sorry that I've fallen in love with you, and all I ask is that you trust me. Let me go with Orm and get the trident."

"I'll grant your request, but I won't be happy about it," Kai said, motioning one of his men forward.

Kai gestured to the dagger and sheath tied to the man's middle, and he quickly took it off and handed it to his captain. Kai lifted my shirt, his fingertips brushing across my skin. Warmth blossomed in my chest, and my skin broke out in goosebumps as Kai strapped the dagger to my waist.

"If he even looks at you wrong, I want you to carve out his heart," Kai asserted loud enough for Orm to hear, which, judging by his face, was the intended effect.

My eyes flicked to Orm, who waited in the water. "You have my word," I promised Kai as I shed my clothing, walked over to the railing, and dove overboard.

My body sang as the cool water encircled me, hydrating my parched skin. I swam back to the surface to find Kai with his hands braced on the railing, tension evident in his taut muscles.

"I'm ready," I called to the sea witch.

A wicked smile tugged at her lips as she shot her magic toward me.

A scream ripped from my throat as the transformation started. Tears of pain leaked from my eyes, and I wished Kai had changed me instead of the sea witch, but I could deal with the intense pain if it kept his true identity safe.

I breathed deeply, thankful that the whole ordeal was over. My tail ached, and the thought of using it to swim all the way to Aquarius felt like a daunting task. The sea witch's skill in the transformation process seemed inferior to Kai's, or she intentionally heightened the pain. Given her nature, the latter was likely the case.

The water beside me rippled. I turned to see Orm's hand reaching for my shoulder, concern lining his expression.

"Touch her, and I will cut your heart out myself and feed it to the gulls," Kai warned from above.

Shock rendered me speechless as Orm lowered his arm back into the water. I had never seen Orm back down from anyone or anything. I glanced up at Kai. His dark, unruly hair blew in the wind, and the menacing set of his stubble-lined jaw promised death and danger. Even in his weakened state, he was a force to be reckoned with. I could easily understand Orm's hesitation.

Kai's gaze raked over me, and I felt a tug in my chest, pleading for me not to leave his side.

"Let's go," I said to Orm as I dove beneath the waves before my emotions argued me out of my mission.

I plummeted deep, hoping the cold water would numb the ache in my heart. The thought of Kai dying before I returned clawed at my mind, making my thoughts dizzy.

Orm caught up with me quickly. He had always been faster than me with his powerful tail. "You think your father will just hand you his trident?" Orm gripped my arm, forcing me to stop.

I knew my father would never give up his trident, and the

fact that I would have to put him under the persuasion of my siren song a second time made my stomach sour.

I tore my arm from Orm. "You have no right to ask me anything after what you did."

"After what I did." Orm scoffed. "You went to see the sea witch too, and don't try to deny it. She told me you did."

"That's the problem, Orm. I went to see her to save everyone. You went to her to save yourself."

Orm grabbed for me again, but my senses were on high alert, and I easily avoided him, which seemed to ignite the fire raging inside him. "Don't you dare judge me for trying to save myself. What you've done is much worse."

"Please tell me what I've done that is so bad?" I questioned with a lift of a brow.

"You fell for a land dweller. A killer of our kind. Both of you should be put to death." Orm rushed forward, gripping me by the shoulders. The force he applied was painful as his breath bubbles flew across my face. "How could you choose him over me?"

My hand went to the blade at my side. I snatched it from the sheath, slicing it across Orm's face. The water around us turned crimson with his blood. He released me, reaching up to cover his wound. A dazed and angry look crossed his features.

"Be careful," I warned. "The siren princess you used to know died along that treacherous journey. She is no more."

Orm's eyes swept over me in disbelief. "What has he turned you into?" He sneered at me, showing his pearly white teeth.

I returned the dagger to its sheath. "A stronger being who relics on no one."

Orm held his ground, and so did I. I fully expected him to attack me for carving a notch in his pretty face, but instead, he swam off in the direction of Aquarius, still cradling his cheek with his hand.

I followed behind him at a distance, still not trusting him not to retaliate. The swim after our encounter was blessedly quiet and gave me a chance to decide what I was going to do. I could try reasoning with my father, but from past experience, that had never gone well. We were too alike and known for our short tempers. He would banish me for treason if I even hinted at the fact that I wanted his trident to save the notorious Blackheart Kai.

I stalled in the water, emotion rising up my throat as I took in all the destruction. Dark Water wasn't here anymore, but it had left behind its carnage. Everything that once lived, fish and sea vegetation, was charred, blackened with death and decay. My once beautiful kingdom was just a shell of what it used to be.

I continued forward, dreading what my eyes would behold next. The massive kingdom of Aquarius came into view. The smooth, shell-colored towers of the palace that once reminded me of sea glass on the ocean floor when the sun's rays hit just right were now dull and dingy. Dizziness overtook me as I realized how close Dark Water had come to swallowing up my home.

My gaze sliced to Orm as he looked back at me. "Do you see now why I did what I did?"

"I understand," I conceded, "but all this does is prove how much of a coward you truly are. You abandoned women and children to save yourself."

I rushed past him, disgust churning in my stomach. The

thought of going through my home's gates made fear rise inside me like waves in a squall. What I was getting ready to do was treason, and by the looks of it, Aquarius had been through enough.

CHAPTER 32
RHEA

It was quiet—too quiet. Aquarius used to buzz with vivaciousness and life, and now everything seemed muted and dead. I swam through the once lively village that encompassed the palace, immediately missing the sound of young sirens at play. Debris littered the sandy bottom like everyone had packed up and left in a hurry. As I passed through, a few sirens that had stayed behind emerged from their homes.

"It's okay. Dark Water is gone," I promised as I lifted my hand, urging a small female from her home.

She rushed from the interior, looping her arms around my middle. Tears stung my eyes as a tremor overtook her body. I held her close as she released her fears.

"It's over. You never have to worry about Dark Water ever again."

"You found her, Orm! What would we do without you?" one of the nearby males said as he ventured from his home, commending Orm's heroics.

Orm smiled at him, and I had to physically hold back the sneer that pulled at my lips. I plastered on a smile for appearance's sake. Orm was anything but a hero, but I refused to correct the notion as it seemed to lift morale. More sirens ventured from their homes, crowding the courtyard.

Orm slowed, basking in the glow of the sirens's praise. I rolled my eyes as I picked up my pace, hurrying through the crystal doors that led inside the palace.

Once inside, the sparse guards's eyes trailed over my body, their scrutiny leaving a sense of unease in its wake. Their stares lingered on the newly acquired scars on my chest and back. I had been through a lot since meeting Kai, but the scars were just physical reminders of when the world tried to break me and failed. I ignored their gawking, focusing instead on the sandy floor that was the purest of white.

"They're not in there, Princess." Roland, one of the palace guards, spoke up as my hand reached for the heavy doors that led into the throne room.

I turned to him, my hand drifting back to my side. "Where are they?"

Roland nodded his head to the left. "In the dining hall."

I slowly swam in the direction of the dining hall. The thought of food had my stomach grumbling in protest, reminding me that I had not eaten all day. I hovered in the water outside the hall, mentally preparing myself for what I had to do. With a trembling hand, I reached up and pushed the doors open.

Time seemed to move as slowly as a sea snail as all eyes turned to me. My mother dropped the dainty piece of fish she had been devouring, and my father sat up straighter.

"Rhea!" Meleea cried, shoving away from the table. She latched her arms around me before I could swim through the doors. I returned her bone-crushing hug, gathering her closer in my arms as she laid her head on my chest. "Where have you been? We thought you were dead!"

I smiled at her. "I'm fine, and it's a long story."

Meleea moved aside as my mother swam toward me. Her face was solemn, the perfect mask of a queen, but her eyes betrayed her feelings. They glistened and sparked with disbelief.

"My little sea nymph." Her voice broke as she opened her arms, inviting me in.

I rushed forward, momentarily getting lost in the comfort of my mother's arms and her soothing, familiar scent.

"I would like a moment alone with Rhea." My father's deep voice broke the serene moment, and I pushed away from my mother's embrace.

My mother ushered my sister out of the room. "Don't do anything foolish, Manta," my mother warned him as she closed the door behind her.

To my surprise, my father eased toward me, cupping my face in the palm of his hand. "I thought I lost you."

I shook my head. "It's over, Father. Dark Water is no more. We have nothing else to fear."

Something flashed across his eyes, and it wasn't relief or joy. He dropped his hand from my face. "You could have been killed."

"But I wasn't, and everyone is safe."

Everyone except Kai. The thought resurfaced, reminding me of what I was here to do.

A rare smile tugged at my father's lips. "I'm proud of you, Rhea."

A piece of my heart felt like it broke off and floated away in the current. My father never told me he was proud of me, and here I was, getting ready to betray him yet again. Tears clouded my vision. I blinked, and they blended with the salty sea.

The smile on my father's face quickly faded as he glanced down at my waist. "What is this?" he questioned, reaching for the dagger hanging from my middle.

I closed my eyes, scolding myself for not hiding it before entering Aquarius. A million lies flooded my brain, tempting me to take the easy way out, but I grew increasingly tired of lying to my father. I wanted him to know the truth—even if it meant breaking his heart and mine—but I knew that wasn't an option.

"The important question is *who* gave it to her." Orm's voice slithered into the room, and I turned to find him hovering in the doorway.

Instead of slicing his face, I should have carved his heart from his chest just as Kai had told me to. If I had heeded his words, I wouldn't be in the situation I was in now.

My father's glare ventured between Orm and me. The hue of his irises turned a deeper shade of jade, and the vein above his forehead started to pulsate, hinting at his building rage. I felt a chill crawl up my spine as he focused on me. "Who gave you this weapon, Rhea?"

I glared at Orm, desperately wishing he would drop dead in the doorway to keep me from having to tell my father the truth. Lying was out of the question. No matter what I said at this point, Orm would argue.

I inhaled a shaky breath, meeting my father's scowl. "Blackheart Kai."

I eased back as my father's face reddened to the point it appeared purple. I genuinely feared he might implode. Time seemed to freeze, and its icy fingers gripped my chest as I witnessed every emotion sweep across my father's face simultaneously.

"What...is...he...saying...Rhea?" My father ground out every word like his tongue had swollen in his mouth.

Orm ventured into the room, stopping beside my father. "Yes, what am I saying, Rhea? Tell your father why we are here."

I couldn't even acknowledge Orm or his taunts at the moment. I was too afraid to take my eyes off of my father. Emotion rose with a lump in my throat, and I swallowed. I took my eyes off him for one second to glance at the foreboding golden trident he had a death grip on.

"I came for the trident, Father. I need it to save Kai."

Power exploded from the trident, taking out a column and a chuck of the ceiling, and I ducked. Debris crashed to the ocean floor, engulfing me in a flurry of sand. I was too frightened to move. I had never seen my father lose it like that. He had often lost his temper with his words, but nothing this violent. I blinked up at the hole in the dining hall, still not believing he had destroyed the roof.

My father was directly in front of me and gripping my arm before I could evade him. "How could you even consider betraying your people like this?" he roared in my face, and I just swayed there, taking in his fury. "How could you even speak to someone like Blackheart Kai, let alone try to save him? It was probably he who killed Valeria!"

"It wasn't," I said breathlessly.

My body trembled uncontrollably at his harsh words. I

knew he would bring up my elder sister's death. She was his everything, and to him, my actions murdered her all over again, but Kai was not responsible for her death.

"Will you at least let me explain?" I pleaded, hoping for an opportunity to douse some of his rage.

My father released my arm, and I fell backward before catching myself. "No words you speak will ever persuade my forgiveness." Hurt penetrated my heart as his words turned into a spear, making my chest feel like it was being punctured. My father turned to Orm. "Take her to the dungeons and out of my sight before I forget she is of my blood."

Orm rushed forward, gripping my biceps, and leaned forward to whisper in my ear. "Maybe some time in the dungeon will give you a chance to reconsider which male you want to spend the rest of your life with. I would rather see you dead than with anyone other than me."

My body jolted at his words. I knew he wanted the kingdom, but I had no idea that his power-hungry lust had transferred to me. I turned to him, my face calm and utterly void of emotion. "When Kai comes for you, don't beg me to save you. I expect you to die like the strong male you claim to be."

Orm went slack, his eyes boring into mine. "He's not coming for you. In fact, he's probably already dead. No man can survive Dark Water." Orm began dragging me toward the door.

"I'm giving you one last chance to hear my petition," I said, angling my body toward my father as I pulled against Orm's death grip.

He refused to even look in my direction. "Get her out of my sight," he whispered.

Orm pulled harder against my arm, his fingers digging deep into my skin with the promise of leaving behind bruises.

My lips parted, and my siren song hummed in my throat as it left my lips, casting an invisible tether to me and anyone within earshot. Orm's hand fell from my arm, and his head swayed to the side as he went slack-jawed. I focused my attention on my father.

"Don't do this, Rhea," he gritted through clenched teeth as he tried to fight my song.

I eased closer to him. "You gave me no choice." I intensified my song, strumming every note in perfect melody, weaving it through my father's mind. His eyes glazed over, and his body relaxed as I bewitched him with my song. Tears stung my eyes even as I tried to fight them back. I reached for the trident clutched tightly in my father's fist. My hand touched the cool metal, and I snatched it back as power surged against my skin. I hoped I wasn't making a mistake. I quickly grasped the trident, pulling it from my father's hand before I lost all my nerve.

The trident was much heavier than I expected. Father carried it around like it weighed no more than a sand dollar, but I could barely keep the thing from dragging the sandy ocean bottom. I held it close to my body as I eased toward the door, never stopping my song or taking my eyes off of my father or Orm.

"Rhea! What have you done?!" Mother's voice shook me to my core, sending blasts of ice water into my bloodstream. I gripped the trident tighter as I turned to see her in the doorway.

"Mother, please," I begged, choking on a sob. "Don't try to stop me. I have to do this." The thought of bewitching my mother with my song on top of what I had already done was too much for me to bear. If she forced me to, I would, but it would crack my already injured soul in two. "Please trust me."

Her face softened when she took in my pain and sorrow. She reached up, brushing her hand against my face. "I will always trust you. You are my daughter."

Her warmth soaked through my cheek, and I smiled at her. "Thank you."

She dropped her hand, looking back at my father. "I always knew your song was special. I just never realized how powerful it was." She glanced down at the trident in my hands. "I hope you know what you are doing."

"I don't," I answered honestly, "but I have to stop the sea witch and save the one I love."

My mother smiled at me, her eyes—the same color as mine—reflecting a hint of mischief. "Then what are you waiting for?"

I leaned in, brushing my lips across her cheek. A moan escaped my father, telling me he was coming out of his trance.

I turned back to my mother with a sense of urgency. "Don't let him follow me. I—"

"Rhea…" my mother interrupted, her brows scrunched together in concern.

"Give me a week," I pleaded. "If I'm not back by then, he can send his whole brigade to hunt me down."

My mother's eyes flitted between me and my father. She was the only one who could keep him from doing anything he was determined to do. "I'll do everything I can, but you must hurry. I won't be able to hold him back for long."

"Oh, don't worry," Meleea chimed in, brushing past our

mother with an innocent yet determined grin. "If necessary, I'll find a way to anchor him to the throne."

A comforting warmth filled my chest at the love and trust they displayed. While I understood the impossibility of tying my father to his throne chair, their willingness to attempt it was a testament to their loyalty and support.

CHAPTER 33
KAI

I gripped my pounding head. It felt like a tavern full of barmaids were dancing to the sea shanty across my skull. I breathed deeply, hoping the fresh salty air would alleviate some of the pain, but at this point, I was sure nothing would stop the aching in my chest. I had yet to decipher if it was from Dark Water edging closer to my heart or the fact that Rhea had disappeared with that sea dog beneath the rippling waves.

I forced myself to stand, waiting a few seconds to get my balance before walking up to the helm. *Sink me.* My legs were like that of a land dweller who had never been on the sea.

"Where is she?" I asked Cael as I stopped beside him.

Cael turned to me, his eyes full of concern. "Still lurking below. She hasn't left in days."

I glanced over the railing to find the sea witch circling below like a shark. She smiled up at me, showing off rows of razor-sharp teeth. The thought of blasting her out of the water with one of my cannons was all-consuming, but that hadn't worked so great the last time I tried it.

"Cap'n." Cael gripped the sleeve of my shirt, pulling my attention to the stern of the ship.

Relief flooded through me when Rhea broke through the surface. Her crimson hair flowed around her like a halo in the water as she swam in our direction. The trident she held in her hands caused a different sensation to rise in me. The sea witch was already powerful, and Rhea was getting ready to hand her an object that would make her invincible.

"I was starting to think you double-crossed me," the sea witch said as Rhea stopped before her. "Where's my little minion?" The sea witch glanced behind Rhea.

"I'm not in charge of your pets," Rhea hissed.

The sea witch held out her hand. "It doesn't matter. Hand me the trident."

Rhea pulled the trident closer to her chest. "Not until you remove the Dark Water from Kai."

The sea witch rolled her eyes, irritation evident in her expression. "Fine."

"And I want my legs back so I can be with him," Rhea added.

The smile that rendered the sea witch's face had me longing to pull my sword from its scabbard at my hip and slice her lips from her face.

Rhea swam over to the rope ladder as the sea witch shot a burst of magic through the water toward her. Rhea's face scrunched in pain, but she did not cry out this time, much to the disappointment of the sea witch, judging by the scowl on her face.

Rhea slowly made it up the ladder, and I was there waiting at the top to pull her over the railing and wrap her in my shirt. I swallowed her in my embrace, burying my face in the crook of her shoulder. "You have thoroughly wrecked me. I haven't had a moment's peace since you left," I whispered in her ear.

Rhea pulled away, her honey-colored eyes shining with emotion. Her smile touched my very soul, further breaking through its darkness.

"Isn't this sweet? The reunion of the monster and the monster hunter." The sea witch's bone-grating voice cut through the air as she hoisted herself over the railing.

I extended my shirt to Rhea, inviting her to slip her arms through. My gaze snared on the deep purple blemishes that marred her otherwise creamy skin.

"Who did this to you?" I growled, lightly gripping her arm.

Rhea pulled her arm from me, slipped it through the shirt, and began working on the buttons. "It's nothing."

I stepped closer to her. "It looks like a handprint." The words came out more of a snarl than actual words.

"I had a little problem with Orm," she barely whispered.

"Did you carve his heart out like I told you to?" I secretly hoped that was why he was not here.

"No." She exhaled as her eyes finally climbed to meet mine.

"Good." I pulled her closer. "That means I will have the pleasure of doing so."

Rhea shivered as fear shot through her eyes. I didn't need to turn around to know that the sea witch was lying in wait behind me. An unreadable emotion flashed across Rhea's face as she gripped the trident tighter. I angled my body toward the sea witch.

"Make no mistake. I am my father's daughter. If you do not remove every drop of Dark Water from his veins, I will turn you into sea foam," Rhea threatened, making her point as the trident in her hands started to glow. Her threat enticed a smirk of pride from me. She was certainly not the same unsure princess I had picked up off the beach all those months ago.

The sea witch's face scrunched with anger as she slid toward me. She rubbed her hands together, and a hazy dark smoke rose from her palms. "Don't say I didn't warn you. I very seriously doubt you will survive this."

Before her threat took root, she plunged her sharp nails into my chest, digging into my skin. A roar of pain ripped from my lungs as her nails dug deep, nearly grazing my heart. The sea witch cackled with malice as the mist poured into my body.

Rhea stepped forward, as did Cael and my entire crew. I managed to lift a shaky hand, staying their attack. The extraction was excruciating, but I could feel it working. The lesions the sea witch caused in my chest started to leak a combination of my blood and Dark Water. I glanced at Rhea, who had tears pouring down her face. To alleviate her fears, I nodded once.

I felt it the moment the last drop of Dark Water left my body. The sea witch ripped her claws from my skin, and I fell back onto the deck. My back and head slammed against the railing.

"Kai?" Rhea questioned. Her eyes flitted between me and the sea witch like she didn't know whether to hold her ground or hand the trident over.

I reached up, wiping a hand across my chest. All that was left behind was the crimson stain of my blood. "It's done."

Relief flashed across Rhea's face before she tossed the sea witch the trident.

The sea witch hugged the trident to her chest in a fit of hysterical glee. "It's mine! It's finally mine!"

Rhea fell to her knees beside me, her face hovering nervously above mine. My skin pulled together, healing the holes created by the sea witch. Energy surged through me, pounding with relentless power, making the glow of my skin return.

Rhea smiled, tucking her hair behind her ear before leaning down and brushing her soft lips against mine. "I thought I lost you."

"Never."

Rhea's eyes roved over my face. "How are you feeling?"

"Good as new," I answered, sitting up straighter.

The sly smile that brushed against Rhea's lips had me wanting to do unspeakable things to her. "Good, then go get my father's trident back."

Heat flooded my body as I realized this was her plan all along. Blackheart Kai may not be able to stop the sea witch, but Kai, son of Poseidon, could. "As you wish, my little sea demon."

I stood, immediately ensnaring the attention of the sea witch. Her glare brushed across my chest before an angry sneer tugged at her lips. "How is this possible?"

I swaggered closer, stopping mere inches from her, bending and whispering in her ear. "Did I fail to mention I was the son of Poseidon?"

The sea witch reared back so violently she would have snapped her spine in two if she had one. "Poseidon had no heirs." Fear engulfed her entire body as she gaped at me in disbelief.

"None that he acknowledged," I assured her.

The sea witch eased back, and I allowed her to retreat. There was nowhere in the Seven Seas she could hide from me if she chose to flee. "I will not allow the bastard son of Poseidon to stop me," she wailed, moving closer to the railing.

"Then do your worst," I baited her. "You got the upper hand last time, but I assure you it will not happen again."

A screech rose from her throat, signaling the onset of battle. The trident glowed in her grasp as she unleashed its power upon me. It streaked through the air like a bolt of lightning, but I invoked the ocean, swiftly conjuring a watery barrier to block the blow. The trident's force rebounded off the water, hurtling back in her direction. She tried to evade the blast, but it singed off one of her tentacles, leaving behind a black nub. The air turned putrid with the scent of burnt flesh.

An angry whoosh of air left her as she stared down at the severed tentacle. I smiled in amusement when the thing didn't immediately grow back. "Apparently, sea magic has a different effect on you than the blade of a man. How about I remove the other seven?" I threatened, my tone laced with a hint of danger.

Panic rendered her features, causing her to shrink back. "I have just the thing for someone like you." She cackled, engulfing herself in inky black magic.

I rushed forward, but she'd disappeared. The only thing that met me was the spark of magic as it sizzled through the air, tingling against my skin. I gripped the railing, scanning the ocean for any signs of her. She reappeared a few feet away from the ship with an onyx blade as black as a moonless night in her hands. I stared at the weapon. I didn't know what it was, but I could hear the whisper of evil and taste the promise of death in the air.

She held the dagger up, the ebony blade reflecting the sun's rays. "Do you know what this is, son of Poseidon?"

Rhea stepped up beside me, concern lining her features.

"This is the Obsidian Blade. Gifted to me by Hades himself to kill his brother Poseidon," the sea witch purred.

My blood ran colder than the water in the Mariana Trench. *The sea witch was responsible for the death of Poseidon?*

The sea witch smiled. "And now I am going to use it to kill you. A fitting sentiment, don't you think?"

"There's only one problem with your plan," I countered, leaning against the railing of the ship like her threat bored me. "I am not my father's son. He created sea creatures for his glory. I, on the other hand, kill monsters for the pleasure. Rest assured, I fully intend to adorn the bow of my ship with your wretched carcass!"

The sea witch's pale gray skin blanched, making her look even more grotesque.

"Fighting positions!" I bellowed, and the crew jumped into action. The cries of war hummed in the air, a sweet melody to my ears. My eyes never left the sea witch as she blinked at me in animosity. "I am also not alone."

"Fire!" Cael bellowed.

The water around the sea witch exploded, the force sending salty water in my face. I stepped off the railing as the ocean rose to meet me. I rushed toward the sea witch, who was still dazed from the carcass shot. She recovered quickly from the strike. More of the dark mist billowed from her palms as she used it to meld the Obsidian Blade and Manta's trident together. The trident's middle prong dissolved, and in its place emerged the dagger. An electric shock ran through me, causing me to freeze in place, as the once-golden trident transformed into the purest of onyx.

Power exploded from the tip of the blade, sending a bolt of black energy in my direction. I brought up another wall of ocean water, but this time, the magic effortlessly passed through, slicing through my forearm. I hit the waves hard, sinking into the sea as the magic seared my flesh.

CHAPTER 34
RHEA

Another round of exploding cannons drowned out my scream. I gripped the railing, watching in desperation as Kai sank beneath the waves. Horror took hold of me as I watched the sea witch send another dark jolt of magic through the water with my father's tainted trident.

As I prepared to hoist myself over the railing, Cael yelled, "Rhea, don't," and bounded toward me.

I stopped when Kai resurfaced, using the might of the waves to hoist himself back up. He was favoring his left arm. Angry, welted skin showed where the trident had hit him.

I knew Kai could triumph over my father's trident, but Morgana had combined it with a blade that had killed Poseidon. I had put Kai in mortal danger with my plan.

Kai glowed brighter, and the sea around him rippled in all directions, sending his power through the water. I waited, but nothing happened, and the sea witch took the opportunity to strike again. This time, Kai was prepared for the blow and evaded it. He reached up, calling down all the might of a tempest. The sea roiled in a furious, unforgiving frenzy, as lightning and wind conjured a swirling cyclone. With immense power, he flung it at Morgana, sending her tumbling into the raging depths of the ocean.

Whatever flicker of hope I clung to faded into the abyss as the sea witch resurfaced, like an unending nightmare, now in her massive kraken form. Kai glared at the beast, fury etching every sharp angle of his face.

"Reload those cannons!" Cael thundered, his voice commanding as he seized the wheel, steering the ship directly into a head-on collision course with the sea witch.

I wove around the bustling crew, making my way to the bow of the ship. I gripped the railing, legs apart, to steady myself as the boat rose and fell in the midst of the typhoon. I delved into the depths of my being, summoning my most lethal siren song. Kai needed a diversion, and I was going to give him one. The only problem was if I called upon this lethal song, the entire ship would be at my mercy, but I would deal with those consequences later.

My song cut through the roar of the storm that Kai created, hooking itself through Morgana's ears. My song distracted her momentarily and the trident's black power ceased as she turned her ire to me. Commotion behind me confirmed my fears. The crew, ensnared by my enchantment, were driven to madness, each one determined to eliminate the others just to get to me. During the chaos, one crew member was thrust overboard, his body catapulting over the railing and into the swirling waters below.

Kai's eyes met mine across the distance and then traveled to his crew member who sank beneath the waves. Kai reached out, hurling a wave in his direction and sweeping the man back on deck. Kai turned to Morgana, sending blue bolts of lightning through the water. I marveled at the beautiful but deadly rays as they glided through the sea toward their target. The screech that left the kraken when the blaze of energy tore through her flesh was so loud that my song died on my lips.

I spun around as the crew swayed on their feet, coming out of my trance. I couldn't risk doing that again without jeopardizing Kai's entire crew, so I prayed that the final blow from Kai was enough to end Morgana. Blood so blue it almost appeared black stained the water, but she was still upright.

"Bravo, son of Poseidon. You have proven to be a worthier opponent than your father, but your luck is running out," Morgana boomed in an unholy, monstrous voice that shook me to my very core.

My stomach clenched as I watched her weave more magic into my father's once majestic golden trident. The weapon began to glow red as evil radiated from it. Kai held his ground, and I marveled at the strength he portrayed.

"Oh, bloody hell."

I turned at Cael's stricken voice.

Blood rushed through my veins, drumming so loudly in my ears that it drowned out the sound of the squall and battle. A helpless feeling seized me, and my stomach bottomed out as I watched sea creatures of every size, shape, and hue rise from the depths of the ocean. I could barely believe my eyes. Leviathans, dagons, ebirah, and a slew of other creatures I had scarcely seen in my entire life waded close to the ship, all with a particular interest in Kai. There had to be over a dozen lurking on the horizon.

Morgana froze as she took in all the sea creatures and their tentacles, razor-sharp teeth, and claws, and the tightness in my chest eased.

"Blast these things from the very sea!" Cael thundered.

I lashed out, gripping his arm in desperation. "Wait!"

My focus shifted to Kai, who rose higher and had an air of calm serenity about him. He was glorious and easily the most beautiful thing I had ever seen with the water billowing around him, perfectly matching the shade of his vibrant eyes. The spritz of salty water etched a path down his brawny chest, adding a sheen to his already impressive abs. His skin glowed, and the untamed strength of his power surged through him.

A smile pulled at my lips. Kai was at peace with who he was and the beasts he once hunted and slayed. Realization dawned on me as I recalled the ripple of power he had sent through the water and how he had done the same thing with the creatures of the trench.

"Kai controls these sea creatures," I said without ever taking my eyes off his glorious form.

The muscles relaxed in Cael's arm, and I dropped my hand, easing closer to the railing. Kai's hands flew forward, and all the beasts immediately rushed toward Morgana. The fear that skipped across her face was paralyzing, and I was almost sorry for her. *Almost.* She sent everything she had at the creatures, but there were too many, each as massive as her kraken form. Her dark, evil blood polluted the water as they tore into her flesh, maiming her. Her tentacles were severed and ripped from her body. A leviathan latched onto her arm, and I watched as the trident slipped from her hands and fell beneath the bloodied waves.

I dove off the ship's bow, plummeting deep to reach the trident. Kai's magic caressed my body as my legs pulled together as one, and my tail appeared. I smiled to myself. Even amidst the gory battle, he was still protecting me. My eyes adjusted, warding off the sting of the salt water as my siren vision returned. The trident had already reached the bottom, its prongs lodged deep in the sand. I reached for the blackened metal, stalling when the sting of evil vibrated through the current. I didn't know what would happen if I touched something like this, but I couldn't risk Morgana getting her hands on it again.

I gripped the cool metal, closing my eyes as I prepared for the worst, but nothing happened. I used my powerful tail as a counterweight to dislodge the trident from the ground. Once it was free, I rushed back up to the surface.

A blood-curdling scream ripped from Morgana as my head broke through the surface. She was all but dead at this point. Kai's eyes raked over me, and I tossed him the trident. He stalked toward Morgana.

"Please, call off your beasts," she whimpered as blue-tinged blood spewed from her mouth.

Kai lifted his hand, and all the sea creatures retreated. Morgana would have sunk below the waves, but Kai held her upright with his swirling waves.

Morgana's eyes met Kai's, hazy with pain as death crept into her body. "You truly are the king of the Seven Seas."

"No, I am Blackheart Kai," Kai growled, sinking the trident deep into Morgana's abdomen.

The sea witch tried to cry out, but her voice was strangled as her throat filled with her blood. Morgana exploded into a surge of black sea foam. I ducked below the rippling waves as her inky darkness sprayed across the sea, tainting the waves. The current roared around me and lifted me from the sea. Kai pulled me into his arms with the force of his mighty waves. His power encircled us in seawater as he embraced me and brought his lips down to meet mine. His kiss was needy and rough, with a heavy dose of power and salt. It was perfect and sent an electrical jolt coursing all the way down to my tail fin.

Kai pulled away, and we stared at the black trident that began to glow in his hands. In a puff of smoke, the Obsidian Blade separated from my father's trident, undoing and marking the end of the sea witch that plagued these waters.

"What are you going to do with that?" I hesitantly asked, looking toward the evil, dark dagger.

Kai held it up, turning it in his hand. "I can't destroy something like this. I can only hide it and hope no one ever finds it."

His power surged, creating a strong current in the waves before forming a whirlpool that engulfed the sword. It disappeared beneath the waves.

I looked up at him. "Where did you send it?"

"To the deepest, darkest place in the Seven Seas."

I smiled, knowing nothing could go that deep and be able to ward off the trench creatures, no one except Kai.

My father's trident gleamed, reflecting the sun's rays across my face. I looked at it as my trepidation rose.

Kai's arm tightened around my waist. "We better get going. We need to return this to your father before he comes looking for it."

"We?" I asked, gazing lovingly at him.

"Yes, we. I have no intention of making you face your family alone again. I saw the pain and hurt in your eyes when you returned. No matter what happens, I'll be by your side."

"I love you, Blackheart Kai," I whispered as I laid my head against his chest. Fear snaked its way through my body as I looked out over the horizon in the direction of Aquarius. I knew Kai sensed my rising dread by the way his muscles tensed, mirroring his concern for me.

Kai gently lifted my chin, his touch tender as he pressed his lips against mine. "And I, you, my little sea demon." A hint of playfulness shone in Kai's deep blue eyes that swirled with all the colors of the sea.

I didn't know what would happen once I returned home and faced my father after what I did, but I knew I could face him because I had the love and the strength of the Seven Seas going with me.

CHAPTER 35
RHEA

Kai swam beside me in silent support. He seemed to know when I needed words of encouragement and when I needed solitude to wrestle with the thoughts screaming in my head. My worst fear was that my father would attack Kai on the spot, and he would retaliate, striking down my father. I hoped it wouldn't come to that, but knowing my father's temper, anything was possible.

"Quite a city." Kai's deep voice interrupted my thoughts as Aquarius loomed in the distance.

I swallowed the bile that burned the back of my throat as my apprehension increased tenfold. Kai's warm hand grazed against mine as he intertwined our fingers, and I turned to him.

I motioned to my father's trident. "Do you want me to take that? I don't know how everyone will take the sight of a man swimming into Aquarius with our kingdom's emblem in his grasp."

Kai shook his head. "No, it was my fault we had to take the trident. I intend to take full responsibility and return it to your father."

I gulped. "That's what I was afraid of."

I continued toward the gates that led inside. The guards hovered at the entrance—visible concern and confusion pulling on their facial features.

"He's with me," I said, motioning to Kai.

The guards glared at Kai, but they didn't move aside. News of how I betrayed my father must have traveled over the entire kingdom. I was sure I was no longer welcome in my own home. I eased forward with the intention of begging, but before I opened my mouth, power pulsed through the water, tickling against my skin.

The guards parted ways for us to pass so quickly that I was confident they got whiplash. Kai's fingertips brushed against my back as he pushed me forward through the gates.

"What did you do?" I asked, glancing back nervously at the guards.

"Nothing." Kai shrugged innocently. "I just introduced myself."

I blinked a few times, wanting to know more, but apparently, his ripple of power through the water had *introduced* him to more than just the guards. The sparse kingdom left after the wake of Dark Water crowded around us as we ventured toward the palace.

"Poseidon."

"King of the oceans."

"Master of the Seven Seas."

The voices rose in unison, reverberating through the current as they pressed forward to see him. I couldn't disguise the laughter that trickled from me when I looked over to Kai, whose lips were pulled tight into a sneer. He spun around, and the entire horde fell back in fear when the name Poseidon rose again.

I pulled on his arm, gaining his attention. "Apparently, you weren't clear when you introduced yourself." I snickered, and Kai rewarded me with his glare. "In all fairness, no one here knows what Poseidon looks like, so to them, you are him."

"Then I better correct them," Kai grumbled.

"Maybe later." I pleaded with my eyes. Kai's face instantly softened as he let his anger go with the tide.

My heart lodged in my throat as the doors to the castle crashed open. The flighty muscle increased its rhythmic beat when my father rushed through the doors, murder in his eyes.

"What is the meaning of this? Who is this man, Rhea?" my father bellowed.

I opened my mouth to answer, but Kai shoved me protectively behind him and swam up confidently before my father. I was not the fainting type, but at that moment, my head was dizzy, like the anxiety in my body was too much for it to bear.

Kai held the trident out toward my father. "I came to return this."

My father snatched it from Kai's grip, his face pinched with anger. "Who are you?"

Kai straightened, stretching to his full height that towered over a man even as magnificent as my father. "Blackheart Kai."

The entire ocean seemed to gasp at Kai's admission. I glanced at my father, whose bloodshot eyes were filled with rage. Every muscle in his body tensed as he raised the hand clutching his trident.

"Manta!" My mother's voice was a small mercy, cutting through the tension. She rushed through the doors with my sister in her wake and latched onto my father's arm. "He has come all this way to return your trident. The least you could do is hear what he has to say."

My father pulled his arm from her grip, turning his blazing eyes in my direction. "Is this what you wanted my trident for? To make it easier for this murderer to slay our kind? Have you taken leave of your senses?"

I eased forward. "Father, please."

His face was so red it turned a purple hue as he swam closer to me.

Kai moved in front of my father, blocking his path. "With all due respect, Your Majesty. Rhea didn't make me like this. My father gave me these abilities."

My father stayed his anger, if only for a fleeting moment. "And who is your father?"

"Poseidon."

An unreadable emotion flicked across my father's expression. "He would be ashamed of what you have become." My father jabbed Kai in the chest with an emotional knife and twisted.

Kai never backed away nor took his eyes off my father. "We were ashamed of each other." Kai inhaled. "We don't get to choose our family, and if it were up to me, he would have never been my father, but life often deals a dirty hand. I'm not trying to make excuses for what I have done. I have been running from my responsibilities for a long time, but Rhea helped me see past some of that rage." Warmth blossomed in my chest as Kai glanced back at me. "I don't expect you to understand, but I will not stand here and watch you take it out on Rhea when all she has done from the beginning was try to save everyone from the Dark Hydra, and she did so by abolishing the darkness that resided in me."

My father blinked like the words Kai spoke were foreign,

and his brows drew together in confusion. "You expect me to believe all of this?"

"I don't, but I do expect you to have faith in the strong daughter you have raised. Because of her, the Dark Hydra is dead, and so is the sea witch."

"The sea witch is dead?" My mother gasped, easing around Kai and embracing me.

I met my father's gaze, which had softened slightly. "That's why I wanted the trident. I needed it to save Kai so he could defeat the sea witch."

My father pressed his lips into a thin line. "I understand what you did and why you did it, but stealing the trident from me and putting the ruler of Aquarius under your siren song is an unforgivable offense."

"Manta, don't you dare," my mother threatened, but her words fell upon deaf ears.

"You are hereby banished from this kingdom." My father's words rang in my ear, sending a jolt of anguish straight into my heart. I swallowed as emotion crawled up my throat.

Kai was by my side in a matter of seconds, wrapping an arm around my waist and pulling me close. "I had no intention of leaving you here anyway. I need you by my side."

My father's banishment and Kai's declaration of needing me had my emotions all mixed up. I was happy but had a broken heart at the same time.

My father eased forward, watching Kai with careful eyes as he approached me. He gripped my chin and stared deep into my eyes. "This doesn't mean that I am not proud of you. You never belonged here anyway." My father smiled at me. "Your place is by his side, ensuring the Seven Seas are safe for all creatures."

I flew into my father's arms. "Thank you, Father." His hand reached up, gripping the back of my head, his long fingers stroking my hair in a soothing motion I remembered from childhood.

My father's eyes climbed to Kai's. "I will bless this union, but you must swear to protect her."

"With my life," Kai's voice echoed through the water, touching my very soul.

My father pulled away, running his fingers down my cheeks. "Then it is done. This union that I have ordained, let no man nor creature come between."

"You can't be serious! Treason like this is punishable by death!" Every fiber in my being tensed as Orm rushed from inside the palace. He had his war trident gripped tightly in his fist, waving it around like a man possessed.

My father released me, and Kai latched onto my wrist, pulling me protectively behind him. "Oh yes, I almost forgot about you." Kai's lips twisted into the slightest hint of a grin that brimmed with all the evilness in the world, promising death.

I reached up, squeezing Kai's biceps as I pushed around him. "Allow me to face my accuser?"

My eyes beseeched Kai, and his expression softened, but his muscles tensed as he turned to me.

"If he touches a single hair on your head, I will rip him in half whether it's your fight or not," Kai growled in my ear, sending goosebumps across my flesh.

"He won't get the chance," I promised as I turned to face Orm. "I had a good teacher."

"You have to be joking," Orm scoffed. "The princess

against the captain of the guard?" Orm stalked closer. "I will slaughter you before you take your next breath."

"I wouldn't be so sure about that. She has faced greater monsters than you." Kai's whiskers brushed against my cheek as he leaned over my shoulder. "No mercy. You end him this time."

"With pleasure."

I turned to my father, who was holding the crowd at bay with the might of his trident. "Orm betrayed you, Father. He made a deal with the sea witch to be her servant in exchange for protecting him from Dark Water."

"I am not completely clueless, Rhea. Why do you think I am allowing this battle?" My father smiled, handing me his trident.

I reached for it, my hand brushing against the cool metal. "You want me to use your trident?"

"You are my daughter," my father answered with pride beaming in his eyes.

Orm rushed toward me like the coward he was, taking me by surprise. He raised his trident high, preparing to sink it deep into my skull. I glimpsed Kai out of the corner of my eye as he readied to end Orm, but I raised my father's trident, blocking his blow.

Orm's trident was so close to my face that the tip brushed against my cheek, drawing blood. I ignored the sting as I shoved against his suppressing weight. Orm's face blanched to the same color as his pale hair, and his eyes simmered with anger as he realized his adversary was more predator than prey.

Orm attacked again and again, but each time I was ready for him. Kai's words rang in my ears about studying my opponent, and this particular rival had a telltale sign of arrogantly curling his upper lip before he struck. Orm was quickly losing patience as I evaded each blow, and his anger engulfed him.

"I will not be made a fool of by a mere princess," Orm declared.

The smile that curved my lips was more deadly than sweet. "Haven't you heard? I'm not a princess. I am a sea demon."

Orm's tail muscles tensed, a coiled spring of fury, as if the very currents themselves trembled in anticipation of his attack. The water around us seemed to hum with the impending strike.

But I was ready.

As Orm surged forward, his movements swift and lethal, I danced with the fluid grace of a seasoned warrior. With a deft twist, I parried his blow, narrowly evading what could have been a fatal strike. In that split second of vulnerability, I seized the opportunity presented to me.

With a surge of determination, I struck first.

The look in Orm's eyes betrayed his surprise as my weapon found its mark. His pupils dilated, mirroring the shock that rippled through his body as I drove the three prongs of my father's trident deep into his abdomen. The water around us momentarily stilled, as if even the currents themselves paused to witness the outcome of our clash.

Gasps resounded in the water from the sirens, and my body began to tremble.

Orm sputtered as the water turned murky, tainted with his crimson blood. A tiny thread of guilt wove its way through my conscience as his body stiffened and sank to the ocean floor. I had never killed another siren, and even though Orm deserved it for everything he had done, I still felt guilty.

"Remove this bilge from my sight," my father called to the guards, who quickly rushed forward to dispose of the body. He smiled as I handed the trident back to him. "You have impressed me today with your strength."

I looked at Kai whose face seemed to beam with pride. "We should go."

Meleea rushed to me, enveloping me in a tight hug. "I'm going to miss you, but at least now I can be queen."

"Aquarius will be much better off with you as queen." I smiled, gently pulling away.

"Yes, with me as the queen and you as their protector, along with that gorgeous being." She winked, nodding toward Kai, and I laughed at her remark.

My heart dipped as my mother approached and crushed me to her chest, holding me like she never intended to let me go.

My father pulled her away, hugging my sobbing mother to his chest. "Just because she is banished doesn't mean we'll never see her again." His words held a promise that had a smile blossoming across my face.

Kai pulled me to his side, wrapping his arm protectively around my waist.

"I love you all," I exclaimed before Kai shot through the water, pulling us back to the surface—and to our destiny.

THE SUN HAD SET by the time we reached the Wraith. The skeleton crew on deck greeted Kai and me as he sat me back on the deck. Cael rushed forward, offering me his shirt as Kai gave me back my legs.

Sorrow weighed heavy in my chest as I wondered if and

when I would ever see my family again. I was banished, so I couldn't just show up whenever I missed them. Kai's eyes bored into mine, concern reflecting in them. He pressed his lips lightly against my forehead before heading below.

I hugged the white shirt tighter as the cool wind blew across my exposed limbs. I should follow Kai below and change into suitable clothes, but my tattered emotions would not let me go down, not yet.

Cael stood at the wheel as I approached the helm to join him.

"Your mission was a success?" he asked. I leaned onto the railing as he guided the ship farther away from my home.

"If you call being banished from your home a success, then yes, it was."

"Don't worry. Rulers can always change their minds. Look at Kai."

I smiled at Cael's words. He was the epitome of knowledge and always knew what to say to make me smile. I may not have my blood family, but I had something just as good in my unlikely but loyal crew.

Strong arms encircled my waist, and my worries skipped right out of my mind as I was engulfed in Kai's warmth and salty, masculine scent. "You'll see them again. Even if I have to go there and drag them to the surface. I promise you, you will see them again."

I smiled as his words soothed my soul. We both straightened, and I rested my back and head against Kai's chest, gazing across the moon-drenched sea.

"What are your plans now? I don't think we can continue hunting sea creatures after that statement you made," Cael said, turning to Kai.

"We're going to do what we should have done all along. We're going to be a bridge between the land and sea dwellers and ensure that one does not hurt the other." Kai's voice rumbled in my ear, and I wasn't sure if it was his deep baritone or his words that made my flesh break out in goosebumps.

"I'm proud of you both," I said, smiling at Cael, who was trying to hide the elation from his impassive face.

"You're going to have to give up your lavish life. I don't think people are going to pay well for you to protect sea creatures instead of killing them," Cael said.

Kai's deep laughter vibrated in his chest. "I don't see why. That's what this little sea demon is for. She knows where all the sunken treasure ships are. The ocean will provide for us." Kai turned me in his arms, his deep blue eyes swirling with longing. "Besides, I do believe you owe me one sunken ship already."

My pulse skidded to a halt under his gaze that heated my body to an uncontrollable temperature. "About that…" I ran my fingers lovingly up his chest. "I may have exaggerated a bit about the worth of that cargo." I rewarded Kai with an innocent smile that was anything but guilt-free.

Kai's vibrant eyes were ablaze as he bent low, whispering in my ear. His stubble brushed against the shell of my ear, sending bolts of energy to my heart and turning me to sea slush in his arms. "I'm going to take that out of your hide, sea demon."

A screech escaped my lips as Kai tossed me over his shoulder and started toward the lower deck.

"I hate to interrupt this little tryst, but what's our heading,

Cap'n?" Cael bellowed, and Kai spun back around. My body swayed helplessly in his arms.

"Turronto Port. I still have a bone to pick with Dante, especially if he's still entrapping leviathans and using them to do his dirty work."

"Aye, Cap'n." Cael chuckled.

I sat up with a victorious smile etched across my face, bracing my elbows on Kai's shoulders and resting my chin in my hands.

The scuff of Kai's boots across the deck and stairs had my heart tripping over itself the closer we came to his cabin. He eased me from his shoulder, my body pressing against his as my feet hit the floor. Kai bent down, brushing his lips across my cheek. The light touch sent shivers to all my extremities and made my entire body tremble. Then he ventured to my lips. The kiss was like pure lightning, backed by all his power and might, scorching its way through my body.

My knees weakened and buckled, but Kai's grip around my waist tightened. "Do you remember when we first met and I swore to you that I would never touch a creature like you in that way?"

My brow scrunched in confusion as to why he was bringing up the horrid way we met and how he practically spat in my face that he would never desire a creature such as me. "Yes?"

Kai backed me toward the bed. "I lied."

THE END

LEAVE A REVIEW

I hope you enjoyed Of Song and Darkness!

Please consider leaving a review for my book on your
preferred platform! Thank you!

About the Author

By day, I work as a Registered Dietitian at a health department. By night, I escape into the fantasy worlds in my mind and bring them to you through my writing. I began my writing career on Wattpad, where you can find the first books I have written. I write closed door romances with strong female leads and swoon worthy alpha males. I live with my husband and two German shorthaired pointers on the family farm. I am an avid baker and enjoy living off the land.

ALSO BY JESSICA SPRUILL

Claimed by the Sicilian Mafia

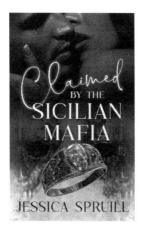

The Alpha's Huntress

Court of Nightmares and Ruin

FOLLOW JESSICA SPRUILL

Stay connected with Jessica at the following places:

Subscribe to my readers list:
www.jessicaspruillauthor.com

Instagram:
https://www.instragram.com/jessicaspruillauthor

Made in United States
Troutdale, OR
11/15/2024